R.A. Γ

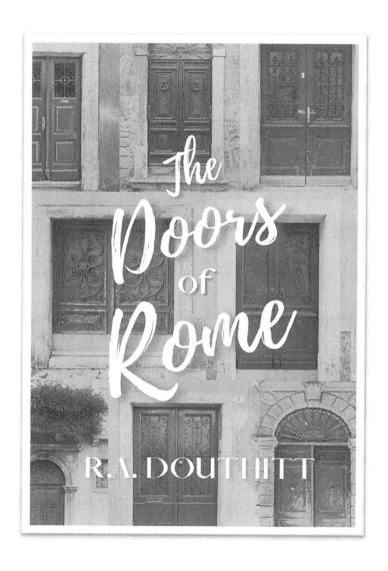

The Doors of Rome

R.A. DOUTHITT

The Doors of Rome is a work of fiction. References to real people, events, establishments, organizations, or locales are intended only to provide a sense of authenticity and are used fictitiously. All other characters, incidents, and dialogue are drawn from the author's imagination.

Printed in the U.S.A.

Other books by R. A. Douthitt:

Fantasy Adventure
The Dragon Forest
The Dragon Forest II: Son of the Oath
The Dragon Forest III: The King of Illiath
The Elves of Vulgaard: The White Wolf
The Elves of Vulgaard: Dragon Games
The Elves of Vulgaard: Dragon Riders
Here There Be Dragons Coloring Book

Mystery Thriller
The Children Under the Ice
The Children in the Garden
The Children of Manor House

Contemporary
The Cafeteria Club
First Christmas at War
The Road to Home
The Fine Art of Love
Journeys of Forgiveness

Nonfiction
Seek Him Prayer Journal: 25 Prayers of HOPE

DEDICATION

To Scott.
Thank you for our time in Rome.

ACKNOWLEDGEMENTS

I'd like to acknowledge my editor for her excellent work and
unending patience.

I thank my dear friend, Dana McNeely, for her helpful feedback as
a beta reader. Her insights have made this a much better story.

I thank my husband for our time in Rome together and for
patiently waiting for me while I ran the 2018 Rome Marathon.
Seeing you at the finish line made it all worthwhile.

You are an inspiration to me, and I thank you for 35 years of happy
endings.

Lastly, I thank God for seeing me, hearing me, and blessing me
with His presence daily.

CHAPTER ONE

Doors open.
Doors close.
That's what doors do.

To open a door without knowing what's on the other side requires courage.
To close a door that never should have been opened requires faith.

∽

Photography contest. Enter today.

Millie remembered well the day she read those words online.

She glanced in the mirror and inspected her hair, pulled back into a ponytail. The gray at her temples reminded her of her age. *It's now or never, Millie . . .*

"Heading out now?" asked Sister Margaret, approaching Millie.

She spun around. "Yes. I'm meeting a friend for a quick run."

"Enjoy this break in the weather before the rain returns." Sister Margaret leaned down to glance out the nearby window of the homeless shelter.

"I will. See you tomorrow." Millie handed the nun her apron.

"You are such a blessing, Millie. The Lord appreciates your faithfulness in serving the poor here at our shelter."

"It's my pleasure," Millie said, and she meant it.

Bustling down the street like a leaf on the breeze, Millie waved to strangers as they passed by. One lady pushed a stroller with a toddler inside, who was munching on what looked like dried cereal.

"Hello there," Millie said to the child. He grinned back with red cheeks, round like apples.

As mom and child passed, the toddler's pacifier plopped out and bounced on the ground.

"Oh, miss!" Millie shouted after her. "Your child dropped this."

With a grateful smile, the mother took the pacifier. "Oh, thank you. You're so kind."

"No problem." Millie patted the boy's head of tight blonde curls. "Have a great day!" With a wave, Millie jogged off to meet her friend.

Busyness kept Millie sane. Running kept her trim. And photography kept her happy. The clouds parted to reveal a glorious blue sky. Millie removed her phone and took several photos of the cloud formations and the sunlight bathing the flowerbeds along the sidewalks.

Lovely. She sighed and posted it on her social media page with the message, "So glad for the break from dreary rainy weather."

Edith Engram stood on the corner, waiting for Millie. She pointed to her watch.

"Yes, I know I'm late." Millie held out her hands. "Forgive me." She bent down to grab some trash off the grass and tossed it into the nearby trash bin. "But I have some news."

"What's that? You have news? Did something newsworthy happen at the homeless shelter?" Edith Engram smirked. The bestselling author of suspense and romance novels in bookstores and library shelves all over the world loved teasing her best friend Millie about her simple and uncomplicated life.

"No, silly." Millie put a cap on and tucked her bangs

underneath it.

"I'm just glad you showed up." Edith sighed.

Millie's wide smile lit up her face.

Edith turned to her. "You're in a chipper mood."

"I am. I have big news and—"

Edith sighed. "Not me. I need this run today."

"Don't worry. Our run will be therapeutic for you." Millie offered her a brave smile.

Edith winced. "But painful therapy." She bent down to adjust the laces on her running shoes then tucked her short, snowy white hair underneath her cap and faced her friend. "Your cheeks are red. You look flushed. What's going on, Mill? What's your big news?"

"A photography contest." Millie removed a magazine clipping from the pouch of her running belt and thrust it at Edith.

"What? A contest?" Edith asked.

"Look." Millie jiggled the clipping she had seen months earlier. "What do you think?"

Edith's eyes darted back and forth as she read it. "Great. I think you should enter."

"I did." She hoped her wide smile would give it away. Millie couldn't help but smile.

"You did?" Edith grinned. "Look at you being adventurous and bold. Good for you, Mill. Did you tell Walt yet?"

"Walter," Millie replied. "And not yet."

"Better get on with it." Edith stretched her back. "I'd hate for you to enter and then face his disappointment about it. Especially if by chance you win. Just think of the look on his face if—"

"I won."

Edith stopped stretching and jerked toward Millie. "You what?"

After hopping up and down a bit, Millie nodded. "I won. Can you believe it?" She shoved the clipping at Edith again.

"Me. I actually won! And look at the prize, Edith. Just look at it."

With wide eyes and a shocked expression, Edith did read it. "A trip . . . to Rome?"

"Can you imagine?" Millie clapped her hands at the thought. "An all-expenses-paid trip."

All her adult life, Millie had yearned for adventure. She had never traveled outside the country before. In fact, she had never traveled anywhere because—*No. Don't go backwards. Stay in the present,* she told herself. *Celebrate today!*

"An all-expenses-paid trip to Rome . . ." Edith sighed and closed her eyes. "Ah, Rome. It's been decades since I've been there. Went on a research trip for a romance novel some time ago. You'll love it."

"I'm . . . gobsmacked." Millie laughed.

"I'm not." Edith crossed her arms. "I know you're that talented, my friend. Known it all along. This is amazing. I'm so happy for you." She reached out and hugged Millie's neck.

"It's a dream come true." When they parted from the hug, Millie folded the magazine clipping and carefully placed it into her runner's belt as if it were made of rare and precious parchment. It was rare and precious to her. Zipping the pouch closed, she patted it as though thanking it for the joy it brought her. "Me and five other winners will—"

"Five other winners and you," Edith corrected.

Millie sighed and tossed her head back. "Will you ever stop being a writer?"

"Never. Now go on."

"Five other winners *and I* will travel to Rome to take photographs for a calendar coming out next year." She glanced upward. "I can't imagine the scenery. The fountains. The ruins. The food."

"You've Googled Rome, have you?" Edith giggled.

Millie nodded and clasped her hands together, fluttering

her eyes like a girl in love.

"But . . . you haven't told Walt yet?" Edith curled her lip. "When are you going to tell ol' Walt?"

"Walter," Millie corrected. She slowly exhaled. "Tonight."

"Ah . . ." Edith raised an eyebrow. "What's the plan? I know you have one. You always do."

"Well, I'm making his favorite meal, a chocolate cake for dessert, and then I'll tell him when he's nice and satisfied."

"I thought he had a work meeting tonight."

"He does, but he said he'll be home in time for dinner." Millie rubbed her hands together. "It'll work out."

Edith turned and started to jog off. "If you say so."

Millie knew what Edith meant.

Walter wasn't known for taking adventures. Careful and cautious, he calculated his every move in life, love, and business. One thing Edith often complained to Millie about was Walter's lack of spontaneity.

It never bothered Millie before. In fact, Walter's steadiness always made her feel safe. She supposed that was why she married him.

A thunderclap from above startled her as she ran.

Mother once called her desperate for marrying in her late thirties, but Millie called it wisdom.

Walter was safe, and Millie felt safe with him.

But as she ran, she thought more about her life with Walter. After fourteen years of marriage, safe wasn't working anymore. She and Walter were getting older, and life was passing them by.

A few raindrops hit her exposed arms.

She sensed what Walter's answer would have been had she told him about the photography contest and entering it.

"Absolutely not," he'd say. "We can't afford it."

Then she would have explained how it didn't cost anything to enter.

"You'll never win," he'd say.

But I did win. Millie's heart skipped a beat as she ran faster.

Next, she would have to explain what an all-expenses-paid trip meant, to which Walter would have replied that nothing is ever free.

So not telling him that she had entered the contest seemed the wisest move. She knew once she won the contest, she would explain that she had to go, and he would have to come with her.

He'd go with me, right? The raindrops spattering the running path interrupted her thoughts.

She slowed down to jog alongside Edith, doing her best to ignore Edith's descriptions of Walter that came across as offhanded and harsh.

Millie imagined every word of Walter's response and facial expressions as he spoke. She knew she'd have to be prepared with a defense for her actions and detail just why he had to come with her, no matter what the cost.

Besides, not coming with her would prove much more costly.

He just *had* to come with her to Rome.

Her eyes welled with tears. In her heart, Millie suspected it was their last chance to rekindle the tiny flame left in their marriage.

"Are you even listening to me?" Edith interrupted.

"No. And just so you know, if Walter refuses to go, you're coming with me."

"What?"

Millie sprinted down the path with Edith shouting after her.

The dining room table was set. Lace tablecloth, Walter's

mother's china, crystal wine glasses, and Millie's grandmother's silverware completed the scene. Lit candles rested on the credenza to create a more romantic mood.

Using candles would please Walter, because it meant saving money on their electric bill.

She glanced at herself in the mirror by the kitchen. Tall and trim, Millie looked a good ten years younger than her fifty-two years. Many people told her so. Still, she longed for those younger days. Her wide shoulders aligned with her wide hips. But her once slim waist had thickened. She sighed in bereavement, remembering her slim waist.

The door creaked open. "Millie?" Walter shouted.

"In here, dear. Dinner's ready," she called from the kitchen.

He plopped the keys onto the table near the door and hung his wet coat on the hook. The rain outside had slowed down a bit.

"Cold outside? It's so rainy for March, don't you think?" Millie asked as she placed the pot roast onto the serving platter. His favorite dish. The heavenly aroma made her smile. *This will warm him up.*

"You'll never guess what happened." His voice raised.

"Something wonderful, I'm thinking." Millie came into the dining room carrying the roast and set it on the dining table. She was tempted to say, "Ta da!" at the lovely setting that was worthy of being photographed for House Beautiful magazine.

"Yes. Something absolutely wonderful happened today." He pecked her cheek, then sat down, whipping the linen napkin off the plate, snapping it, and placing it onto his lap. "I mean, absolutely perfect."

Relieved to see him in such a good mood, Millie sat down at the opposite side and rested her elbows on the table. "You mean as perfect as this dinner?" She wiggled her eyebrows up and down as her mouth formed a playful grin.

"Huh? What?" Walter glanced at the feast before him.

"Oh, yes. This is wonderful. Smells fantastic too. Pot roast. My fav—"

"Favorite, I know." Millie winked and gently placed her linen napkin onto her lap, folded her hands, and bowed for Walter's dinner prayer, thanking the good Lord for all His provisions.

Amen.

She handed him her plate, and he served the roast, a dinner roll, and a scoop of salad as he explained in detail about his day.

"And the candlelight?" Millie asked as she watched him salt the roast and butter his roll.

"Yes, brilliant. Will save us money on the electric bill. We should light candles more often. Oh, and we'll light a fire tonight and turn off the furnace."

"Of course, dear."

He gestured wildly as he spoke. "The chief corporate officer came to visit the bank just to congratulate me on the new system of data gathering that I developed. Can you believe it?" He pointed to his chest. "He came to thank me. *Me.*" A monumental moment for Walter, indeed.

Speaking between bites, Walter's pitch rose. Millie patiently waited for him to finish telling the story about his day.

Her plate was clean by the time he finished.

"Dessert?" She raced to the kitchen before he could answer.

"What? Uh, sure," he said from the dining room.

Millie re-entered with the delicious chocolate cake atop the crystal cake serving dish his mother had left them. "Ta da!" She managed to sneak the exclamation into the conversation after all. "What do you think?"

"Chocolate cake?" He dabbed the corners of his mouth with his napkin and stood to assist her. "Why, I am speechless. What's the special occasion?"

Millie returned to her seat and watched him slice the cake

for her, thinking of how she would bring up the subject. "Well, I have some big news of my own."

"You do?" He set a slice of cake onto a small dish and handed it to her.

"I do. Don't act so surprised." Millie giggled.

His eyes widened as he sat. "Oh, I'm sorry. I didn't mean to—"

"It's all right. I'm only kidding." She took a bite of the sweet cake. But everyone knows there is always a hint of truth behind every joke, no matter how trite.

"Go on. What's the big news?"

With that question still lingering in the air, Millie hopped up and pulled open a drawer in the dining room hutch. Inside was a file folder containing the photographs she had entered along with the notification letter. With trembling hands, she held it for a moment, remembering the excitement of the day she had read the letter. She didn't want anything to ruin that significant moment.

She turned to face Walter. *No matter what he says or does. Don't let anything ruin this for you.*

She handed him the file folder.

"What's this?" he asked.

"Open it." Her face was adorned with the widest smile she could muster since their wedding day.

He carefully opened the folder, almost as if something would pop out. "Oh, your photographs. Yes. I've seen these. They are lovely." He handed her the folder. "I thought it was a card congratulating me or something."

Millie frowned and gently urged him to continue inspecting the folder. "No, Walter. Keep looking."

He did and removed the stack of photos to the table next to his dinner plate. She watched his face as read the letter.

He furrowed his brow and slowly looked up at his wife. "What? What is this now?"

Millie pulled out the chair next to him and sat with hands folded as if in prayer. Millie did pray inside.

17

She prayed to the good Lord that Walter would understand.

"Walter, dear. It's a letter of notification about a contest I entered. See here?" She pointed to the heading.

He reread the letter. "A contest?"

Millie tapped the stack of photos. "Yes. A photography contest." She hopped up and down on the chair, waiting for him to see the last paragraph.

"Ah, now I understand. You should have explained it a little better before you—"

"I won." Millie just couldn't wait any longer.

His body jerked. "What?"

"See here?" She pointed to the last paragraph. "I won!"

Silence.

"Can you believe it?" Millie stood, gathered the photographs, and grabbed the letter from his hand before he could crinkle it up. "I'm just as shocked as you are."

He sat back with his mouth open. "I am shocked. I mean, congratulations, Millie."

"Thank you, dear." She carefully returned the letter and file folder to the drawer, then began clearing the table.

"That's . . . that's quite an accomplishment." He remained seated.

"Again, that tone of surprise?" She managed a fake giggle, but she was serious.

"Well, yes. I mean, since I've known you, you've never done such an extemporaneous thing as enter a contest." He chuckled, and Millie did her best to remain calm. "Or anything like that."

She set the plates onto the kitchen counter and took deep breaths. "I know. Isn't it wonderful? I feel like I'm growing as a person . . . as a photographer." She returned to the dining room and sat by him again, studying his shocked face.

"And you won?" He stared at the place where his plate used to be.

"Yes, dear. I won." Millie reached for his hand and

squeezed it. "I, along with five other people, won the main prize."

"Which is what?" When his eyes lit up, she knew exactly what he was thinking. Prize money.

"Well, it isn't money, so to speak."

A frown appeared on his face. "Oh, camera equipment?"

She poured more wine into his glass. "No. Much better than that, dear."

"Really?" He took the glass and leaned in. "What is it?"

Millie clasped her hands together again with joy. "Ready?"

He nodded.

"An all-expenses-paid trip to Rome!" She clapped her hands. "Can you believe it, Walter? We're going to Rome, Italy. The two of us. Can you picture it? Us walking through the streets of Rome?" The images she had seen on the computer appeared in her mind, and goosebumps rose on her arms. She rubbed away the chills.

A look of horror came to Walter's face.

Oh, Walter.

Since Millie had known him, Walter's focus in life had been to save as much money as possible for retirement.

Retirement.

That word sounded so final, so permanent. So stagnant.

"No, we can't go to Rome."

"What? Why not?"

"We'll travel when we're retired," Walter said as he stood and headed to the kitchen. "You know that."

"But why can't we go now?" She blew out the candles and turned on the dining room light. "They leave in three weeks."

"Three weeks?" Walter said. The sound of crashing dishes alarmed her.

"Yes. I already have our passports ready and everything. We are all set to go." She helped him clean up the broken dish from the kitchen floor.

"We can't possibly afford to go to—"

"All-expenses-paid trip, Walter." Millie tossed the broken pieces into the trash.

"No, I can't sit on an airplane for six or seven hours." He wiped off his hands with the dish towel.

"Two first class seats." Facing him, she was prepared for any rejection. "They'll pamper us, and the time will fly by. You'll see."

"No." He stormed past Millie. "We can't go. Not now."

"Walter . . ." She followed him. "I don't see why we can't go to—"

"I'm up for a promotion, Millie." He turned and grabbed her shoulders. "A big promotion. Don't you understand?" His eyes were wide with excitement. "To go away now while the Chief Operating Officer is inspecting us is insane."

But not to go is dangerous . . . She shook her head and pulled away, wilting like a parched plant. "I understand." Of course, she understood. She always understood.

He patted her shoulders. "You'll see. I'll get this promotion and save our money. And soon, we'll travel the world once we—"

"Retire." Millie's shoulders sank, and she turned away.

"Exactly." Walter removed his tie. "You'll see."

As she made her way back to the kitchen, something inside her tugged at her middle and prevented her from moving. She clenched her fists. *No. Walter makes me feel safe, but I'm tired of safety. There's no adventure in safety.* Her heart pounded and made her dizzy. Walter had become blind and deaf to her needs. But she had allowed this to happen. Millie had allowed herself to blend into the background and disappear.

Well, no more.

Spinning around to face him, she inhaled courage. "No."

Walter picked up the newspaper from his chair, right where Millie placed it every day. "Excuse me?"

"No, Walter." Her eyes filled with tears. "I don't

understand."

He made the "tsk" sound with his mouth and held out his hands. "Millie, be reasonable."

"I'm afraid, Walter." Her nails dug into her palms.

"Afraid? Of what?" He winced and half chuckled.

"I'm afraid of being left behind. I'm afraid of waiting too long. I'm afraid that if we put off living our lives, we'll have missed out." She swallowed back tears, trying not to weep. "I'm afraid if we wait until we retire, we'll never have an adventure."

"Oh, please," he said as he plopped down onto the chair. "Don't be so dramatic. We'll be fine."

"What about Charlie?" Millie hugged herself as she thought of Edith's late husband. "He put off many trips with Edith until the time was right. And then he passed away suddenly."

Walter glanced out the window. "He had heart problems. I'm fine. We're both healthy."

"But my point is, you just never know." Millie rushed toward him. "We aren't guaranteed tomorrow, Walter. All we have is right now."

He exhaled and rolled his eyes. "Millie, I've waited so long for a chance like this. A chance to earn real money." He stood and slammed his fist into his palm. "I'm up against Harvard grads and other college boys. Yet the COO is looking at me for this position, Millie. Me." With intensity in his eyes, he pointed to his chest. "It's too good an opportunity to miss out on. I just can't leave work right now." He patted her again as he made his way to the stairs.

"I'm going, Walter." Millie's eyes followed him. "I'm going to Rome with or without you."

Walter stopped mid-step up the stairs. Without looking at her, he muttered something under his breath.

"Please come with me, dear. Please." Millie grabbed onto the stair rail with a white-knuckle grip. "I know your work is important."

He remained still, avoiding her eyes.

"But our marriage is important too." Her voice quivered. "Don't you see?"

Silence.

"I'm afraid, Walter. I'm afraid that this trip is our last chance. *This trip* is too good of an opportunity to miss out on."

But Walter continued up the stairs, slowly ripping apart Millie's heart with each step he took.

CHAPTER 2

Two days later, Millie spotted Edith sipping coffee at her favorite café in town. The rain had ended, and the sun shone brightly, causing everyone to venture outside again.

As she approached her friend, Millie anticipated all the sarcastic responses Edith would have to Walter's reaction. She'd badmouth Walter, remind her of his stubbornness, mock his frugal ways.

But Millie didn't care. Today she needed to be with someone who was on her side. She needed to tell her friend the news.

"Hello." Millie stood before the table wearing her favorite cotton floral print dress and a lavender cardigan sweater over her shoulders. The way she gripped her purse strap, one might think she was afraid it might be stolen.

"Millie! You look nice. Your favorite dress…I take it things went well?" Edith grinned.

But Millie didn't smile. "I needed to wear it. I needed the confidence."

"Uh oh. Here . . ." Edith scooted out the chair from underneath the table. "Sit! Tell me what happened."

"He's not going." Millie sat, gripping her purse even

tighter to her body like a shield.

Edith frowned and leaned back. "Oh no." She shook her head. "I suspected as much but had hoped deep down inside he'd change his mind."

Millie wept in her hands. "Oh, Edith."

Scootching closer to her friend, Edith rubbed Millie's back in a comforting way. "Now, Millie. Come on, girl. Stay strong. We'll get through this."

"I don't know what I'm going to do. I fell asleep on the couch last night, and when I woke this morning, Walter had already gone to work."

"I'm sorry."

She lowered her hands and wiped the tears off her face. "He didn't even say goodbye. Why can't he understand?" Millie shook her head. "I seriously have no idea what to do."

"Yes, you do." Edith scowled. "You know exactly what you're going to do."

Millie sniffled. "I do?"

"Yes, you do." Edith handed her a napkin to wipe her eyes. "Say it."

Millie tilted her head. "No. I don't know what—"

"Say it."

"I don't know—"

"Yes, you do." Edith leaned in closer. "Say it."

"I'm . . ."

"Yes?" Edith touched Millie's hand.

"I'm . . . I'm going to Rome."

"That's it!" Edith leaned onto the table and stared at Millie with piercing blue eyes. "That's it exactly."

"I'm going to Rome?" Millie smiled. "I, Millie Devonshire, am going to Rome!"

A man and woman at a nearby table turned around.

Millie pointed to herself. "I'm going to Rome."

The man smiled. "Good for you. You'll love it."

Edith chuckled and glanced upward with glossy eyes. "Ah, Rome. So lovely. The sights, sounds, food and wine."

She ran her hand along the tabletop. "It's magical."

"And you're coming with me."

Edith chortled.

"I'm serious. You can conduct research for your next book while I'm photographing the city." Millie waved the waitress over and ordered coffee.

"I don't think so." Edith shook her head. Millie knew Edith had to write the book the publisher requested. But Edith was successful enough to write whatever she wanted.

"Yep. You're famous enough to tell your publisher what you want to write." Millie nodded. "And you are writing a romance set in Rome."

Edith's mouth dropped open to say something, but she hesitated.

Millie laughed.

"What's so funny?"

"I remember how shocked I was when you moved back home to North Carolina after making millions by selling novels and having them made into movies."

"Why?" Edith tilted her head.

"I figured you would settle in L.A. or New York, but move back home and buy a ranch? And not just the ranch but the whole town?"

Edith shrugged her shoulder.

"Oh, come on. You're a rebel. You always do what no one ever expects." Millie nudged her friend. "You've been to Rome before. You can show me the sights. Otherwise, I'll get lost—you know that."

Edith's eyes narrowed as though studying Millie. "I do have another romance novel inside me just begging to come out."

"Just tell your publisher you're heading to Italy for research." Millie nudged her. "I don't know Rome like you do. I need you there."

Edith remained silent for a few uncomfortable moments.

"You're so brave, Edith. I've always admired you for

that." Millie smiled. "I remember how you once told me that you always wanted to buy Hopkins, fix it up, and make it a tourist attraction with bed and breakfasts, a French bakery, and a museum dedicated to her life. You did just that."

"Remember when that horror film was made in town a few years back?" Edith chuckled.

"Filmed in the woods right behind our house." Millie giggled. "Now the tourists love the area, especially at Halloween. Walter, on the other hand, hates all the traffic every fall. He blames you, you know."

Millie didn't hate it, though. She loved the excitement.

"Whaddaya say, huh?" Millie smiled widely and took the coffee from the waitress. "You're the adventurous one."

"I could use a break." That faraway look returned to Edith's face. "I suppose I could tell my publisher I'm researching for a new romance. I'm tired of writing suspense."

"See? Now you're talking."

"You write one New York Times bestselling suspense novel, and everyone just assumes that's all you want to write. Now that I have fifty of them published, it's time for a change." Edith pounded the table in protest. "I'll just tell them that I'm heading to Rome to write a romance, and that's that."

Millie hopped up and down in her seat. "Yay."

"Besides. I enjoy writing love stories. It's been a long time since I published a romantic novel. There's just something refreshing about it. And it doesn't get more romantic than Rome in spring." She spread her hands through the air as if painting the sky. "I see a story of a young girl searching for adventure in Italy. An artist, perhaps. She finds herself stuck in Rome, where she encounters a gorgeous Italian boy willing to show her the sights." Edith winked. "If you know what I mean."

"Sounds wonderful." Millie lifted her shoulders. "So . . . you're all in?"

"I'm in."

Millie shrieked with joy and clapped her hands. "I'm tickled pink. We leave in three weeks. I've already started packing and will need to buy some—"

"On one condition," Edith said as she scrolled on her phone.

"One condition? What condition is that?" Millie leaned over.

Holding out her smartphone, Edith smiled widely. "You're going to love this."

Straining to read the screen, Millie shrugged and took a sip of her coffee. "The Maratona di Roma? And?"

"I'll go with you if you will run the Rome Marathon with me."

Millie spit out her coffee, then covered her mouth. "What?" She coughed and used a napkin to wipe the spittle off her chin. "Are you serious?"

"Yes." Edith set down the phone and crossed her arms. "Completely serious. I've always wanted to try a marathon, and well, here's my chance. *Our* chance."

Millie dabbed her mouth. "Edith, come on . . ."

"When you mentioned Rome the other day, I wondered. So I looked it up, and sure enough. There's a marathon in April."

"But a marathon in Rome?" Millie crinkled up her face.

"Why not?" Edith laughed. "It's fate."

"There's no way we can run a marathon." Millie shook her head. "Do you know what it takes to finish a marathon?"

"Running. A lot of it. I think we can do it."

"It takes months of training . . ."

"We run every day."

"To build up endurance."

"We have endurance."

"Please." Millie rolled her eyes. "We run three miles here and there and then six miles on the weekends. That's not nearly enough training for a marathon."

"Millie." Edith turned in her seat to face her. "You've

been a runner for decades. You've run many marathons. You'll just rely on muscle memory."

"Muscle memory." Millie rubbed her forehead and chuckled. "Edith, I haven't run a marathon since I was in my twenties. I'm fifty-two now. And you're fifty-six, for crying out loud." She stood and grabbed her purse.

Edith handed the waitress some cash and followed after Millie. "Wait! I'm totally serious."

"If you don't want to go with me, just say it." Millie stomped off toward her car. "Don't make these ridiculous demands because you don't want to go."

"I do want to go." Edith reached out and grabbed Millie's forearm, stopping her mid-stride. "And we can do it. Look, you want adventure, right? You want to see Rome? What better way to see Rome than running through the city streets?" She ran her hand through the air again. "We start at the Colosseum."

Millie's eyes twinkled. "The Colosseum?"

"Yes! Then we run by the ruins, the many fountains, and even Vatican City," Edith said in a dreamy voice. "And through the fashion district." She held out her phone again. "Just look at the photos from last year's race."

"Oh, great." Millie rolled her eyes and searched for her key fob. "That's just what I need. All sweaty and stinky in running shorts, running by all those millionaires wearing Versace and Armani and sipping their cappuccinos. Are you kidding me?"

"It'll be magical." Edith grabbed Millie's hand and squeezed it. "You wanted adventure, deary. What greater adventure than this? Running through Rome . . ."

Staring into Edith's penetrating eyes, Millie was drawn in. "Adventure . . . running through Rome . . . but can we do it, Edith? Twenty-six miles of running?"

"Hey, if we need to walk, we'll walk. No big deal." Edith hugged her friend. "I'll take care of everything. I'll pay for the registration. You'll need a doctor's signature on the form, and voila! We are ready to go."

"Well, I'll need new shoes and a runner's belt and—"

"Millie, I'll take care of all that." Edith spun around to head to her car. "This will be the adventure you've been wanting all your life."

"All my life," Millie said in a small voice. "I wish Walter would be there to experience it with me."

"Hey. He made his choice. Now you must make yours. Okay?"

"You're right. It's my choice." Millie raised her chin. "My choice is to do this."

"All the way!" Edith used the keypad on her phone. "Now to call my publisher and tell her I'm writing a romance set in Rome."

"Will they let you do it?"

"Hon, when you've sold over 10 million books for them, they let you do what you want, my friend." Edith pursed her lips and held the phone up to her mouth. "Hello, Darla?" She waved goodbye to Millie and walked off. "I've got some interesting news for you . . ."

Millie watched her friend walk off for a moment, then sat inside her car, listening to soft music playing. *This is really happening.* She smiled and surveyed herself in the rearview mirror. The chestnut hair remained thick, but a few wrinkles under her eyes and around her mouth reminded her of her age. Still, she was healthy and strong. *I still can't believe it. I guess I won't believe it until I am standing on the streets of Rome, looking at the Colosseum through my camera lens.* She brushed aside her bangs and smiled. *And running through the streets of Rome.* She giggled, but the thought of leaving Walter behind made her smile disappear. Her shoulders sank as sorrow filled her insides. "No," she said to the mirror. "Don't let the what-ifs ruin this for you."

She started the car. *You're going to Rome.*

∞

At the airport terminal, Edith tapped her foot on the tile floor.

"Nervous?" Millie asked.

"It's been a while since I've flown overseas." Edith sighed. "Hanging over the Atlantic Ocean in a metal tube makes me nervous."

"We'll be fine." Millie hugged her shoulder. "We'll be in first class! I still can't believe this is really happening."

"Now boarding Flight 1131 first class for Rome, Italy," the announcement came.

"Here we go . . ." Edith motioned for Millie to follow her.

Once seated on the plane, Millie sank into the soft leather seats. "Wow. This is amazing."

"Would you like a mimosa?" the attendant asked. Her perfect hair and makeup made Millie shrink a bit.

"Uh, no thank—"

"Yes. Two mimosas, please," Edith interrupted. She playfully slugged Millie's arm. "You are going to relax and enjoy yourself. Have a mimosa. Have two, for crying out loud. This is a once-in-a-lifetime experience. Enjoy it."

Millie exhaled. "You're right. You're absolutely right." She took the glass from the attendant and sipped the champagne and orange juice. "Delicious."

"Cheers." Edith raised her glass. "To our adventure in Rome."

The glasses clanked together, making Millie giggle and cover her mouth with embarrassment.

Before they knew it, the plane was in the air. Millie gripped the chair arms during the turbulence.

"It won't last long. Only until we rise above the clouds. You'll see." Edith smiled.

To pass the time, Millie removed a journal from her backpack and started writing.

"Journaling your adventure? Good for you." Edith sipped her mimosa.

"No. Just writing a letter to Walter."

Edith jerked around. "A letter to Walter?" She crinkled her nose.

Millie nodded as she wrote. "I told him I would write, and I will. Once we get to the hotel and I can use my laptop, I'll write him emails each day, detailing what occurred throughout the day so he feels he's with me."

Edith smiled. "Why don't you just call him?"

"I did. Three times. I left three voicemail messages and three text messages." Millie looked up from her journal. "What?"

"Nothing. I just think that's sweet."

Millie sat back. "I know you don't like Walter, but he's a very—"

"I like Walt."

"Walter."

"I just think he needs to relax a little. Let go and enjoy life before it's gone, you know?" Edith sipped more mimosa.

"I know. I think so too." Millie glanced out the window. "I reminded him about Charlie."

"Hmm." Edith shifted in her seat.

"It was no use. He's set in his ways. I suppose I am, too." Millie sighed. "But he makes me feel safe."

"Safe is good."

"And secure." Mille smiled. "He's a lot like my . . ." Her voice trailed off.

"Father?"

Millie nodded. Her father's hardened face appeared in her mind. There he was, standing by the car door and slamming it closed. Her body shivered from the sound and his scowling face as he stormed over to her. "Except my father never made me feel safe."

"Then how is Walt like him?"

"Walter is frugal and practical like my father was." Millie chuckled. "At first, I really liked that about him."

"I suppose we all marry someone like our fathers." Edith

sighed as she studied the champagne flute in her hand. "Charlie was a lot like my mother."

"Really? I didn't know that."

"She always had to be the life of the party, and so did Charlie. I suppose that's why they got along so well." Edith chuckled as if remembering something.

"You ladies headed somewhere special?" a man across the aisle asked.

"Rome," Millie replied.

Edith nudged her. "Shh. Don't go telling total strangers our business."

"Oh, he's harmless." Millie leaned over Edith. "We're running in the Rome Marathon."

His eyes widened, and his mouth dropped open. "No kiddin'. That's incredible—two older ladies like—"

"I beg your pardon." Edith shot him a harsh look.

"I mean . . ." He held out his hands as though directing someone to stop. "I didn't mean it that way. It's just that you both don't look like typical marathoners is all I'm saying."

Edith smirked and sipped more mimosa. "I suppose." She pointed to Millie. "But Millie here has run marathons before."

"Well . . ." Millie glanced upward with embarrassment. "A very long time ago."

"She made it to the Olympic trials." Edith nodded with pride.

"Seriously?" a woman in front of them turned in her seat.

"Again . . . a very long time ago." Millie laughed.

"When she was in college." Edith provided clarification.

"No foolin'? That's amazing." The man across the aisle held out his hand. "Name's Ted. I'm flying to Rome on business."

Millie stretched across Edith's lap to shake Ted's hand. "I'm Millie, and this is Edith."

"Pleasure to meet you." Ted offered a smile. "What do you do, ma'am?" he asked Edith.

She finished her mimosa so quickly, she almost belched

before answering. "I'm a novelist."

Millie giggled again.

"What books do you write?" The woman in front stood and leaned on the back of her seat.

"She's the best-selling author Edith Engram." Millie jabbed her thumb at her friend.

The woman's eyes widened, and then she reached down to retrieve a paperback book. "You mean . . ." She turned it over and studied the author photo, then returned her gaze to Edith, who did her best to avert the stare.

"It's you!" The woman smacked her husband, who was reading his own book. "Harry! It's her. My favorite author!"

Others turned in their seats to see what the commotion was about.

"Oh my goodness," the woman said, placing her hand over her heart. "I cannot believe this. I have read everything you've ever written. I have all your books. I brought about ten of them with me. The Seaside Murder series . . . the Lighthouse Mysteries series . . . the Doors of India series . . . I have them all at home. And here you are. In person. Oh my! I think I'm going to—"

"Calm down," Harry muttered from his seat.

The woman thrust her novel at Edith. "Can you please sign my book?"

Millie giggled under her breath. She knew Edith hated such attention.

Edith cleared her throat. "Ahem, sure."

The woman handed her a pen and the paperback.

"What's your name, dear?"

"Susan Miller." She clasped her hands together like a little girl about to see Santa Claus. "Can you write a personal note or something?"

Edith exhaled and raised an eyebrow.

Millie knew that look. Edith was irritated.

"Certainly." She scribbled something, then signed the book with her usual autograph. "Here you go."

"Stay out of trouble. Edith Engram," Susan Miller read. Her husband snickered.

Susan turned around and sat down with a confused look on her face. Millie couldn't stop giggling.

"What?" Edith asked.

"Nothing." Millie giggled until she snorted. "I don't know why you became a writer if you don't like to meet your readers."

"I like to meet my readers." Edith crossed her arms. "At book events or conferences, but not on vacation," she whispered. "Oh, miss." She waved over the attendant.

"Another mimosa, ma'am?"

"Yes, please." Edith jiggled her champagne flute in the air.

CHAPTER 3

When night fell and everyone was asleep, Millie reached up and turned on the small light above her. She removed her journal and wrote to Walter.

Dear Walter-

So far, the trip has been ordinary, and I'm thankful for that. We made our flight on time, got seated in first class right away, and even talked with the other passengers. We met Harry and Susan, a married couple headed to Rome for the wedding of a friend's daughter. Susan is a huge fan of Edith's books. She got an autograph out of the old bird. I was impressed. Edith's getting soft in her old age. Or maybe it was the mimosa? Ha ha!

We met Ted, a businessman from Texas, and June and Marty, a couple on their honeymoon. They are so young and dreamy-eyed for each other.

Remember those days?

Everyone is asleep now, so I thought I'd write you a note so you know I am thinking of you and you are with me. I miss you. I wish you were here next to me instead of Edith. Not that I don't appreciate Edith coming with me, but I'd rather have you here.

First class is everything I imagined it would be. We had mimosas, croissants, and jelly. Fresh strawberries and Danish. I had roasted chicken for dinner and a freshly baked brownie for dessert. Edith opted for the cheesecake. Anyway, we are eating like royalty! The seats are large and very soft.

I hope your time with the CCO went well. I know we didn't say much to each other before I left, but I just wanted you to know that I am not angry with you at all. I kept away from you because I sensed that you are angry with me. I know one day you'll understand why I had to go on this trip. It's an adventure that God blessed me—us—with. My prayer is that someday you'll see it that way.

Love, Millie

Millie closed the journal and held it close to her heart for a bit, almost hoping that magically, Walter would reply. She glanced out the window at the full moon high in the navy-blue sky. All she could hear was the nasal droning coming from Ted across the aisle.

Pillowy clouds spread across the horizon like a blanket that Millie had wrapped herself in as a little child.

A little child.

She shivered at the memory.

"Do you need a blanket?" the attendant asked.

"Sure." Millie reached up and took the downy blanket. Spreading it out, she reclined her seat and covered her chilled body—chilled from painful childhood memories and not the temperature of the plane's cabin.

As she rested in the warmth of the blanket, Millie thought more about Walter. In many ways, he was like her father. He had never been cruel and controlling like her father had been. The weight of Walter's past debt pressed upon him, even though they both worked hard to pay off that debt. The fear of losing everything controlled his life. Millie knew this. But Walter was never abusive like her father had been.

Walter was kind and considerate. He was just too frugal and cautious. Overly cautious.

With closed eyes, Millie silently prayed a prayer of thankfulness to God that Walter was responsible and safe. But she also thanked God that Walter was not exactly like her father.

Her father.

A memory of her college running days made her shiver, so she pulled the blanket tightly around her legs and torso.

"Running is ridiculous," her father had yelled. "You should be working or married and having children."

Twenty-year-old Millie stood on the grassy field in the center of the track that early June morning at Northern New Mexico College. Susanna, her running coach, stood before her. "Ignore him."

Millie nodded and stretched her arms across her chest, imagining herself in the upcoming race.

"I told your mother this." Her father paced back and forth in the bleachers opposite Millie. "What can running provide? A living?" He laughed. "I doubt it."

Susanna turned to face him. "Do you mind? We're trying to get ready for a meet!"

"Don't." Young Millie took her coach's arm. "It's not worth it. He won't listen to you anyway."

"You just focus on the race, got it?" Susanna squeezed Millie's shoulders.

"Got it."

Millie shut her eyes and remembered that race. It was an Olympic qualifier.

"Runners ready?" the announcer asked.

At the start, young Millie could feel the weight of her father's stare on her back. *Brush it off, Mil. Just brush it off.* She dangled her arms at her sides to loosen up her tight shoulders. Before her was the track that she would lap twelve times before heading out onto the streets to run the rest of the marathon, culminating in a finish back on the track. Deep inside, she hoped her father wouldn't be there for the finish.

The gunshot jolted Millie, and off she ran.

"You're wasting your life!" Her father's shout was the last thing she heard as she raced down the track that day.

Now fifty-two and sitting in first class on a plane headed for Italy, Millie chaffed her arms and glanced out the window. *I won't waste my life any longer.*

She sighed and stared at the moon gently illuminating the blanket of clouds.

When the plane landed, the passengers headed down the tunnel to the gate.

Edith grabbed Millie's arm. "This way to the van."

The ladies hustled through the airport to a counter where

vans waited to pick up traveling parties.

"There they are!" Edith shouted and waved to a group of puzzled people. "Clearly, they are Americans. Hello."

"Hello," replied a woman. She stood by a younger woman who resembled her. "Are you two contest winners too?"

"Yes. How do you do?" Edith firmly shook the woman's hand and then offered her hand to the younger woman.

"I'm Joy, and this is my daughter Jamie." The woman turned to her thirty-something–year-old daughter, who adjusted her backpack.

"Hello there," Edith said with a smile.

"You don't seem tired at all," Joy said.

"Not at all. I'm used to traveling." Edith made her way toward another set of contest winners.

Millie yawned. "I'm not used to traveling, and I am tired."

"I could use some coffee." The young woman yawned in reply.

"Me too," Millie replied. "How was your flight?"

"Wonderful," Joy said with a wide smile. "A couple of other winners were in first class with us. Our plane landed over an hour ago."

Jamie pointed. "Those two over there were with us on our flight."

Millie turned to see a young man with an older man. "Oh, really?"

"Father and son," Joy said. "Very nice."

"This way!" Edith waved Millie and the others over. "This is the driver taking us into the city. Did you already change over your phone coverage?"

Millie removed her phone and saw that she did have internet and coverage. "Yes. I called my provider before we boarded the plane."

"Is everyone here?" an Italian man asked. "We are ready to go, yes?" By his uniform, Millie suspected he was the van driver.

Joy and Jamie stood with the young man and his father. Two couples approached.

"We are ready to start this adventure," one woman said.

Edith led the way. "Yes, we are too. Let's go, Millie."

Still yawning, Millie was very glad Edith took charge. "Coming . . ."

In the van and seated next to the window, Millie took in the sights of the rolling hills passing by. "I can't believe we're in Italy," she said.

"Just you wait until we enter the city." Edith smiled. "It's all coming back to me now."

Little did Millie know, but fate was already laying the groundwork for drastic change not only in her life, but the lives of all the contest winners on board.

The van turned into the city streets, and many small cars, mopeds, and motorcycles flew by, weaving in and out of traffic. Millie clutched her chest, nervous for them. The van stopped to make a right turn, then a left. Suddenly, everyone in the van gasped and let out a series of "oohs" and "aahs".

"What is it?" Millie asked, turning in her seat.

"Over here." A man waved to her.

She sat up and craned her neck to see. When it came into view, Millie's mouth dropped.

Ahead of them was the Colosseum.

"There it is!" Edith tapped her shoulder.

Millie swallowed back tears of joy. "I can't believe I'm seeing it."

The van turned left down the street named Via Cavour to their hotel. When the van stopped, everyone scurried to the exit to see the hotel and surroundings.

"Whoa . . ." muttered the young man as he looked both ways. "This is a terrific location."

"Isn't it?" Millie asked as she set down her bag at her feet.

He pointed across the street from the hotel. "That's the

Basilica di San Pietro."

Millie waited.

"You know it, right?" he asked. When she remained wide-eyed and silent, he rolled his eyes. "That's where Michelangelo's Moses statue is."

Millie's eyes widened even more. "I had no idea." She smiled. "I've never been to Rome or read much about it. In fact, this is my first trip outside the United States."

"Well, you are in for a treat!" The older man appeared next to the young man. "My name is Ben Colorno, and this handsome young man is my son Michael."

"How do you do, Mr. Colorno?" Millie shook Ben's hand. "Which one of you won the contest?"

"Please, call me Ben." Ben nudged his son's shoulder. "And it was Michael who won. My son is a very talented photographer. He just doesn't know it. I made him enter, and now he has won! I hope he knows now that he has talent."

Ben's thick accent made Millie think he was Italian.

"Come along, Father." Michael helped him up the steps and through the revolving glass doors of the Grand Hotel Palatino.

Millie thought the boy was kind to not only bring his father with him, but to gently assist him.

Staring in amazement at the lovely hotel façade while the bellhops took in their luggage, Millie and Edith smiled at one another.

"This will do nicely." Edith nodded in approval at the hotel. She took Millie's arm, startling her out of her amazement. "Come inside."

In the hotel entry, all the contestants stood in awkward silence, but Millie continued to inspect the surroundings. The chandelier lights glistened in the marble tiled floor, polished to a mirror-like shine. Across the way, Millie spotted the entryway to the restaurant and a sitting area decorated with modern furniture. "This is so beautiful. I feel like I'm in a dream."

"Buongiorno!" A neatly dressed woman with impeccable makeup approached. With her dark blonde hair pulled back into a neat bun, her green eyes left quite the impression on Millie. "She must be a fashion model," Millie muttered to Edith.

The woman's arms opened wide. "Benvenuti a tutti. Welcome to Italy, everyone."

Ben approached her and rattled off a few sentences in Italian. The woman gladly greeted him with a kiss on both cheeks and an embrace.

"My name is Claudia, and I am your representative for the publisher. I am from Rome but moved to New York City years ago, and now I am back in Rome. Welcome to my beautiful city!"

Everyone clapped enthusiastically except one woman. Millie noticed the woman frowned and crossed her arms. She reached up and stopped her husband from clapping.

"What?" he asked her.

"Don't be ridiculous," his wife said through pursed lips.

"Come," Claudia said. "Let's get you settled into your rooms, and then I will show you the Via dei Fori Imperiali."

"What's that?" Millie whispered as she and Edith approached an elevator.

"A most beautiful street where you can see the Colosseum and ancient ruins." Edith narrowed her eyes and rubbed her chin as though thinking of something. "A street with a very interesting history, indeed."

"Really?" Millie chuckled. "I'm not used to streets that have interesting histories."

"Millie, we live in North Carolina. The town we live in was involved in many Civil War battles," Edith whispered.

Millie shook her head. "You'd think I'd know that. I need to read more history books."

As the two exited the elevator, Edith continued with her banter. "I think there might be ample material here for a book. I'm still studying our fellow travelers."

"Oh, really?" Millie glanced behind her at the older woman standing with a younger woman plus the husband and his grumpy wife. "Will all of them make it into your book?"

Edith pulled Millie toward the hotel room door. "Not sure yet. But here's our room."

Claudia exited another elevator. "Please meet me in the lobby in fifteen minutes for your tour to begin. Spero di vedervi tutti presto!"

"What did she say?" Millie whispered to Edith.

"She said she hopes to see us there quickly." Ben smiled and walked off to his room with his son.

"Hello. I am Joy, and this is my daughter—"

"Mother, you already introduced us at the airport, remember?" her daughter replied curtly, then took her mother's arm.

"Oh yes. I forget. See you soon," her mother said with a giggle.

Edith and Millie watched from the hallway as each of the contest winners and their guests disappeared into their hotel rooms, leaving the two friends alone. "Interesting characters, all of them," Edith said.

"So I suspect you have your stories for each couple, yes?" Millie placed her hand on her hip.

"I do." Edith tapped her chin.

"The wife who scolded her husband for clapping? She's miserable in her marriage. I suspect he's been unfaithful, and she's making him pay for his actions."

"Wow." Millie leaned in close to listen. "What else?"

"The young man . . ." Edith squinted. "I suspect he wasn't too thrilled that his father entered his photo into the contest without his approval."

"Ah." Millie nodded. "I can see that."

"But the father is Italian, so the son agreed to come with him. Why?" Edith turned to Millie.

"Is he a widower? Where's the wife?"

"Divorced?"

Edith shook her head. "Catholic."

Millie raised her finger. "Yes."

"I look forward to hearing their story." Edith raised an eyebrow.

"And the mother and daughter?"

"Not sure yet, but the daughter seems too stern and not at all excited about this trip. Makes me wonder if her mother entered the contest for her just like that father did for his son."

"Meddling parents?" Millie laughed.

"Probably." Edith removed the room key card from her purse. "Joy is happy to be here, though. I like that. Makes me think something happened to the daughter, and the mother convinced her to come along."

"Something happened? Like what?"

"Don't know yet." Edith used the key card to open the door to their room. "First, we unpack."

Millie gasped when she entered the room. "It's perfect!" She raced to the window and threw open the curtains. "And we have a view."

Edith rushed over but frowned when she looked out the window. "Not much of a view."

Their room from the fourth floor overlooked an alleyway. The building across the alley had windows with baskets that held small pots of red geraniums greeting them. Some clotheslines stretched from one building to another, and sheets hung from the lines.

"It's straight out of a magazine ad for Rome!" Millie laughed. "I love it." She pried open the window and stretched her neck to see all the way down the alley to a few buildings in the distance. "I love the architecture."

"That's a church over there, and the piazza is over that way. Come on, let's get unpacked and see the sights." Edith made her way to the luggage.

Before Millie closed the window, she heard shouts and

singing coming from below. "Listen . . ."

Edith paused. "That's coming from a bar in the alley. I suspect they are watching a football game."

"Soccer?" Millie unzipped her suitcase.

Edith nodded. "The Italians are fanatics about soccer." She giggled. "And about spirits."

"Spirits?"

"Various kinds of liquors." Edith winked.

"Ah. Yes." Millie winked back.

As she unpacked, Millie soaked in all the details of the room and view. She couldn't wait to write to Walter about everything she'd learned so far. She removed her laptop and plugged it in to charge for when they returned after their excursions. But before grabbing her digital camera, Millie checked her emails to see if Walter had responded to any of her emails. Then she checked her phone for a text message.

Nothing.

"Ready?" Edith asked.

Millie placed the camera around her neck and joined Edith in the hall.

"Buongiorno, everyone. I will be your tour guide this afternoon. Are you ready to see parts of Rome?" Claudia smiled. "Pronto . . ."

Millie followed Claudia through the revolving doors without checking for Edith.

"Wait for me." Edith chuckled. "Are you excited or what?"

"I can't wait to start this adventure."

Edith took Millie's shoulder and turned her left. "That way leads to the metro. We'll take a train later to the Vatican City. I got tickets for the tour online. And we'll also head to Florence for the day to see—"

"David!" Millie exclaimed. "Oh, I can hardly wait."

"Yes. I bought tickets for that too." Edith raised her chin as though proud.

"My goodness, you thought of everything, didn't you?" Millie smiled.

"I did. And I'm amazed at how simple it is to plan a trip nowadays with the internet and all. Come along, let's go." Edith led her down the street. "As that young man pointed out, across the street is the basilica with Michelangelo's statue of Moses. We'll see that later. Gelato shop up ahead. We'll definitely visit that place later."

"Absolutely."

A man stood on the sidewalk, holding a restaurant menu, and waved to them as they approached. "You come and eat, yes?" he asked as he waved.

Another young man waved at them while he thrust a menu in their faces. "Delicious food. You come in?" he asked.

"I've never seen anything like this before," Millie whispered to Edith. "They really want us to eat there."

"All of the restaurants do this. They can be very persuasive. We'll try them all soon enough. Let's go."

Finally, they stood on the corner of Via Cavour and the Via dei Fori Imperiali. Spinning around, Millie saw beauty in all directions.

The ancient ruins were in front of them, the Colosseum was down the Via dei Fori Imperiali a short distance, and the magnificent Vittorio Emanuele II Monument at the Piazza Venezia square was in the opposite direction. The streets, burdened with shoppers and tourists, came alive. Sunlight bounced off the windows of buildings. A slight warm breeze gently touched her face. Spring wrapped its arms around Rome . . . and Millie.

And her heart filled with joy. *Thank you, Lord, for giving this gift to me.*

"It's spectacular," Millie said. "Absolutely spectacular." She pointed her camera at the scene and shot a dozen photographs. *If these ancient ruins could speak, what would they say?*

"It sure is." Ben stood with his hands on his hips. "I never tire of this view."

"Pops grew up near here," Michael said.

"Is that right, Mr. Colorno?" Joy approached. "I can't imagine growing up near Rome."

"Prego, call me Ben." He placed his hand over his heart. "Yes, it true and this place is as beautiful as I remember. Here, let me take your photo."

Joy shook her head. "Please no. I look a fright." She frantically smoothed out her hair.

Ben laughed.

"Let me take your photo, Ben." Millie waved to him to stand aside.

An older portly gentleman barely above five feet tall, he did his best to pose while Millie took his photo.

"I can't wait to take photos of Rome," Joy said. "We're going to walk throughout the city, aren't we, Jamie?"

"Yes, Mother." Jamie rolled her eyes as she clutched her backpack.

"How can she roll her eyes while in Rome?" Edith pursed her lips.

"Well, maybe she's jetlagged?" Millie offered.

"She's a young woman in the most romantic city in the world." Edith crossed her arms. "I don't know about that. How can she be so—"

"Hello again, everyone." Claudia stood before them and clasped her hands together. "Congratulations for winning the Millview Publishing photography contest." She clapped for them, and passersby turned to see what was happening.

Millie's face grew warm.

Was Claudia aware of the direct and indirect effects Millview Publishing had on each person before her? Could she know?

"You should be very proud of yourselves. Thousands of

people entered, but the five of you were selected as winners. What an accomplishment!"

Edith nudged Millie. "Told you so."

Millie nudged her back.

"Why don't we go around and introduce ourselves? I'll start." Claudia straightened and used her hands to smooth her tight pencil skirt. "As I stated before, I was born in Italy, then moved to New York, where I worked in the Millview Publishing offices. Today, I work for Millview but from Rome."

"How do I get a job like that?" Jamie asked her mother.

Claudia continued. "I'm married to Freddy, and we have a bellissima bambina. A beautiful little girl named Frederica."

"Congratulations to you. Well . . ." Millie stepped up. "My name is Millie Devonshire, and I live in North Carolina. I'm married to Walter, and I entered the contest for an adventure."

"So . . . where's Walter?" Judith asked with squinted eyes.

"Well, he couldn't get the time off from work, so I asked my friend Edith to come with me." Millie waved Edith over.

"Hello, everyone." Edith waved to the group, then stepped back.

"Wait a minute," Joy said as she leaned in close to Edith. "Wait just one minute." Her eyes widened, and she reached into her bag to pull out a paperback novel. She studied the back photo, then stared at Edith and back again.

Millie covered her mouth and began to chuckle.

"You're . . ." Joy pointed, then turned to her daughter. "This is Edith Engram, Jamie." She showed Jamie the book. "It's her. It's you!"

"Who is this Edith Engram?" Ben asked his son.

Michael pointed to Edith. "Her."

"She's a world-famous novelist. And she's here! She's right here with us." Joy clutched the paperback book to her chest as though it were a rare treasure, and her eyes filled with tears.

"Easy there, honey." Edith patted Joy's shoulder. "That isn't the Bible, you know."

Millie laughed.

"But you don't understand. Your stories have meant so much to me. I just adore them." Joy sniffled. "And here you are, right before me."

"I thank you." Edith smiled. "Yes, I am a novelist, and I tagged along with Mille to do some research for my next book. Nice to meet you." Edith stepped back again.

"Benvenuta," Claudia said. "We are blessed to be in your presence."

"Saint Edith." Millie shoved her. Edith shot her that look.

"Uh, my name is Michael, and this is my father." He pointed to Ben, who nodded. "We both live in Brooklyn. Pops is from here, like he said. My mom's still back home, working in our bakery. I love to take photos, and Pops here entered one into the contest, and well . . ."

"He won!" Ben exclaimed.

Everyone in the group clapped for them.

"That's wonderful," Millie said.

"I had to enter the contest for him. He took this magnificent photograph of the bridge back home. It's perfetto." He made the chef's kiss gesture and laughed.

"Thanks, Pops." Michael cleared his throat. "When I heard I'd won, well, I wanted the whole family to go, but Mom insisted I bring Pops."

Ben hugged his son's shoulders.

"Mom's back home taking care of the bakery."

Edith nudged Millie and nodded toward Jamie, who stared longingly at Michael. Millie nodded back at Edith because she understood.

"Love is in bloom," Edith whispered. "I don't blame her. He's a good looking young man and also a caring son."

Michael stood well over six feet and had chiseled good

looks that any red-blooded young woman would be attracted to.

"I don't have much time left on this earth, so I thought, why not come back to Roma one final time, si?" Ben laughed and patted his son's back.

"One last time." Michael glanced down at his feet.

One last time? Millie wondered.

"My name is Joy, and this is my very talented daughter, Jamie. I begged her to enter the contest because I just knew she'd win." Joy gently touched her daughter's cheek. "She's a talented artist and—"

"I'm right here, Mom. I can speak for myself." Jamie moved away from her mother's touch.

"Is this your first time in Roma too?" Claudia asked.

Jamie nodded and adjusted her eyeglasses on her delicate nose.

Millie thought her beautiful in a gentle, minimalist way, yet the chip on her shoulder might make her unattractive to some. A side glance toward Michael showed her that maybe he thought the same thing about Jamie? His eyes practically sparkled as he looked at her.

"How wonderful." Claudia turned to the next couple. "And you—"

"My name is Judith," she said, interrupting Claudia, "and I entered the contest because I'm a very talented photographer. I could go pro if I wanted to." Judith crossed her arms. "We've been to Italy before, but this is our first time to Rome." She glanced around the area with a look of annoyance, as if at a used car dealership.

Her husband stood expressionless, carrying his wife's camera bag. Everyone stared at him. He simply sighed and licked his lips out of boredom.

"Oh, this is George." Judith jabbed her thumb toward him.

"Hello, George," Claudia said.

It became evident to Millie that Judith not only felt she

was above everyone else but they would probably be her competition. Especially when Judith, a taller woman, looked down her slim nose at everyone.

"Hi there, everyone." The wife of the other couple stepped up. "My name is Betsy, and this is my husband, Hank."

"Hello," Millie said.

"Hank convinced me to enter a photograph of our granddaughter, and I won. I couldn't believe it. I've never won anything before in my life." Betsy took hold of Hank's arm and pecked him on the cheek. "He's the best. He's always believed in me and my photography. He even made a studio for me out of our garage back home in Indiana."

"That's so sweet," Joy chimed in.

Millie's stomach burned with jealousy. She could see the love in Hank's eyes as he gazed at his wife. *They're so in love.* She exhaled. *He sees how important this trip is. Why couldn't Walter?*

Millie removed her phone from her pocket. No text or voicemail messages from Walter showed on the screen.

"How long have you been married?" Claudia asked Betsy and Hank.

"Thirty-nine years," Betsy said with a giggle. "And it feels like only yesterday we were married. We never had a honeymoon, so this is it."

Hank took her waist and pulled her toward him. He planted a kiss on Betsy's lips, and everyone clapped again.

Everyone but Millie.

Edith leaned over her shoulder. "You all right?"

"Perfect." Millie nodded and shook off her feelings of envy. She was in Rome, after all.

"All right, everyone." Claudia waved her arms. "We go see the sights now. But tomorrow, you work. I have your assignments."

Suddenly the group grew quiet and serious as they gathered around Claudia.

"You will select a theme and photograph Rome using that theme. Whether you choose the food, the wine, the ruins, the people, the architecture, or whatever. You will spend the rest of your time here photographing Rome." She raised her arms.

"How fun." Joy bounced up and down on her toes. "What theme are you going to choose?" Jamie shrugged.

"So be thinking about it as we see the sights today," Claudia ordered. "For now? We head to the Colosseum."

Millie walked along the road in silence. Her eyes wandered up to Betsy and Hank holding hands as they walked and talked together. She looked down at her empty hand and sighed.

"Thinking about a theme to select?" Edith asked.

"Yes," Millie said in a flat voice.

"Hey." Edith playfully smacked Millie's arm as they walked. "Knock it off."

"What?"

"Sulking like that." Edith held out her hands as if surrendering. "For crying out loud, Millie. Look up. You are in Rome! You're having that adventure you always wanted. For the first time in your life, you weren't left behind, huh? You are here."

"You are absolutely right. I'm here." Millie smiled.

"Yes. Now be here!" Edith walked past her. "Be in the present, okay?"

"You're on." Millie rushed to catch up with her.

CHAPTER 4

As they entered the Colosseum, Claudia explained the history of the ancient ruins and how the church saved it from being destroyed once the rule of the Caesars ended.

"Hard to imagine what occurred in these amphitheaters," Edith said. "The games, the theater . . . amazing."

Millie snapped many photographs as the tourists walked along the halls of the massive structure. When Michael and Jamie came into view, Millie got Edith's attention. "Look."

Edith turned and watched the two young people walking together, deep in conversation.

"Well, what's their story?" Millie asked.

Edith squinted as though thinking about it for a moment. "I see him as a long-suffering son. He has to take over the business for his father but has nourished dreams of being a photographer or musician or something in the arts. There's a calm creativity about him. She, however, is a brokenhearted girl. Probably jilted by the boy she had loved. Now, in the most romantic city in the world, chance has placed them together."

"Oh, Edith. You're so observant. I can hardly wait for you to write this story." Millie closed her eyes and slowly shook her head. "So romantic."

"We shall see what happens with those two." Edith grinned.

"Now, what about the bitter wife and her husband?" Millie pointed to Judith and George up ahead. Judith with her arms crossed, snickering, and George studying the ancient structure.

"She's bitter, all right. Not sure why just yet, but I have my suspicions." Edith took hold of Millie's arm. "Come along."

"Tell me," Millie whispered.

"Well, like I said before, I bet George had an affair a while back, and that's why Judith is so unhappy." Edith snapped her fingers.

"But why didn't she divorce him?" Millie tilted her head.

"Not all women file for divorce when they discover their husbands have cheated." Edith leaned on the rail overlooking what was left of the Colosseum floor. "Some stay in the marriage and make the husband suffer."

"Oh, that's awful." Millie scrunched up her face as though she'd eaten a lemon.

"It is." Edith turned to her. "That's what my mother did."

"No."

Edith nodded as she walked off. "She stayed with Dad but made his life miserable."

"What did she do?" Millie followed after her.

"What Judith is probably doing to George," Edith chortled.

Millie chuckled under her breath. She knew one of Edith's many assets was her unvarying way of judging people. Millie was just glad she'd never been on the receiving end of that judgment.

"She's making him pay for what he did by forcing him to spend his money on her, buy her things, take her on trips all over the world." Edith shook her head. "Mom made Dad buy her mink coats, fancy cars, and diamond bracelets while we kids barely had food on the table."

"That's horrible. How could she do that?"

"It was easier than being a divorced single mother. At least we had a nice house and went to good schools." Edith made a clicking sound with her mouth. "I have a feeling that's what Judith is up to. Punishing George for something."

"What a shame."

They headed to the ruins by the Colosseum. They weaved in and out of the temple ruins and listened to the tour guide explain the excellence of Roman engineering of the structures, roads, and aqueducts.

Next, they ventured to Parco del Celio and hopped onto a tour bus that took them by the Circus Massimo grounds, fountains, churches, and more temples.

As the many sights passed by, Millie took dozens of photos, still unsure of what theme to settle on. *Should I photograph the people?* Many locals rode their bikes along the roads. *Or the fountains?*

The tour bus stopped at the Trevi Fountain, and the group stepped off to act like tourists and toss a coin into the water famous for making wishes come true.

"Will we run by this fountain during the marathon?" Millie asked.

"I think so. And we'll run by some others too. We'll run along the Tiber River and see some stunning architecture." Edith gave her a thumbs-up.

"You're running the Rome Marathon next weekend?" Michael asked.

"We sure are!" Edith replied with a bright smile.

"Yes . . ." Millie bit her upper lip. "That's the plan."

"Your reply wasn't as enthusiastic as hers." Michael chuckled.

"I was coerced into doing it." She frowned.

"Nonsense," Edith said. "She's a runner. She knows she can do it."

Millie shrugged.

"She made it to the Olympic trials when she was in

college." Edith playfully shoved Millie.

"Wow. Well, I'm impressed." Michael offered a slight bow.

"Don't be until we have finished." Millie raised her camera and took a few photos. She heard languages from all over the world and saw people of all ages and nations taking selfies and group photos in front of the fountain.

"I think I'm going to take photos of the fountains," Jamie announced. "For the calendar."

"That's your theme?" her mother asked.

"Yes." Jamie's eyes followed the Trevi Fountain from bottom to top. She stood with her hands behind her back, rolling back and forth on her heels. "I've decided."

"Good for you," Michael said as he stood next to her. "You'll do well."

"I will?" Jamie tilted her head.

"I saw your winning photo. You are very good with outdoor lighting. I can't wait to see what you come up with." Michael offered her a wink and a smile.

"Thank you, Michael." Jamie shyly glanced away. "What will you photograph?"

"Not sure yet."

"You should photograph the people." Jamie slowly lifted her gaze. "I saw your photographs on your website. They are very good."

"You went to my website?" He placed his hand on his heart.

Jamie nodded and offered him a slight smile.

Millie turned to Edith. "It's happening . . ."

"I think you're right." Edith admired the couple as they stood side by side. "They are a good match. He's slightly taller than she is. They are both good looking and about the same age. This will be interesting."

"Indeed," Millie replied. "You're too funny. You describe them as if they are a couch and loveseat you want to buy."

Edith smirked then made her way toward Ben, who leaned

against a lamppost as he watched his son talk with Jamie. "What are you doing over here so far from the view?" she asked.

Millie followed along.

"I'm admiring the view very well from here." Ben smiled.

Suspecting he wasn't talking about the fountain but about his son, Edith patted his shoulder. "We were admiring them too."

"You write romance, Ms. Engram?" he asked.

"I used to, but because I am here in Rome, I feel it's time to return to love stories now that one might he happening right before our eyes." She turned to Millie. "Right?"

"Right."

"Well, I wish my son would read romance novels. He needs to learn more about romance." Ben jabbed his finger toward his son still admiring the fountain with Jamie. "He needs to remember how to trust love. They look good together."

"That's what we think." Millie smiled. "Trust love again? Did something happen that made him no longer trust love?"

"I'm glad he decided to come on this trip." Ben sat down on a ledge. "A few years ago, he loved a young woman. A baker who specialized in wedding cakes, Isabella was lovely. They dated for a while. Just when he considered marriage, she ran off with another man to live in California." Ben's downturned mouth revealed his feelings. He shook his head. "Since then, Michael doesn't trust love."

"Oh no. That's too bad." Millie watched Michael and Jamie talk. "I hope he learns to fall in love again."

"Ben," Edith began. "May I ask you a question?"

"Certainly." He gestured for her to continue. "Please."

"When you said this will be one last trip . . . what did you mean by that?"

Millie leaned in.

Ben exhaled and rested both hands on his knees. Never taking his eyes off his son, he answered, "I have cancer."

Millie gasped, then apologized when Edith shot her a harsh look.

"I completed treatment, but the cancer has returned. I refused any more treatment." He waved his hand in the air. "No more."

"I don't blame you." Edith sat next to him. "You want to live each day to the fullest, right?"

"Exactly." He pointed his finger at her. "So I entered the photograph, and when Michael won, I said we will go together for one last adventure." Ben smiled.

"One last adventure," Millie whispered.

"That's beautiful." Edith hugged his shoulders.

"See, you understand, Ben." Millie thought of Walter. "You understand about the need for adventure."

"Yes," he replied. "Life is too short not to live . . . not to have adventures."

"I only wish my husband understood the importance of living for today." Millie leaned against the wall.

"Not everyone understands it," Ben said. "But when you hear the doctor tell you how much time you have left, well, that forces you to prioritize your life. Yes?"

"Yes." Millie smiled at him.

"We're glad you're here, Ben." Edith patted his shoulder.

But Millie hoped a tragedy wouldn't have to get Walter's attention. She had hoped his friend Charlie's passing would have opened his eyes.

A door opened and interrupted her thoughts. She turned in time to see a person exit the nearby Hotel Fontana. On a whim, Millie hurried over to the front door and photographed it. When she inspected the photo in her digital camera, she smiled. Next, she walked a bit further and spotted another beautiful door. She photographed that one too. "Lovely," she whispered.

Returning to where she left Edith, Millie spotted yet another beautiful door on the Via di S. Vincenzo. The dark green doors, adorned with an ornate architectural arch and two brass lion-headed knockers, drew her in. Her heart raced, so she photographed it right as Edith approached.

"Ben's story is so inspirational. I'm definitely adding it to my book." Edith studied Millie. "What are you doing?"

"Look." Millie handed her the camera.

"Doors?"

"Yes. Look how beautiful they are." She took the camera back and spun around, searching for more doors. "I love how different they are. So unique. So intriguing."

"Over on the Via della Stamperina, there's another set of lovely doors. Come!" Edith grabbed Millie's arm and away they went in search of more doors.

As they walked, Edith breathed in deeply. "Smell that?"

"What?"

"Each town in Italy has its own smell. Inhale deeply. Go on."

Millie did as commanded.

"What do you smell?"

"Coffee . . . baked goods . . ." She did her best to identify the smells.

"Excellent." Edith breathed in again. "Be sure to use all the senses when in Rome. Most people walk around holding their breath. It's important to remember to breathe in and out and take in the smells as well as the sights and sounds."

In the Piazza Dell Accademia di San Luca, they spotted doors of all kinds in every direction. Millie took dozens of photos. "I love these doors."

"I think you've found your theme for the calendar?" Edith crossed her arms and watched her friend.

"I think you're right."

The group made their way back to the bus stop and waved for Millie and Edith to join them.

"We'll walk back!" Millie shouted to the group.

"We will?" Edith's eyes widened.

"I mean, I'll walk back. You go ahead. I have more doors to photograph."

∞

Alone in Rome . . . Millie's heart raced like it did when she was younger and on a first date with a cute boy. *I still can't believe this is happening.*

Rome was her date that day. And she could hardly wait to get to know it. She photographed the entrances to a government building, a hotel, and a church. The aroma of Italian cooking made her stomach growl from hunger, so she stopped at a restaurant for lunch and ordered spaghetti carbonara.

Sitting in a small table outside the restaurant, she ate and watched people stroll by. Like Edith, she imagined their stories. Where were they going? Were they happy?

How would they imagine my story? She sighed and sipped some red wine. A middle-aged woman in the most romantic city in the world sits alone, eating lunch and sipping wine. *Pathetic.*

Millie had been young once and in love. She still was, but now something tempted her. Not a man, but a way of life. Her new endeavor was to make something of herself. Was it possible at her age?

While she sipped her wine, Millie thought back to her fondest memory of talking with Walter about traveling the world when they were dating. She was in her late thirties, and he was in his early forties. Walter was a dreamer back then. That date remained one of Millie's fondest memories, because that day was perfect: A walk in the park, touring the museums, coffee together, buying old books about art, and then sitting at his apartment dining table while Walter cooked dinner. Laughing and dreaming together, planning their future. *Oh, Walter.* Millie did her best to blink away tears.

Pulling out her phone, she called home and left a voice message. "Hello, Walter. I'm just checking in. Have you received my emails and texts? All is fine here in Rome. Edith and I are sight-seeing and . . . well, I hope you are doing well too. Call me back. Please. Love, Millie. I mean, I love you."

She ended the call and cringed. *Good grief. I sounded strange. He's going to think I'm crazy.*

She ran her finger along the wine glass. *I hope he's all right. What if something happened to him?* Next, she texted her neighbor to ask how things were going and if she noticed anything out of the ordinary at their house. Besides her not being at home like she always was, day after day . . .

"More wine, senora?" the waiter asked.

"No, thank you." Millie set down some euros to pay for lunch. As she made her way down the alley, Walter's young, handsome face flashed in her mind. Although they married late, Millie knew God's timing was perfect. But she didn't know how much it would hurt to forgo children and so many other plans they had made while dating.

She photographed another door. A closed door.

A theme for her life began to emerge.

Doors closed on children.

Doors closed on traveling . . . on adventure.

So many closed doors.

Millie knew she'd have to trust God again and learn to be content. *Be in the now, Millie. Focus on what you do have and not what you don't have.* She smiled.

The door she had photographed opened, and a young woman emerged. Their eyes met, and the young woman smiled, winked, and walked off.

The girl's confident stride sent envy over Millie. She once had been confident as well. Confident in her running, photography, and future.

She strolled down to the next door and raised her camera.

"You know, I should have been the sole winner of this contest," came a voice from behind.

Millie turned to see Judith standing with her arms crossed and lips tightly pursed to a thin line. She tapped her foot for further emphasis.

That woman.

"Excuse me?" Millie squinted with confusion.

"I said, I should have been the sole winner of the contest. Why they selected five winners, I'll never know." Judith approached and used her manicured fingernail to move a strand of hair away from her eyes. She raised an eyebrow when she studied Millie's hands, unkept and calloused from scrubbing the bathtub at home and washing dishes at the homeless shelter. Millie hid her hands.

"What do you mean, Judith? It said on the entry form that five winners would be selected because of the volume of entries. They wanted to give more people a chance to win. How is that a bad thing?"

"I mean, my work is the best, and I should have been the only winner."

Millie sighed as she watched Judith storm off.

"And another thing," Judith said as she returned to make another point, lips still pursed. "I just want you to know that I'm photographing the architecture around the city. If you're thinking of selecting the same theme, you've got some real competition. Got that?"

"I guess."

Judith's husband George appeared from a nearby gelato shop. "Hello," he said to Millie and raised his cone as though toasting with champagne. "I went in there to use the restroom. Strange toilets they have here in Italy."

Judith rolled her eyes. "Let's go, George."

"Have a nice time." He licked his gelato. "See you later at the hotel for din—"

"Now, George," Judith ordered. "Let's go. I have a hair appointment."

"See you later," Millie said as the couple walked off.

She watched them for a moment until they disappeared around a corner. *Oh, Lord,* Millie prayed, *may I never become that discontented.*

✿

Millie smoothed out her blouse and adjusted the comb that held back her hair from her narrow face. While Edith finished dressing, Millie stared at herself in the mirror. She spied prominent new wrinkles under her eyes and a few gray hairs at her temples. Clipping on some gold earrings, Millie hoped people would notice them and not her face and hair.

"She really said that to you?" Edith shouted from the next room.

"She sure did." Millie came out of the bathroom. "What's her problem, anyway?"

"I sensed she was very unhappy. I could see it right away." Edith grabbed her purse. "But I had no idea it was this bad. It's important we do not judge her but pity her instead. I mean, here she is in this amazing city—"

"For free, by the way. Everything is paid for." Millie pointed her finger.

"Exactly. And yet she's incapable of seeing the beauty because she's so unhappy."

"I think God's trying to teach me a lesson in all this." Millie put on her black flat shoes.

"Oh?"

"Yes."

Millie checked her phone. Nothing from Walter, but a text from her neighbor appeared.

Everything seems fine, her neighbor wrote. I saw Walter checking the mail. I waved to him the other day.

Millie sighed with relief, but sorrow filled her as well, making her shoulders hunch.

They both exited the room and made their way down the hall toward the elevator.

"Through Ben's story, God wants me to remember what's important in life, and through Judith, He's reminding me the importance of being content."

"Ah, contentment." Edith pushed the down button. "That's always something I've struggled with."

"Buona sera," Ben said as he and Michael approached.

"Buona sera. Did you all have a nice time today?" Millie asked.

"We did." Michael pushed the lobby button.

"Hold the elevator!" came a cry from the hall.

Michael held open the door.

Joy and Jamie entered.

Millie inhaled Jamie's perfume and smiled at her lovely floral dress. "You look pretty, Jamie, and I love your perfume."

"Thank you." Jamie smiled and awkwardly straightened her long wavy hair. Her eyes gently found Michael's.

"Buona . . . buona sera, Jamie," he said with a nervous stutter.

"You, too."

In the lobby, the rest of the group waited to be seated in the hotel restaurant. Dimly lit by chandeliers, the romantic lighting added to the ambience. The windows overlooked the city streets bustling with motorcycles and cars. As the streetlights came on, the city took on another life.

"I, for one, am starved." Edith craned her neck to see the tables. "Ooh, white tablecloths. Fancy."

"The food here is fantastico." Claudia gestured with her fingers as she approached. "And have some wine too. They have an excellent collection." Dressed smartly in a burgundy sheath dress with hair swept back and eyes enhanced by false eyelashes, Claudia was stunning. Millie thought her to be a professional model.

"What do you recommend we order?" Millie asked her.

"The steak Diane is delicious. It comes with garlic potatoes and asparagus with formaggio cheese on the top."

Claudia continued to gesture like a classic Italian, making the meal sounds even better.

"That's what I'll order then." Millie laughed.

"If you desire something lighter, their parmesan-encrusted salmon is a must." Claudia motioned toward the host making his way over to the group. She said something to him in Italian, and he tossed his head back and laughed.

Millie suspected they were old friends.

"This way." The host led the party to their tables. Edith and Millie sat with Jamie and Joy. Michael and Ben sat nearby with Hank and Betsy.

"Where's Judith and George?" Millie asked as she placed her linen napkin across her lap.

"They said they would eat out." Joy shook her head. "Judith said the food here isn't good enough."

"Of course they said that. Nothing is good enough for Judith." Edith rolled her eyes.

Millie tapped Edith's arm. "Look," she whispered.

Edith spied Jamie giving Michael a sideways glance, and Michael smiling widely. "A story is forming. I must watch them closely."

"Indeed." Millie giggled.

"So what sights did you all enjoy the most?" Joy asked. "We loved the Trevi Fountain."

"That was more beautiful than I had imagined," Millie said.

"I find the Colosseum to still be my most favorite place to visit in Rome. So much fascinating history." Edith munched on some bread. "I never grow tired of learning about Roman history."

"Will it make an appearance in your next book?" Joy leaned forward, resting her arms on the table.

"I believe it will." A studious look came to Edith's face. "You see, I am always researching. The sights, the sounds, the people, the smells, the—"

"The smells?" Jamie crinkled her nose as she sipped some

water.

"Of course." Edith nodded. "When I write, I attempt to include all the senses. It draws the reader into the world I've created. Each city in Italy has its own smell. You'll see when we head to Florence." She tapped Millie's hand.

"Like what smells do you mean?" Jamie asked.

"The flowers, the food, the land . . . even the people." Edith used the piece of bread like a pointer.

"The people?" Jamie winced.

"Yes. Even the streets. Each city has its own smell. One must become fully immersed into the surroundings in order to truly experience it."

"I can hardly wait to experience Florence and see the statue of David." Millie pictured it.

"Us too," Joy replied.

"Ever since I was a young girl and I saw the statue in a book at the library, I dreamed of seeing it in person." Millie's eye shone.

"So will any of us make it into your book, Edith?" Jamie asked with a quizzical brow raised.

"What do you think?" Edith raised an eyebrow.

"I think we will." Michael chuckled. "All of us have stories. We'll provide enough fodder for three novels set in Rome."

"Stories?" Jamie said curtly. "What makes you think we each have stories?" She crossed her arms as if hugging herself for protection.

"Don't we?" Michael replied with a sly grin.

"Look at the view. The sun us going down." Millie pointed to the windows behind them, dutifully changing the subject.

"So lovely. We'll take a stroll after dinner. This city lights up delightfully." Edith gave Millie a thumbs-up. "You'll see."

"We'll get some gelato too. I spied a shop not far from the hotel." Joy wriggled her eyebrows.

"That's a must." Millie smiled at Joy.

"Mother." Jamie frowned. "I'm watching my weight."

"Oh dear. While on vacation?" Millie asked her. "You must allow yourself to enjoy the tastes while you're here." Edith turned in her seat to face Millie. "Wow. We've been here only one day, and you've already changed."

"I'm learning." She laughed.

"Changed?" Joy asked.

"Yes. She's beginning to understand how to embrace her surroundings."

"And be immersed in the experience," Millie joked.

"Mother," Jamie whispered. "Don't forget we have to call Martha tonight."

This seemed to intrigue Edith. She rearranged her silverware near her plate. "So, Joy. What's your story?"

"I beg your pardon?"

Edith chuckled. "As Michael suggested, everyone here has a story. What's yours?"

Joy leaned back and shrugged one shoulder. "My story?" She blew her bangs away from her eyes. "You sure you want to know?"

"I wouldn't have asked otherwise." The side of Edith's mouth quirked upward.

"Well, after thirty-five years of marriage, I find myself single again." She used her hands to smooth out the wrinkles in the tablecloth. "It's not what I had expected, you know?"

"And it doesn't help that my father married a woman younger than I am." Jamie shook her head in disgust.

Millie's eyes widened. "Oh, my . . ." Her thoughts raced, as did her heart. The idea of being alone again so late in life made Millie's palms sweaty. *Is this a sign? Is God telling me something? Did this trip to Rome somehow communicate to Walter that I'm leaving him for good?* She swallowed back the anxiety.

"Take it easy." Edith squeezed Millie's hand as if she knew her thoughts.

Millie nodded and inhaled deeply.

"Now, dear," Joy said to Jamie, "Tiffany is a nice girl." Joy patted her daughter's arm.

Jamie rolled her eyes. "Don't get me started on Tiffany and Dad."

"I'm so sorry that happened to you." Millie meant it. More and more, she appreciated her Walter back home.

"Tiffany, you say?" Edith sat back with a scowl. "And you like her?" She curled her upper lip.

"As much as I can like her, I suppose." Joy managed a fake smile. "It hasn't been easy, but I'm all right. I'm learning to accept it." After a long pause, Joy's eyes met Jamie's. "I have to accept it."

"We're all right." Jamie hugged her mom's shoulders. "We're survivors."

"I'm glad you're here." Millie offered them a cheerful smile.

"And?" Edith leaned in. "What about you, Jamie?"

Jamie jerked around as if surprised by the question.

Edith raised an eyebrow as she waited for the answer.

Jamie reached up and scratched her neck, then straightened as if called on by a teacher. "I don't have a—" Her face turned bright red. "I don't have anything to share."

Edith tapped her finger on the arm of her chair and waited. Millie checked Edith's expression. Her curiosity piqued. Jamie might as well share. Edith would get it out of her eventually. By the determined look on Edith's face, Millie could almost hear the wheels inside her head spinning.

Jamie winced and squirmed in her chair as though she were in a dentist's waiting room. "You don't understand. It's complicated."

"She's a very talented photographer and artist." Joy gazed at her daughter with loving eyes. "I don't think Carl ever truly appreciated that in you."

"Mother . . ." Jamie exhaled. "It's really none of anyone's business."

Michael cleared his throat and nervously sipped his ice water. But he continued to listen, as did everyone else at the table.

"They dated for three years, then got engaged," Joy whispered through the side of her mouth. "And then he left."

"Mother!" Jamie jerked her head around and whipped the linen napkin off her lap. "If you don't stop, I'm going to leave."

"It's true," Joy said. "It's nothing to be ashamed of."

"These total strangers don't need to know all that." Jamie snapped the napkin.

"I'll tell anything you want to know about me," Edith said as she leaned her elbows on the table and laced her fingers together.

"Me too," Millie chimed in.

Jamie looked away with a snicker.

"I was sorry to hear about your husband. Do you plan to remarry?" Joy asked Edith. Jamie shot her mother a harsh look. "What?" Joy waved her hand. "She said we could ask."

"No. I do not plan on remarrying." Edith sipped her water. "Once was enough. No one could ever replace Charlie."

"What happened to your husband?" Jamie asked.

"He passed away from cancer." Edith twiddled her thumbs. "Now. What happened with Carl?"

Jamie used her finger to move her fork around. "He uh . . ." Her eyes met Millie's. "And what about you? Why are you here without your husband?"

Millie offered a smile. "He's up for a big promotion at work and couldn't risk taking any time off right now."

"Interesting," Michael said.

"What's so interesting about that?" Millie asked with a chuckle. "He's a good worker who deserves the promotion."

"Carl was a nice boy," Joy interrupted, slowly shaking her head as though filled with regret.

"Mother, you're interrupting Millie." Jamie frowned.

"Tell us about Carl," Edith said.

"He could be nice at times." Jamie bit her upper lip. "But in the end, he . . . well . . . he chickened out. On our wedding day, he didn't show up."

Millie gasped and covered her mouth.

Edith shot her that look.

"Sorry," Millie said through her fingers.

"You've got to learn to listen without reacting," Edith whispered to Millie.

"Yeah, so," Jamie continued, "I survived."

"Do you plan on trying love again?" Edith asked with a wry grin.

Millie's eyes went from Jamie to Edith to Joy, waiting for the answer.

Slowly, Jamie's eyes lowered. She managed a sideways glance at Michael. "I don't know."

Millie and Edith smiled.

So did Michael.

CHAPTER 5

After dinner, the group made their way down Via Carvour and stopped at a gelato shop.

"I've been dreaming about this," Millie said as she searched for some euros in her fanny pack.

"It's delicious. You'll love it." Edith waved for Jamie and Joy to join them. Ben and Michael did too. "It's creamier than American ice cream."

"I'll have one scoop of vanilla and one of the chocolate swirl, please." Millie pointed to the gelato in the glass case.

"Cone?" the server asked.

"Yes, please." Her mouth watered as she watched him scoop the creamy gelato into the cone. "We'll have to go running tomorrow morning to burn this off."

Next, Edith ordered a small cup, and Joy did too.

When Michael and Ben entered the small shop, Jamie's face lit up.

"Join us for dessert?" Millie asked as she ate her gelato.

"Absolutely!" Ben passed by Michael and made his way to the counter. He ordered in Italian and handed a cup of gelato to his son.

"Hello," Michael said to Jamie. "Did you enjoy your dinner?"

"Yes, I did. It was better than I thought it would be,"

Jamie replied.

The two scooted outside and sat at a small table to chat.

Millie and Edith watched for a moment. "It's happening . . ." Millie whispered.

"Look. Across the street." Edith pointed. "It's Judith and George."

The couple sat at an outdoor table of a nice Italian restaurant, sipping wine.

"Let's go say hello," Ben said. Millie and Edith joined him and crossed the street.

"Why did you not join us for dinner tonight?" Ben glanced around the restaurant. "You prefer to eat here?"

With her usual pursed lips, Judith sneered and set down her wine glass. "Not that it's any of your business, but we wanted authentic Italian food and some wine."

"So you'd rather pay for your food than eat at that four-star restaurant in the hotel?" Edith asked.

"All our meals at the hotel are included, you know," Millie interjected.

"We know." Judith sipped more wine. "We can afford to eat elsewhere."

"You know, people like you really make me angry." Edith scowled.

"People like me?" Judith raised an eyebrow.

Woman looked into woman.

"Yes. People who insist on being ungrateful for things that—" Edith leaned in.

Millie stopped her. "What Edith is saying is that we try to be grateful for all the things, Judith."

"Because some of us have suffered loss," Edith said through clenched teeth.

"And some of us have much to be grateful for," Ben chimed in.

"I find that gratefulness makes my day so much brighter." Millie did her best to add cheer to the moment.

Judith chortled. "That sounds a bit like what a simpleton

would say."

Edith frowned. "I beg your pardon?"

"Come on. Let's go see the city at night." Millie pulled on Edith's arm. "Don't let her ruin our evening."

"She called you a simpleton." Edith waved her hand. "Did you hear that?"

"Yes. Just ignore her." Millie turned to Ben. "Come with us, Ben. We're going to see the sights."

"I'm going to see what Michael wants to do. Buona notte." He smiled, then crossed the street again.

Millie and Edith looked down on Judith and George. "Enjoy your dinner," Edith said with sarcasm dripping off her tongue.

As they walked off, Millie and Edith laughed and finished their gelato.

"Thanks for pulling me away. I was about to get angry," Edith said.

"I could see it in your eyes." Millie tossed the empty gelato cup into a trash can. "Look, don't let her get to you. Judith is a very unhappy person."

Edith inhaled. "You're right."

"We're in Rome on this bella notte." Millie glanced all around the area. "It still feels like a dream."

Once they made it to Via dei Fori Imperiali, Millie stood with mouth agape as soon as she saw the ruins lit, as well as the Colosseum. "How beautiful." She held up her smartphone and took several photographs.

"Shall we start with the Colosseum or the monument?" Edith asked.

"The monument." In the distance, Millie could see the beautiful monument at the Piazza Venezia lit up with hundreds of lights. When they stood in front of the gate before the monument, she sighed. "What a sight."

"It is spectacular," Edith agreed. "They call it the wedding cake."

Millie laughed. "I can see why."

Then she tapped Millie's shoulder. "Take a look over there."

Millie turned and saw Michael walking with Jamie. Joy and Ben followed close by.

"Just look at them," Millie said. Michael walked and gestured, and Jamie listened intently. "They make a lovely couple." She turned to Edith, who was studying them too. "Okay, what's the story you're conjuring up inside your head?"

"Two young people, stuck in Rome, meet up and find they have much in common . . ." Edith squinted. "And many regrets."

"Do they have regrets?" Millie cocked her head.

"Jamie and Michael?" Edith asked. "Not sure. But I was talking about my own characters."

"Ah…well, it's a good start to your story." Millie returned to the monument and continued taking photos as tourists lined up along the fence.

Back at the hotel, Millie checked her phone. No message from Walter and no replies to her emails appeared. She called him, and his phone went straight to voicemail.

"Hello, Walter. It's me. Again." She sighed. "Just checking up on you. I hope everything is all right. Let me know if you've received my message." She hung up and opened her laptop while Edith took a shower.

Dear Walter,
    Our first day and night in Rome is finished. We learned what the publisher wants from us: to photograph Rome according to a theme we select. I selected to photograph the doors of Rome because they each are so beautiful and intriguing—just like the city. And they represent mysteries of life. Some doors are businesses and others lead to residences. My

74

imagination wanders as I imagine what's on the other side of each door.

We toured the Colosseum today and did a quick bus tour. I took many photos of the Trevi Fountain! Oh, Walter, I wish you were here with me. It was magical. You would have loved it. I tossed in a coin and said a prayer for you to get that promotion at the bank.

Our dinner at the hotel was fantastico! That's what Claudia said. She's our guide from the publisher. She's so beautiful, she could be a fashion model.

For dinner, I had a delicious steak, and Edith had salmon. And then we went for some gelato. I figure I can eat what I want since I will run the marathon soon.

The marathon.

What am I thinking? I can't possibly run 26.2 miles at my age. Anyway . . .

Next, I took photos (see attached) of the city at night. It's magical. I still cannot believe I am here.

I wish you were here with me, Walter, seeing the sights, sipping wine, eating gelato. It's better than any ice cream I have ever had. I know you'd love it, what with your sweet tooth. Ha ha!

Tomorrow, Claudia (from the publisher) said we will visit a children's art class at the local community center and then we can take off to photograph the city. Edith wants us to go see the Pantheon! I'm looking forward to it. And I want to have a real cappuccino.

Love and miss you,
Millie

When she finished the email, Millie reread it a few times, attached the photos, then hit send. When it went through, she closed her laptop, knowing Walter wouldn't reply.

"Writing to Walt?" Edith dried her hair with a towel.

"Walter. And yes." Millie made her way to her bed. "I told him all about our first day and night."

"Do you think he'll write back?" Edith asked from the bathroom.

"Walter? Send an email?" Millie chuckled. "No. He's not

one for computers. I mean, he loves using email and Excel spreadsheets at work, but I don't think he's ever sent a personal email to me or anyone."

"Sorry." Edith came out of the bathroom dressed in her pajamas. "But you had a great day today." She plopped onto her bed with a moan. "And I did too. That's the important thing. But boy, am I exhausted."

"Yes. I had a wonderful day, and thank you for coming with me. I don't think I would have had as much fun alone." Millie pulled back the covers of her bed, then grabbed her pajamas. "I'm going to take a shower. See if there's a movie on or something."

In the shower, Millie went through the day's events in her mind. One by one, she cherished the memories, especially all the doors. *Tomorrow, I'll head down more streets and see what other doors I can find.* And then Judith's frowning face appeared. Millie rolled her eyes. *That woman. Edith's right. Judith is an unhappy person.* "Lord, please help me to never be such an ungrateful person as that Judith." She rinsed the shampoo out of her hair. "I mean, how can You stand her? You've blessed her with a nice husband and a free trip to Rome, and she still isn't happy."

After showering, Millie dressed in her pajamas and came back to the room. "That Judith woman. Why do you think she's so unhappy?"

But all she heard was Edith's deep breathing. Because Edith had fallen asleep, Millie decided to just read in bed for a bit.

She flipped through one of Edith's suspense novels, about to settle into the story, when the sound of music filtered in from the open window.

Millie peered out the window and saw some shadows dancing in light coming from the bar below. Cheers and laughter rose to her ears, and the delicious aroma of marinara sauce and baked bread hit her nose, making her smile. *Must be a soccer game on, and the locals are watching.* For a few moments, Millie leaned on the windowsill, taking in the sights and sounds of Rome. Edith always said to try to use all the senses to truly experience a city.

Millie decided she was right.

The sounds of music and Italian men laughing and cheering on their favorite teams relaxed Millie's tired mind and body. *This is it. I'm in Rome.* She listened for a while longer. My *adventure has just begun.* Then she climbed back into bed to read a chapter of Edith's latest bestseller.

∽

The next morning, Millie and Edith arrived at the hotel restaurant for continental breakfast with the group.

"I'm starved after our three-mile run this morning," Millie said.

"I'm starved, tired, and sore after our three-mile run this morning." Edith yawned and rubbed her back. "I need coffee."

"Cappuccino," Ben corrected Edith as he passed by. "It's right over there. Buongiorno."

Inside the restaurant, Millie saw how it had been transformed by the staff from the lovely, dimly lit dinner space to a bright, cheerful breakfast nook complete with all kinds of pastries, jellies, fruits, boiled eggs, cold cut meats, and juices lining the buffet tables in the center of the room.

"Wow. Would you look at this spread?" Millie exclaimed. "Have you ever seen such bounty?"

"Buongiorno," Claudia said as she entered. "Please, enjoy the various pastries, fruits, and salumi. We have eggs over there, along with juices."

"Uh . . ." Edith tapped her on the shoulder. "Where's the coffee?"

"Café Americano?" Claudia gently took Edith's arm. "Or cappuccino? The waitress can bring you what you like, or they have a carafe of freshly brewed coffee right over here with cream and sugar."

Edith waved to the server. "Cappuccino, please?"

Millie chuckled and grabbed a plate. Once she had it filled with strawberries, pastries, a boiled egg, and prosciutto, she found a seat at a table by the window and began enjoying her breakfast. The coffee was strong and began to wake her up.

Edith sat down with a groan. "It's those cobblestones." She pointed out the window. "It isn't easy running on those streets, you know. We should have trained for them."

"We should have trained for the marathon. Period." Millie smirked. "Let alone for cobblestone streets."

"I know, I know." Edith chuckled. "We'll be fine." She inhaled the scent, then sipped her cappuccino. "This is delicious." She frowned when she saw Millie's bounty. "How can you eat so much in the morning?"

"I usually just have a cup of coffee, but this spread is fantastic. I didn't expect all this." Millie bit into her Danish.

Joy and Jamie pulled out chairs and sat down at the table. "Isn't this wonderful?" Joy's eyes were large. "I didn't expect this either when I read they'd have a continental breakfast buffet."

"I know," Millie said between bites. "And I'm not a breakfast eater, but this is just too good to pass over."

"Well, eat up, because we need to get moving," Edith said. "Busy day ahead."

"Why do you think they have us going to the community center?" Joy asked.

"I think to watch children at an art class," Michael said as he sat down with them. "That's what I heard Claudia say."

"Good morning," Jamie said to him with a shy smile. She casually pulled her long hair behind her ears.

"Buongiorno," he replied. His large brown eyes sparkled.

"How was your stroll last night?" Millie asked while holding her coffee cup at her lips. She raised her eyebrows and took a sip.

"Fine," Jamie replied in a flat voice. "It was lovely out.

Perfect weather."

"Yes, it was." Michael looked down at his plate.

"A perfect night for romance." Joy giggled.

"Mother." Jamie spread butter on her roll.

"I agree with your mom." Michael chuckled under his breath and stirred sugar into his coffee.

The group turned around when they heard loud voices coming from the other room.

"And there's Judith, complaining about something." Edith grabbed a strawberry off Millie's plate and bit into it.

Sure enough, Judith loudly complained to Claudia about the late breakfast service to her room, how the coffee wasn't hot enough, and how warm her room was throughout the night. Hardened and mean, Judith seemed indifferent to those she had stepped over on her way to the top.

Claudia, on the other hand, remained kind and graceful as she apologized profusely to Judith, who ignored her as she filled a coffee cup and poured cream into it. "And another thing . . ."

Of the two, Millie aspired to be like Claudia.

"To Claudia," Millie cried out and stood. She raised her coffee cup. "All of us would like to thank you and the hotel for this wonderful breakfast. Cheers."

The group stood and followed Millie's lead.

"Bravo!" Ben exclaimed.

"Grazie," Claudia said with shiny eyes. "Mille grazie."

"Prego." Ben clapped.

"Brava," Edith cried out as she clapped.

Millie watched Judith's nose crinkle and her eyes narrow to slits.

Vittoriosa. Millie smiled and nodded at Judith.

An hour later, the group hopped off the bus at the

community center. A plain brick building with large glass windows along one wall, the center didn't seem to match the splendor of the other architecture they had seen.

The sun shone on another glorious day of spring weather in Rome. Millie inhaled the floral scents deeply. "Perfecto."

"Indeed." Edith led the way, and the group followed her into the center, where a dozen children sat at long tables covered with paper, paints, cups, brushes, and plates. A teacher was explaining to them in Italian the day's project. She spoke so quickly that Millie could only pick out a few words here and there.

Dressed in khaki pants and a light blue blouse tucked in, Claudia finally looked casual instead of like a model from a magazine ad. "This way, ladies and gentlemen." She waved her arms, and the group spread out. "Today, you will photograph the children creating art and then over here"— She made her way to a separate room—"the most excellent Carlo Ricci will discuss his work and take questions."

Millie grabbed Edith's arm as if to keep from falling over.

"What is it?" Edith asked.

"Carlo Ricci?" she muttered. "Did she say—"

"She did," Michael replied with wide eyes. "I can't believe he's here."

"Who's Carlo Ricci?" Joy stood next to Millie.

Jamie scrolled through her phone, found a photo, then showed her mother. "He's a world-famous Italian photographer, Mom."

Millie covered her mouth. "I can't believe we get to learn from him." She blinked back tears of joy. "This trip is becoming more and more of a dream come true."

Edith patted Millie's hand. "I'm so glad. You deserve it, friend."

Soon the group found places around the children.

"All right," Claudia began. "You are to photograph these little artists at work for our online magazine."

Millie removed the lens cap from her digital camera and

began photographing the children at work. Looking through the viewfinder, Millie captured the sunlight streaming through the window, lighting the tables, and the children perfectly. *I feel like a professional photographer.* The wide smile on her face made her cheeks hurt. She touched her face and giggled.

Making her way around one table, Millie focused on a little girl using a brush to paint watercolor flowers. The light from behind her made a halo around her smooth, dark hair. Millie raised her camera and took several photos of the heavenly scene until tears filled her eyes and prevented her from taking any more. She backed away and wiped her eyes.

Edith approached her. "You okay, friend?"

Millie sniffled and nodded. "Yeah. I'm fine."

Edith spotted the little girl painting and giggling with the other girls at the table. "She's adorable."

"She is." Millie grabbed her belly to stop the ache. She had always dreamed of having a girl with dark hair and long black eyelashes.

Edith must have sensed this and hugged Millie's shoulder.

"I'll be okay." She walked off and took more photos of the children hard at work creating masterpieces for their waiting parents, beaming with pride.

"Oh no," came a cry from behind. Millie turned to see that some paint and brushes had fallen to the ground.

"I can help." She set down her camera and raced to the sink for some paper towels.

Together with one of the mothers, Millie wiped up the paint and took the brushes to the sink to rinse them out.

"They have people for that sort of thing, you know," Judith said.

"I know." Millie dried her hands with paper towels. "But I can help too."

Judith looked down her nose at her.

All Millie could think of was Judith's feckless scolding of Claudia and the hotel staff. "We all can pitch in and be kind."

Without saying a word, Judith spun around and went about her business of photographing the children.

Michael and Jamie sat together and helped some boys mix paint on paper plates. Joy used her phone to snap photos of Jamie and Michael working with the children.

Ben sat with some children and chatted with them in Italian. The children giggled, and so did he.

"What do you suppose he's telling them?" Edith asked Millie as they watched.

"Probably a story." More tears welled in Millie's eyes. "Michael is so blessed to have—" She raced outside before she could finish.

Edith found Millie sitting on a bench in the courtyard outside the room, so she sat next to Millie but remained silent as she wept.

For a few moments, Millie was a child again, looking up at her angry father's face. He shook his finger at her, and the familiar sting of pain made her chest tighten.

"What's going on?" Edith broke the silence.

Millie shook her head. "Just envy, that's all."

"Envying what? Those kids?"

"Yeah, I guess them and Michael and Jamie and . . ." Millie wiped her eyes.

"Young love?" Edith handed her friend a tissue.

"No." Millie wiped her eyes. "I envy the relationship Michael and Jamie have with their parents."

"Ah." Edith tossed her head back. "I understand."

"I love how Ben wants the best for his son and Joy is such a caring mother." Millie could see her mother's worried face flash in her mind. "I wish I had parents like that."

Edith rubbed her back. "I know, Millie. I know."

Millie's father's death the previous year continued to haunt her since she hadn't seen him before he died. Walter had decided it was best that they no longer be in contact with her father due to his cruel tendencies.

"I know Walter meant well when he said we'd no longer

visit Mom and Dad, but I . . . I really . . ." Millie's voice trailed off.

"I'm sorry." Edith sighed. "I don't agree with Walt all that often, but I did agree with him about that."

"Walter."

"He was protecting you, Millie. You know that."

"I do. I understand his reasons. It's just hard, you know? To never have resolved anything. Now both my parents are gone." She glanced up and spied another ornate door. "It's like a door slammed in my face and forever locked."

She raised her camera and photographed it.

"I couldn't agree more." Edith sighed.

"But—" Millie stood and glanced upward at the blue sky. "Life must go on." She inhaled the fresh air. "It has to."

"This way, ladies," Claudia shouted from the open door. "Time to go listen to Carlo!" She clapped her hands.

"Yes." Millie wiped her eyes one last time, tossed the tissue into a trash receptacle, then waved to Edith "Let's go. This will be an amazing experience. I just know it."

When they entered the lecture room, Millie and Edith sat in chairs beside Betsy and Hank.

"I just love his work, don't you?" Betsy whispered to Millie. "We saw an exhibit when in New York last year. Fascinating stuff."

"Absolutely," Millie agreed. "I get chills thinking about seeing him."

A few locals entered the room and sat around the group, chatting in Italian. Millie chuckled as she watched them gesturing with their hands and speaking loudly.

"What's so funny?" Edith asked.

"I love to watch the locals converse with each other. They use their hands all the time." Millie imitated them. "It draws me into the conversation."

"Benvenuti signore e signori," a man said from the podium. A screen lowered and a slide appeared with Carlo Ricci's picture on it. The man introduced the famous photographer.

When he entered, the audience applauded and rose to their feet, Millie and Edith included.

"I can't believe it's him," Millie said as she clapped, spilling her camera bag onto the ground. She furiously cleaned up the mess when she sat.

"Oh, Millie." Edith shook her head.

"I know, I know. I'm a klutz."

Carlo Ricci stood at the podium and introduced himself in Italian and then in English. "I'm told we have some American photographers here." He waved at them.

Millie and Betsy giggled and squirmed in their seats. "That's us," Betsy said.

"I welcome you to my beautiful home city. I hope you will find many places to explore and photograph while you are here."

More applause.

Slides of his work appeared as he explained the context behind each one. As she watched, Millie's heart raced. For the first time since her college days, she felt like a student. She filled with pride as he spoke to them as photographers and not tourists. Carlo Ricci spoke to her like a colleague and certainly not like a housewife from a small town in North Carolina.

Each slide showed his brilliant work shot from war zones or small towns across Europe. Photographs of children playing in Kenya, splashing in fountains of Rome, and elderly people smiling for his camera flashed on the screen, one after another.

"So beautiful," Betsy whispered.

"I love his use of light," Millie replied.

"And finally, I see you were asked to photograph the little children in the next room. Budding artists, si?" Mr. Ricci said.

Millie and her group nodded and laughed politely.

"That's good. You must photograph subjects while they

are living their lives. Smiling, laughing, playing . . . living. That's what I have always tried to do." He then explained in Italian and with gestures about his work. "Capture lives worth living."

A life worth living. Millie glanced out the window at the bougainvillea bushes animated by the breeze. *That's all I've ever wanted . . . to see what's behind all those closed doors.*

After the lecture, Mr. Ricci took questions, then meandered around the room while refreshments were served. Millie stood aloof, sipping some punch from a small plastic cup, watching him converse with the guests. She set down her punch, inhaled courage, and crossed the room.

"Where are you going?" Edith asked.

"It's now or never, right?" Millie nodded toward Signore Ricci.

"Mi scusi," Millie said as she approached him. "Mr. . . . Senor . . . Signore Ricci," she began. Her face turned red.

He turned to see who it was. "Yes, miss?"

"Mrs. . . . Ms. Devonshire." She held out her hand.

"Ah, from England," he said as he shook her hand.

"Oh, the name? Yes, my husband's people are from England. Probably took the name of the town they lived in."

"How may I help you, madam?" He bowed.

"Your work—it's greatly influenced my own. The way you use light is amazing."

"Mille grazie." He placed his hand on his heart.

"What I wanted to ask was—" She inhaled more courage. "How do I go deeper?"

He tilted his head as though confused. His assistant translated in Italian. "Ah," he said when he understood. "You must look through the lens, yes? And see more than just the subject. See all around the subject. Tutti quanto, si?" He gestured. "Vieni con me . . . Come with me."

Together they returned to the class where the children were painting.

At the doorway, Carlo paused. Raising his hands, he motioned for Millie to do the same.

She did.

"Look at them. Their innocence." He smiled like a proud father would. "But also look at everything around them, affecting them as they create," Carlo suggested. "The light coming in through the window, the chairs they sit on, the brush in the hand. The air . . . is it hot? Cold? Watch them for movement and expression." He motioned for Millie's camera.

She immediately handed it to him and watched as he lifted it to his eye and took photos of the children.

Millie rubbed the goosebumps off her arms. *He's using my camera. Carlo Ricci is using my camera.* She glanced around the room, looking for Edith. When their eyes met, Edith flashed her a thumbs-up sign.

And then Millie's eyes found Judith, glaring at her through eyes narrowed to slits. Millie raised her chin and grinned sardonically at Judith. *Eat my dust.* Millie chuckled.

"Now let us take a look." Carlo reviewed his photos in the digital camera viewer. "See what I mean?"

Millie's mouth dropped when she saw how superior his photos were compared to hers. "Amazing how you captured the innocence."

He remained silent as he reviewed Millie's photographs until he spotted the photos of doors Millie had previously taken. "Ah . . . these are lovely. Very unique," Carlo said.

"Really?" Millie clasped her hands together. "You think so?"

"The doors of Rome." Carlo continued to scan Millie's photos in her camera viewer. "Bellisimo. What made you want to photograph the doors?" He handed the camera back to her.

"I don't know. I suppose they intrigued me." She replaced the camera around her neck. "The architecture, the colors of the stained wood or painted wood, the brass decorations. All of it, I suppose, drew me in."

But Carlo shook his head. "No!" He jabbed a finger at her temple. "That is what your mind looked for." Then he gently tapped her chest. "What did your heart say?"

Upon hearing his question, Walter's face as well as her parents' came to Millie's mind. "Closed doors."

Carlo crossed his arms as he listened. "Go on."

"You see, I've felt closed out of things all my life. In my own family, I'm the middle child of seven. Always being told no or you can't." She exhaled. "Or that I have to wait . . . drove me crazy."

His translator explained certain phrases to him. He nodded as though he understood.

"I would follow my older siblings around, but they would never include me. They would shut their bedroom doors and lock me out. I never felt included or worthy of my parents' time or attention either." Millie's chest tightened again. "Anyway, closed doors intrigue me. 'What's on the other side?' I always ask myself."

Carlo touched her camera and then her shoulder. "What is on the other side is what you need to discover, si?" He lifted her hand and gently kissed it. "You must come to my villa this Friday evening. I am having many local photographers to my house for wine. You must come." Then he walked off as he listened to his assistant rattle off information in Italian.

Edith approached and playfully punched Millie's shoulder. "Well done," she whispered.

Millie stared at her hand where the great Carlo Ricci had kissed it. She pressed her hand to her chest and sighed. "That was . . ."

Edith laughed at her friend. "Yes?"

"Magical." Millie showed Edith his photographs of the children. "I have photographs by Carlo Ricci on my camera. Just look at them!"

Betsy came to see, as did Jamie and Michael. But Judith

grabbed her husband's arm and raced out of the room after Carlo.

"Woohoo, Signore Ricci," Judith cried after him.

"Millie, these are incredible." Jamie's eyes grew wide.

"What was it like talking to him about photography?" Michael asked.

But Millie couldn't hear anything. Carlo's voice echoed in her mind, clouding out all other thoughts. For all she knew, her feet weren't even touching the ground as they made their way to the waiting bus.

CHAPTER 6

At dinner, Millie checked her phone for a text from Walter. Nothing.

She quickly texted him and then searched for voicemails. Before sitting at the table, she left a quick message asking him to call her.

Once at the table, she sat down with a heavy sigh.

"Nothing from Walt?" Edith asked.

"Walter. And no. No messages or voicemails or anything." Instead of dwelling on Walter's behavior, Millie took out her camera and analyzed the photographs again with the group while they enjoyed antipasto and wine.

"I still can't believe how lucky you were to get him alone." Jamie's smile revealed her joy. "It's incredible."

"I won't sleep much tonight, that's for sure." Millie laughed. "Edith and I strolled through the Pantheon, and I took more photographs. Talk about doors. I had never seen such massive doors, and made of bronze too."

"Oh, I know," Michael exclaimed. "And the architectural engineering. Mindboggling how these structures have remained standing through floods, earthquakes, hurricanes, and wars." He looked at his smiling father. "Our streets back home constantly have potholes and are being repaired, yet some Roman streets we walked on today are almost three thousand years old."

"Not a pothole in sight." Ben winked.

"I've been interested in photography since I was a child, but only today did I actually feel like a photographer." Millie beamed.

Jamie nodded. "I know what you mean."

"How about you all?" Millie asked Jamie and Joy. "What did you photograph today?"

Jamie touched Michael's hand. "Michael and I strolled by more fountains. I took about a hundred photos."

Edith shot Millie a sideways glance.

Millie saw Jamie gently stroking Michael's hand.

"Love is definitely in bloom, I must say . . ." Millie giggled behind her menu.

"Hello, everyone," Judith said as she and George sat down at a nearby table.

"Wow. You're blessing us with your presence tonight?" Edith said.

Millie nudged her. "Edith. Stop."

"We thought we'd eat with the group tonight." With her nose in the air and disdain at her lips, Judith whipped her napkin off the table and placed it onto her lap. "Besides, we have much to tell."

"So does Millie," Jamie replied with bright eyes. "She was able to talk with Signore Ricci after today's lecture at the—"

"I saw that." Judith raised her water glass for the server to fill.

"It was amazing. He took photographs with her camera." Michael pointed at a beaming Millie.

"Yes, well, we had lunch with Signore Ricci." Judith cleared her throat. "At *his villa* by the sea." Lifting her butterknife, Judith used it as a mirror to check her bright red lipstick. When she set it down, she glared at Millie. "It has a spectacular view."

"I bet." Edith rolled her eyes. "Anyway, tell them what he said to you about the doors."

But Millie couldn't take her eyes off Judith. Her insides started to turn. "Um. Yes. Well, he uh . . ."

"Go ahead. It was so interesting," Edith told the group. Judith raised an eyebrow. "Well?"

Millie tried to remember, but envy clouded her mind, and she had a feeling Judith knew this.

"He told me my work is spectacular." Judith smiled widely. "Yes. He used that word, didn't he, George?"

George sipped his beer without expression. In fact, Millie thought he looked annoyed as his eyes searched the room for something to settle on. Anything but his wife. He looked as annoyed as everyone else was, listening to the woman go on.

"We met his wife and his neighbors, who also joined us for lunch. And his neighbor owns a gallery in downtown Milan. He said he wants to see more of my work, to possibly show it in his gallery." Judith watched as the waiter poured her wine. "What do you think of that?"

"What's the name of the gallery?" Edith asked.

"The Largo," Judith replied.

"Ah. I see." Edith glanced over at Millie and the others. "I've been to the Largo. Have you?"

Judith furrowed her brow. "No." She took out her phone and began searching the internet.

"Yeah. Nice gallery . . . of paintings. No photographs, dear."

Judith found the gallery's website, and by the look on her face, she proved Edith right.

"I've seen your work, Judith, honey." Edith scooted her chair back. "And I think Signore Ricci was just being nice. As was his neighbor." Edith stood and made her way over to Judith's table. "So I'll believe it when I see your photos actually hanging in this art gallery that specializes in paintings by local modern artists."

Everyone watched Edith head to the ladies' room, and then they turned their focus on Judith, who stared at her phone, then slowly set it face down.

George continued to drink his beer and munch on the fresh bread the waiter placed on the table. He grabbed the breadbasket, scooted his chair away from the table, and headed to the bar, where a soccer game was playing on the large screen television. "I'll be back later," he said as he walked off.

"George," Judith said with a scowl.

"So what else did Carlo Ricci say to you, Millie?" Betsy asked.

"He explained the importance of capturing everything around the subject and not just the subject only. You know?" Millie used her hands to form a frame as though focusing a camera on Jamie. "For instance, look at the light coming in through the window, framing Jamie's lovely hair and face."

Everyone turned to look at Jamie, whose face turned as red as her wine.

"And look at how those around her are also affecting her," Millie continued. "Her expression . . . her smile . . ."

"Her complexion?" Betsy asked with a wink.

Jamie reached up and touched her cheek. "I'm warm. I mean, it's warm in here, isn't it?"

Michael took her hand and squeezed it. "Millie's right. Everything around you is affecting you." He kissed her hand. "Making you even more beautiful. If that's possible."

Joy covered her smiling mouth. Her eyes shone from tears.

"Puh-lease . . ." Judith made a loud noise by scooting her chair back. She left in a huff, but George stayed behind at the bar, munching on bread.

When Edith returned, she saw George sitting alone, staring at the soccer game on the television at the nearby bar. "What's the score?" she asked him.

"Manchester United one, Spain zero." He raised his

beer as though toasting her and the group.

"So what did I miss?" Edith asked.

"Today was . . ." Millie tried to find the right words.

"Perfecto," Michael said.

Everyone raised their glasses and toasted his answer.

"So what are we eating tonight, huh?" Ben asked.

"I think I will have the penne pasta." Millie set down her menu. "What about you, Ben?"

He opened his mouth to speak but began coughing uncontrollably. Michael gently patted his father's back and handed him a glass of water.

Ben sipped some water, then wiped his brow, shiny from sweat.

"Are you all right?" Joy asked.

"Si, si." Ben waved his hand at her. "I am fine."

"You did too much today, Pops," Michael said.

"There is much to do in Rome," Ben replied. "For dinner, I will have the minestrone."

"That sounds amazing. I'll have the same." Edith waved the waiter over, and each one ordered their meals.

"I worry about Ben," Millie whispered to Edith.

"Nah, he's fine. He's stronger than we think." Edith offered Millie a reassuring smile.

In the hotel room, Millie sat on her bed with her laptop open on her lap. She stared at her email inbox. No messages from Walter appeared.

She sighed and closed the laptop.

"Walt hasn't written back?" Edith asked as she rubbed night cream on her face.

"No, Walter hasn't replied." Millie stared out the window. "But I knew he wouldn't."

"Don't let it ruin your amazing day," Edith said. "All right, pal?"

Blinking back tears, Millie nodded and opened the laptop again. "You're right." She looked at Edith. "It was an incredible day, wasn't it?"

"Absolutely. You should be proud of yourself, Millie." Edith climbed into her bed and adjusted the covers around her. "How did it feel, talking to such a famous photographer?"

Millie smiled widely. "It felt more than incredible." She thought about it. "I felt seen. I felt worthy."

Edith rolled onto her side and listened to her friend.

Running her hand along the soft bedspread, Millie remembered being a child. "With so many siblings, I never felt seen. My oldest brother and sister were like our parents, really. The younger ones were a pain. I changed so many diapers."

Edith chuckled.

"But the older ones had all the attention, both good and bad. They were brilliant in school, and my brother was a star athlete. My sister went on to start her own business and left home. I didn't see her again for decades."

Edith cringed.

"So when Mom went downhill, it was me and the younger ones fending for ourselves." Millie leaned back and stared at the ceiling. "We could never please our father. Nothing I did was ever good enough."

"But today?" Edith pointed her finger at her.

"But today, I did it." Millie patted her thighs. "It really happened."

"It's still happening. Tomorrow, we're off to Florence."

"Yes! The statue of David." Millie closed her eyes. "I can't wait."

"Good night, friend. Well done." Edith rolled over to go to sleep.

Millie opened her laptop again and started an email.

Dear Walter,

What a day! You'll never guess what happened, so I'll just tell you: We went to a class at a community center to photograph some little children painting pictures. I attached some of the photos to this email. This little girl was so precious. I could have taken her home!

And then we attended a lecture with the great Carlo Ricci. That's right! He's the man I told you about. He talked with me about how to take photographs. He actually talked with ME! A housewife from North Carolina. And he used MY camera to take photos. Can you believe it? I've also attached his photos here. I still can't believe it. I've been rubbing goosebumps off my arms all day.

After that, we toured the Pantheon. What an amazing structure. Roman engineering at its best. I wish you were here with me. You would have enjoyed that tour. I feel like I'm in a dream. Tomorrow we're off to Florence for the day to see the statue of David. Another long-time dream coming true.

I hope you are well. Let me know how the interview went! I really want to know. Please answer my texts, and please write to me.

Love,
Millie

∞

At the metro station, Millie clung to the strap of her backpack, nervously waiting for Edith to purchase their tickets to Florence. The stench of oil and engine exhaust permeated the air, humid from the rain early that morning. When Edith approached, the frown on her face matched the odors in the station.

"What is it?" Millie asked.

"They had no tickets in regular seating." Edith tossed up her hands.

"Oh no." Millie sulked. "What'll we do?"

Edith held up two tickets. "So . . . I bought two first class tickets." Her eyes widened.

"Seriously?" Millie hopped up and down.

"Yep. Let's go. It's boarding now."

They rushed to the door of the train car and made their way down the aisle.

"A beverage?" the attendant asked once Millie and Edith sat down.

"Yes, please!" Edith rubbed her hands together.

"First class again." Millie sighed. "What a treat."

Edith nestled into the comfortable chair and sipped her orange juice. "Absolutely."

As the Tuscan scenery passed by the window, Millie sipped her tomato juice and fell in love with the countryside. She used her phone to shoot a few photos of the landscape. "Dreamy, isn't it?"

"I wish we had time to do a wine tasting tour." Edith shrugged. "Oh, well. Next time."

"Next time?" Millie laughed. Then she sat quietly for a moment. "I wonder what he'll look like," she muttered.

"Who?" Edith swiveled in her seat to face her.

"David." Millie giggled. She scooted closer to her friend. "Ever since I saw the statue in an encyclopedia in grade school, I wanted to see it in person." Shaking her head, Millie struggled to say the words. "And now . . . I'm just a few hours from seeing him."

"And he's everything you've imagined him to be." Edith sipped her juice. "And all the other sights in Florence. We'll see the Piazza della Repubblica, the Basilica di San Lorenzo, and the Santa Maria del Fiore. If we have time, we'll cross over the river to see the Boboli Gardens."

Millie looked up Florence on her phone and scanned through photos of the places Edith named. "Sounds wonderful."

"Just look at those gardens." Edith bit her upper lip. "They smell as lovely as they look."

As Millie scrolled, she noticed no new emails filled her

inbox. She frowned and glanced out the window. *I won't let it get to me. I won't. I refuse to let him ruin my day.*

"Still no word from Walt, huh?" Edith nudged her.

Millie shook her head. "Oh, well." She placed her phone in her purse. "I refuse to let it get me down."

"Good for you." Edith nodded. "He had his chance to come along."

"He chose to stay home." Millie nodded back. "Nothing I can do about that."

"Exactly."

"I'm going to buy you something," Millie exclaimed.

"What?" Edith wrinkled her face. "Don't be silly. I don't need anything."

"Yes, you do." Millie patted Edith's knee. "I want to give you something for coming with me and helping me."

"Nonsense." Edith handed the attendant her empty juice cup.

"Well. I'm going to find something to give you because you've helped me so much."

"You have helped you, Millie." Edith smiled.

Once they hopped off the train, they studied the map on their phones and recognized the street names.

"This way," Edith ordered. She strode off with Millie following behind. "Take a deep breath in."

Millie obeyed.

"Smell Florence." Edith waved her hand. "Each town has its own smell. Never forget how Florence smelled."

A mixture of car exhaust, floral scents, and various foods filled Millie's nostrils. *Remember the smell of Florence,* Millie instructed herself.

The two made their way down narrow streets until they made it to the Galleria Dell'Academia, where a line of people waiting to get in had already formed.

"Oh no," Millie said. "Look at that line. It's going to take forever for us to get in."

"Mille . . ." Edith showed her their tickets. "We enter this way."

The two walked into the front doors, showed their tickets, and passed through security. Edith motioned for Millie to follow her. "Get out your phone camera and start a video. It's this way."

Millie started a video on her phone and followed her friend.

She heard diverse languages as she filmed and noticed a wave of tourists headed toward a doorway.

"This way," Edith instructed.

Millie filmed as she walked through a doorway toward a crowded gallery area. "This is it," she narrated the video. "I'm about to see the statue of David for the first time in my—" She turned to the right and gasped. Her heart stopped, and she feared it might never beat again.

There before her was the magnificent statue of David, high on his pedestal and lit by the daylight streaming through the skylight above him.

"There he is," Millie whispered into the phone. "Michelangelo's David."

She raised the phone above the crowd so she could get a good quality video as she walked toward it.

"It's a lot bigger than I thought it would be." Her mouth dropped. Resting on a pedestal of over eight feet high, the statue rose another seventeen feet from there. The natural light coming in from the skylight above him illumined the marble statue, giving it an ethereal quality. The perfect way it was sculpted from a single block of marble sent chills over Millie's body. She rubbed her arms and wiped tears from her eyes.

"Impressive, isn't he?" Edith stood next to Millie with her arms crossed. "I never tire of seeing it." Both women couldn't take their eyes off him. "Sculpted from one block of marble."

Millie read the nearby plaque. "Michelangelo was only twenty-six years old when he created this?" She covered her mouth. "Remarkable."

"He's something, huh?" Edith read the Bible verse on a plaque nearby. "Then David said to the Philistine, 'You come to me with a sword, with a spear, and with a javelin. But I come to you in the name of the Lord of hosts, the God of the armies of Israel, whom you have defied.'"

"Beautiful, the way Michelangelo captured David's youth and confidence." Millie pointed to the statue. "The way he's posed. So original and meaningful."

"Powerful." Edith flipped through the brochure she picked up at the entrance. "The way he's posed sets this sculpture apart from all others. It was controversial yet truly appreciated by critics. The writer of this brochure said the many critics admired Michelangelo's bravery in how he approached David."

Bravery. Millie's eyes followed the statue from its feet to its facial expression. "I admire the bravery of the artist and the subject," she replied. "The intensity of his deep-set eyes and strong jaw."

"Michelangelo was sending a message." Edith raised an eyebrow. "To all artists—be brave, yes?"

Millie smiled at her friend. "Yes."

The two stood with other spectators and admired the statue for almost an hour. Millie took dozens of photos with her digital camera and phone, emailing some to Walter back home.

She knew it was early morning in North Carolina, but she hoped Walter would respond.

So she found a bench by the statue and waited . . . and waited . . . but no response came. Frustrated, she slipped her phone into her purse. "Well, I guess we should—" She looked for Edith.

But she was nowhere to be found.

"Edith?" she asked as she looked left, then right. "Edith?"

Millie walked around the statue, but no Edith. She made her way to another part of the museum filled with sculptures and people, but no Edith.

"Edith?" Millie's heart began to race. *Did she say she was going to the restroom? She must have, and I didn't hear her.* Millie asked a museum worker where the ladies' room was. When she entered, she searched the area. "Edith?"

No answer.

Where did she go? She couldn't have left.

Millie headed to the opposite side of the museum, which had smaller rooms filled with statues, paintings, and tapestries. "Edith?" she said in a loud whisper.

A group of students touring the space turned to her.

"Hello," she said to their surprised faces.

Clutching her chest, Millie searched the museum repeatedly. "Edith?"

No answer.

Finally, she thought to look at her phone.

A text from Edith. *Oh, thank God.*

"I'm in the front picking up a book from the bookshop," she had texted Millie twenty minutes earlier.

Millie rolled her eyes and took deep breaths as she raced to the bookshop. When she found Edith perusing the many books about David, she took her arm.

"I've been looking all over for you," Millie said.

A few patrons turned to her.

"Why? Didn't you get my text message?" Edith wrinkled her brow. "What's the matter? You're pale. You should go sit down."

Millie took her advice and sat on a bench, desperately trying to catch her breath. A little boy sat with her. He played with a yo-yo.

Beads of sweat formed on Millie's forehead. She took deep breaths in and out to calm her racing heart.

"Seriously, are you all right?" Edith handed her a bottle of water.

Millie nodded as she sipped. "Yes. I just need to sit for a moment."

"I'm going to pay for my books. I'll be right back."

"No. Let me buy them for you." Millie reached for her purse.

"Don't be silly. Sit here and rest."

As she watched Edith pay at the register, Millie's heart rate returned to normal. She turned to the little boy next to her, playing with his yo-yo.

Gesturing to him, Millie asked to use it for a second.

The boy handed it to her, and Millie performed a few tricks with the yo-yo. Walking the dog, round the world, and rock the baby.

With wide eyes, the boy watched her.

"Playing with a yo-yo? I take it you're feeling better?" Edith asked.

"Yes, thanks to him." Millie laughed at the boy's reaction. She handed him the yo-yo and hugged his shoulders.

"All right. Let's go get some lunch." Edith stood by.

The two walked the streets of Florence, searching for a place to eat. A few sprinkles hit their arms.

"Let's sneak in here before it pours." Edith motioned toward a small restaurant as the rain began.

The waiter sat them in the back, near the kitchen.

"I can smell bread baking." Millie inhaled and closed her eyes. "With this rain coming down, I'm having soup. What about you?"

"I'm having lasagna." Edith chuckled. "And some wine." She waved to the waiter.

"I'll have the Toscana soup and some bread, please. Oh, and we'll have a bottle of wine." Millie nodded to Edith. "This is my treat, by the way."

"What?" Edith shook her head.

"Yes. Let me do this." Millie raised an eyebrow.

"Oh, all right." Edith rolled her eyes.

After the waiter took their orders, the waiter went outside to assist some people who sat at tables on the sidewalk. Covered with plastic, the patrons were protected from the rain.

"He's busy," Millie said as she sipped her water.

"Even on a rainy day." Edith glanced around the space. "This place must have good food."

Deep in thought, Millie ran her index finger alongside her glass.

"What's the matter?" Edith snickered. "You're in Florence, Italy. Nothing is the matter, right? How could it be?"

The waiter brought their wine glasses, and with a delighted expression, poured the wine for them. "This is a refreshing sweet wine. Enjoy." He set down a basket of fresh bread on the table.

Millie inhaled the aroma, then tore into the bread and spread butter onto it.

"Well?" Edith sipped her wine.

Millie ate more bread. "He still hasn't responded to any of my emails."

"You expected him to?"

Looking out the front door, Millie watched people pass by. "No . . . but I hoped he would." The wine in her glass sparkled. "There's nothing wrong with that, is there?"

"You know him. You know he's probably upset that you went without him. Don't expect him to reply. That way, you won't be disappointed."

"I know." Millie drank some wine. "Oh, this is good."

"I agree." Edith smiled. "Warms my belly."

"Mine too."

After a few minutes of silence went by, Edith finally asked, "What happened back there?"

Millie set down the piece of bread and covered her face with her hand. "I panicked, Edith." Millie peeked between her fingers.

"You didn't see my text?"

"No." Lowering her hand, Millie glanced away, embarrassed to look at her friend.

"So you panicked because you thought I'd left or something?" Edith tilted her head.

"That or you were taken." Millie rubbed her aching temples. "Or worse."

"Taken?" Edith's face crumpled. "What?"

"You know, like in the movies."

"Like in the movies . . ." Edith rested her elbows on the table and exhaled as though frustrated.

"The point is," Millie continued, "I couldn't find you, and I totally panicked." She repeatedly rubbed her hands on her jeans. "You know I don't get out much, and I purposefully avoid crowds. When I didn't see a reply from Walter, I put my phone away, so I didn't see your text. And I tried to find you, but—"

"You thought about what happened to you when you were little, didn't you?" Edith shook her head. "Millie. Breathe, okay?"

"I know, I know." Millie hung her head in shame. "I overreacted. I'm such a chicken."

"Drink some wine and relax."

"Relax. Yes." With head buzzing, Millie sipped more wine.

"Slowly." Edith reached across the table and touched Millie's forearm. "Small sips. All is well now."

"All is well." Millie set down her wine glass. "Breathe . . . in and out."

"Sorry about that." Edith scratched her scalp. "I should have made sure you knew where I was before I took off." Edith patted her friend's hand. "Sorry, friend."

"No. It's me. I need to learn how to be social again and relax in public. I need to learn to let go of what happened and live in the present." Her gaze returned to the people passing by the restaurant. "Do you know who I admire, besides you, of course—"

"Of course." Edith chuckled. "Who?"

"I really admire Joy."

"Joy." Edith nodded.

"I mean, here she is, a lovely middle-aged woman who's been jilted, and she's traveling with her daughter. She laughs, she smiles, she's out there touring Rome and living life. She's getting on with her life." Millie waved her hands. "I really admire that."

"Me too." Edith glanced upwards as though thinking about what she'd heard. "I mean, I lost my Charlie, but to be jilted like that after so many years of marriage, and to have him leave for a young woman?"

Millie turned to her. "I know, right?"

"I would have gone to bed and stayed there for the rest of my life." Edith shook her head.

"Me too." Mille pictured Joy in her mind. "Yet she didn't. She carried on."

"Hey," Edith said. "What happened to you when you were young matters. It explains a lot of things. But yes, you don't want to stay in the past. We learn from it, and then we move on."

"Move on." Millie saw the look in Edith's eyes, and she suspected her friend was thinking of Charlie's last days. "I didn't mean to make you think of Charlie's passing, Edith."

"I know you didn't." Edith offered her a playful wink. "It doesn't take much to think of him, you know. Just being here reminds me of him. Especially the food."

The waiter approached with their meals, providing the perfect transition.

"Aha! Time to move on to lunch." Millie grinned ear-to-ear once the scent of her soup hit her nose.

Edith smiled and rubbed her hands together. "Oh, yum."

Taking a spoonful of her soup, Millie blew on it, then slurped it down. "Fantastic. I need the recipe." She dipped some bread into the soup. "Mmmm. Just what my frantic mind needs. Comfort food."

"Take it all in, Millie. The city, the restaurant, the food, the wine." Edith chuckled. "Feeling better?"

"Better."

"I am sorry that your viewing of David was ruined." Edith frowned.

Millie almost choked on her soup when she heard those words. "No, not at all." She coughed into her napkin. "Are you kidding? Nothing, and I mean nothing, ruined my experience. Nothing *could* ruin it. It was . . ." Millie looked away as she tried to find the right words. "Simply divine. It will remain in my mind as a perfectly divine experience."

"I'll add the scene to my book." Edith removed a small notebook from her pocket and scribbled in it.

"Ooh, please do." Millie leaned in to read what she was writing. "Don't leave out any details."

"In fact, that's how the hero and heroine will meet." Edith waved a hand through the air as if revealing a painting. "Picture the scene: the heroine can't find her friends in the galleria. She panics, searching frantically. Coming around the corner in a huff, she accidentally crashes into the hero, who steadies her and then asks if she needs help."

A smile slowly appeared on Millie's face in between spoonfuls of soup.

"As she explains what happens," Edith continued, "he falls in love with her. To calm her, he explains in a thick Italian accent the history of the statue of David."

"I love it."

"As he talks, she falls in love with him." Edith rubs her hands together in victory. "Done."

"That's a great scene." Millie ripped more bread apart and buttered it.

"A good writer can use any real-life experience and make it an even better experience in the story." Edith used her fork as a pointer. "I'll add the senses to the scene—what was she feeling with her hands? Smelling with her nose? What sounds were heard? And on and on."

"Tomorrow is the Vatican City?" Millie's eyes lit up. The food and wine relaxed her. She sat back in her chair.

"Yes. I have our tickets. We'll take the metro to the city, then walk a few blocks. You'll love the sights. Wear your most comfy shoes. We'll be doing a lot of walking." Edith clicked her tongue. "And maybe I'll get another scene for my book from our experience there, yes?"

Millie laughed. "Probably. And all that walking will help us prepare for the race next week. We haven't run as much as I would have liked us to." Millie raised an eyebrow. "A marathon is a lot tougher than you think it is."

"Don't worry about it. We'll be fine out there. When we can't run, we'll walk. No big deal." Edith took a bite of her lasagna.

Millie frowned.

"What?" Edith asked.

A voice from Millie's past came to her mind. She was always told by her coach that a runner never walks in a race. To do so means defeat. It's an embarrassment to the team.

"Nothing." Millie ignored the voice in her head and ate more soup.

"Okay, then." Edith raised her glass, and the two toasted their lunch. "Cin-cin," she said. "To your health. Cheers."

"Cin-cin." Millie grinned.

CHAPTER 7

Later that day, Millie and Edith made their way through the famous Boboli Gardens to burn off lunch calories.

The floral scents of the garden made the air come alive. The delicate anemones bloomed spontaneously among the grass. At the top of the hill, Millie could see the city of Florence behind the Pitti Palace. A slight breeze animated the anemones.

"The Italians call these the flowers of the wind," Edith explained.

"They're so delicate and lovely." Millie bent down to photograph them. They seemed to smile for the camera.

As they made their way around the Neptune fountain, the sun warmed Millie's exposed arms. After the rain in town, the warm sunlight felt like an embrace.

Various pathways bursting with flowers greeted them at every turn. Azaleas, lilies, irises, and petunias with yellow centers and blue petals bloomed on the edges of vast green lawns. Arranged in large ceramic pots were pink, white, red, and purple petunias and sweet alyssum with its tiny white flowers smiling at them as they passed. Creamy white carnations peeked out of flower boxes, and of course, Millie's favorite, bright red geraniums, welcomed her. The intoxicating scent enthralled her, so she sought out a bench to sit and enjoy the pure pleasure of the gardens.

Tourists gathered near the famous Fountain of the Fork near the palace. "The fountain is very popular." Edith wandered to the basin. "King Neptune," she cried. "We salute you."

"Edith." Millie looked left, then right. "What are you doing?"

"This is the famous fountain. Didn't you know that?" Edith said without looking away from the statue. Created in 1565 by sculptor Stoldo Lorenzi for Duke Cosimo I de' Medici, the water feature was always considered the central feature of the expansive gardens. Beloved by locals.

"Pay your respects. Go on," Edith urged her.

Millie rolled her eyes. "We salute you," she said.

Edith smirked.

But loud laughter rose on the breeze, causing the women to turn and follow it.

"This way." Edith waved to her. "A wedding!"

They made their way through the lavish vegetation of the gardens to a bright green lawn, where a wedding was about to begin. Delicate bamboo chairs adorned with white tulle bows were set out in rows, forming a center aisle. A white arch made of tiny white roses stood at the end of the aisle.

"We should leave," Millie whispered.

Edith agreed and gently pulled on her arm to leave the space, but the music from a string quartet, seated in the shade of the trees, made them both stop.

"Canon in D," Edith whispered. "My favorite."

"Hello." A woman's voice stirred them both.

"Uh, hello. Our apologies. We heard the music and laughter, so we—" Millie tried to explain.

"You are Americans?" the woman interrupted.

"Yes," Millie said in a voice slightly above a whisper, gently placing her hair behind her ears. "We'll leave you to it."

But as she turned to leave, the woman pointed to Millie's camera. "You are photographer?" she asked in a thick Italian accent.

"Well . . . yes, I am." Saying it out loud made Millie's chest swell with pride. "I'm in Italy to take photographs for an upcoming calendar. You see, I w—"

"Come with me." The woman, portly and dressed in a burgundy sheath dress, her thick brown and gray hair combed and styled for the wedding, waved them over to a waiting man. "Vene . . . come with me."

Edith turned to Millie. "Why not?"

"No, Edith. We're intruding on these kind people," Millie resisted.

"You wanted adventure . . ." She chuckled.

"Please. You stay?" The older woman smiled. "I am Ginny. My granddaughter is the bride. We are so happy to be celebrating." Ginny pointed to the camera around Millie's neck. "You do photography, yes?"

"I do." She jiggled the camera. "That is why I am in Italy with my friend. I am photographing the various cities."

"We need a photographer. The one we hired called us this morning and is very sick. Now we have no one." Ginny placed her palms together as though praying, and her downturned mouth broke Millie's heart.

"Oh no. I'm so sorry, but—"

"And now God has sent you to us." Ginny smiled a wide-tooth smile.

Millie's eyes widened, and she raised her hands out as though halting traffic. "No, I'm just a tourist. I have never photographed a wedding before."

"Hello." A debonair gentleman approached. "My name is John, and I am the bride's uncle. Please, you can assist us this special day by photographing the wedding."

Ginny's eyes shone with tears as she motioned her hands toward Millie.

"I'll do my best." Millie offered a weak smile.

Edith hugged her shoulders. "You wanted adventure."

"Will you quit saying that?"

"You can do this. I know it." Edith scooted away and sat in the back row. She wriggled her fingers at Millie as if to say 'Go on, and good luck.'

Millie shot her a sardonic look, then removed the camera from around her neck and began taking photographs of the guests as they laughed and talked with each other, gesturing wildly as always.

The soft music from the string quartet called to Millie, so she photographed the musicians as they played. Because they were in the shade of the many trees, she had to adjust the exposure. As she took the photos, she heard Carlo Ricci's voice in her head. *Consider all that is affecting the subject . . .*

She stood before the rose-covered arch at the end of the aisle where the wedding party would stand, pointing her camera down the aisle. The groom and his groomsmen approached from her left.

"Hello," the groom said. "You are the photographer?"

Millie nodded and smiled weakly. "Yes. I believe so."

Dressed in black tuxedos, the groom and his men looked very attractive. Their attention turned to an arched entrance to the garden, walled by perfectly trimmed privet hedges, festooned with tiny white flowers.

Ginny, the grandmother, entered, escorted by a young man. The bride's family were seated, and so were the groom's family. Millie worked hard to ensure they all were photographed.

The music changed to a rendition of Bach's "Jesu Joy of Man's Desiring," and the bridesmaids stepped through the archway entrance one by one.

Each wore a tea-length lavender gown with her hair swept up.

When the music changed to the wedding march, all the guests stood and faced the back. Millie stood in front and shot dozens of photos of the bride as she made her way down the aisle on the arm of her father, Millie assumed.

Stunning in a strapless white ball gown with a diamond tiara in her dark hair that held her tulle veil in place, the bride's beauty made guests gasp. She seemed to float down the aisle, making eye contact with her guests and then her groom. Joy lit up her face. In her hands, she held a bouquet of spring flowers, complete with anemones.

The flowers of the wind.

After taking photos of the bride, Millie turned and photographed the reaction of the groom as he watched her approach. He smiled through tears of joy.

The priest began the ceremony, so Millie dashed to the back of the space behind the guests and photographed the couple as they took hands and recited their vows to one another.

"Hey, great job," Edith whispered from her seat in the back. "Let me see what you have so far."

They both admired the photos through the camera's digital screen.

"Wow, what a stunning bride." Edith tilted her head.

"She is, isn't she?" Millie watched the ceremony. "Look how young they are. So in love. Their journey is just beginning." She thought of her wedding day with Walter, and her heart raced.

Soon the ceremony was over, and the priest gave his blessing on the new couple. They turned and made their way up the aisle arm-in-arm as everyone applauded.

Millie shot several photos as the couple approached her. A woman gasped, and the bride and groom stopped walking, staring straight ahead.

Millie turned to see what everyone was staring at.

When she turned around, Millie saw a young man standing in the archway leading out of the garden space.

The bride covered her mouth as her eyes never left the young man.

His eyes filled with tears, and he opened his mouth to speak, but said nothing.

The bride lowered her hand and then extended her arms out, as if wanting an embrace.

The young man rushed to her and scooped her up into his arms. Many guests stood, clapped, and wept. The groom smiled through his tears too.

The young man twirled the bride around and then set her down by her new husband. The three hugged as though long-lost friends.

Millie photographed them and then watched them walk through the archway, arms around each other.

"What was that all about?" Edith asked.

"I have no idea."

The guests began to file out behind the bride and groom toward the reception area.

"It is her long-lost brother," John, the bride's uncle, explained as he approached. "They have not seen each other since their mother's death three years ago. There was a falling out, and well, it seems all is forgiven."

"As it should be," Edith said in a soft voice.

"That is amazing." Millie showed John her camera's screen. "I was able to capture it."

"Bravo, thank you. Well done."

"Thank you." Millie watched the wedding guests head toward the reception area by the fountain. "So her mother is . . ."

"Passed away, yes." John faced Millie. "As you can see, this day is very special. My sister would have loved to have been here. Thank you for showing kindness to our family." He placed his hand over his heart and bowed.

"The pleasure is all mine." Millie smiled warmly.

"You both come to the reception, yes?" He waved his arm toward the area.

Millie shook her head. "I don't think we can—"

"Of course, we can." Edith motioned for Millie to follow her. "More adventure . . ."

Millie smirked.

By the fountain, Millie took photos of the bridal party, the new couple with their families, and alone together as the sun lowered in the sky.

Finally, as the bride stood alone, a slight breeze animated her veil, spreading it to her left, where it floated on the breeze.

"Gently look toward the veil and raise your arm as if trying to touch it," Millie ordered.

Ginny translated, and the bride raised her long arm as if a ballerina, gently touching the veil. Millie couldn't resist taking dozens of photos of the scene and the bride's gown as it sparkled in the soft sunlight.

"Spectacular," John said.

"She is simply stunning," Millie said. "I'm just here to capture it."

When the photoshoot was finished, Millie made her way to the tables at the reception, where she found Edith. Already enjoying the food and wine, Edith had a sparkle in her eye.

"Come sit with me." She pulled out a chair for Millie. "You must be tired."

Millie sat down and exhaled for the first time since the wedding began. "I am exhausted." Relief washed over her.

"You wanted—" Edith handed Millie some wine.

"Adventure?"

"No, to be a photographer."

"Haha. Don't remind me." She took it and sipped.

"You have been so kind," John said when he approached. "Here is my business card. My family and I own restaurants in the city. I would love to have your photographs hanging on the walls. Please send me some when you send me the wedding photographs."

Millie's eyes widened. "Are you serious? I most absolutely will. Thank you for the opportunity and the honor."

"And let me know how much I owe you for today, yes?" he asked with a grin.

"Oh, you don't have to pay me for—"

"She will let you know tonight," Edith interrupted.

"Grazie. Please, enjoy the food and music." John spun around and greeted guests at another table.

"You are here for vacation?" Ginny appeared at the table.

"Yes, we are." Millie turned in her seat to face her.

"You must see Rome." Her eyes sparkled.

"That is where we are staying."

"Wonderful." Ginny took Millie's hand into hers and kissed it. "Mille grazie for everything today. God used you to answer our prayers."

"It was a pleasure, really. I am glad I was able to help." Millie patted Ginny's hands.

She and Edith watched Ginny walk off and hug the bride and her groom.

"What a day." Millie turned to face Edith. "Never in my wildest dreams did I expect that."

"Nor did I." Edith ate some bread. "Another scene for my book."

Millie laughed.

∽

Later that evening, the two headed back to the hotel, where they ran into the others waiting in the lobby.

"What's going on?" Millie asked. "Are you all headed to dinner?"

"Hi there, ladies. We all decided to eat in an authentic Italian restaurant tonight," Betsy said with a twinkle in her eyes. "Care to join us?"

Edith rubbed her tired shoulder. "Well, we ate at an authentic Italian restaurant today in Florence and walked a lot afterwards."

"Sorry. We're exhausted." Millie vented air between her lips. She and Edith waved to the group as they headed out the hotel revolving door.

"They'll have fun. It's a gorgeous night." Edith hit the elevator button.

Inside the elevator, Millie rested her back against the wall and exhaled. "I don't have the energy to head out tonight." She blew her bangs away from her face.

Back in their rooms, Millie set her camera and purse down on the desk in the corner.

"I'm going to rest. After all that walking around Florence, my feet ache."

"We'd better go to sleep early if we're going to walk through the Vatican all day tomorrow." Edith removed her sneakers and massaged her feet.

The two took naps, then watched some television.

"I'm going to take a hot shower. Are you hungry? How about we order room service?" Edith grabbed the menu off the nearby table.

"That sounds like a great idea." Millie sat on the bed and loaded all her photos from her camera onto her laptop. As she browsed through them, a smile came to her face. Each set of photos evoked so many emotions. She scanned through the photos of the view from the Ponte Vecchio as they headed over the glistening river toward the Piazza della Signoria after lunch. Crowded with many people, the famous piazza made for interesting people watching.

"Giotto's Bell Tower," Millie muttered as she remembered when they came upon the Cattedrale di Santa Maria Fiore. The remarkable marble façade had left her speechless. Made of green, white, and red marble, the monument rose from the piazza floor over eighty meters into the sky. Millie was able to capture it once the rain stopped and the sun came out. Sparkling in the sunlight, the marble made for quite the spectacle.

Next, photos of the lovely Boboli Gardens and the wedding they accidentally intruded on appeared. When the grandmother of the bride asked her and Edith to stay for the ceremony, a wave of romance flowed over Millie. She scanned through the many photos she took of the wedding. In her purse, she located the business card of the bride's uncle. Millie had promised to email him the photos.

"What part of Florence did you like best?" Edith said from the bathroom. "Besides David."

"The Piazza del Duomo," Millie said with a sigh. "But that wedding in the Boboli Gardens was most memorable."

"Weren't the people so kind to invite us to stay?" Edith plopped onto her bed and put on some socks. "The bride was so beautiful in her white ball gown."

"Dreamy." Millie's eyes smiled.

"Get any good shots of doors?" Edith dried her short gray hair with a towel.

"Nope. Only doors of Rome, remember?" Millie held up her finger.

Grabbing the phone and a menu, Edith gestured to Millie. "What do you want for dinner?"

"Something light. Lunch was plenty for me."

"Salad?" Edith pointed to the menu.

"Perfect."

As they ate in their room, the sounds of men cheering at the bar downstairs made for their entertainment.

"Sounds like their team is winning . . . again." Edith turned her head to listen.

"I love it." Millie picked at her salad. "Makes everything feel so real."

Edith studied her friend's expression for a moment.

"What?" Millie stopped before eating a cherry tomato.

"Have you heard from Walt yet?"

"Walter? No." Millie chomped on the tomato. "But like you said, I don't expect to."

"Why do you think"—Edith motioned with her hands as though searching for the words—"Walt is the way he is?"

"Walter had a rough childhood." Millie pushed around another tomato with her fork.

"What happened?"

In her mind, Millie saw Walter sitting in his chair, reading the paper while the news played on the television. His calm expression with his reading glasses resting on the bridge of his nose brought a smile to her face. "Walter's childhood was good, normal. His father worked and his mother stayed home with him and his sister. But when he turned fourteen, his father fell into financial problems and filed for bankruptcy."

"Oh no." Edith rested her elbows on the desk they were using as a dinner table.

"His father abandoned the family, so Walter had to go to work." Millie took a bite of her salad. "He never forgot that feeling of abandonment."

"At fourteen, he went to work? What about school?"

She nodded. "Yes. He had to drop out of school and work. He became the man of the house." She used her fingers to make air quotes. "And his mother relied heavily on him, because after his father left, she sort of went, well, mad. Like my mother, Walter's mother also suffered from mental illness."

Edith leaned back. "I see."

"Anyway, I think he's very frugal and practical because of what happened." Millie used a napkin to wipe her hands. "And of course, after what happened last year."

"Remind me what happened again?" Edith drank some water.

"Remember? His boss, whom he trusted and tried so hard to impress, was arrested for embezzling funds from the bank." Millie folded her arms. "That really hurt Walter. Dennis treated him like a son, and he promised Walter that promotion. Instead, some Harvard graduate got it."

"That does explain a lot." Edith stood and gathered their plates. "I can definitely understand why he's so cautious with money."

"Me too." Millie thought about it. "I liked that about him when we got married. He taught me how to handle money and invest."

Edith returned to her chair. "Why did you leave your job after you two married?"

Gripping her water bottle, Millie reflected on the conversation she and Walter had on their honeymoon. "He told me how important it was for us to have a comfortable home. I felt bad for him not having his mother there. She got a job, too, and worked a lot of hours at night. So I decided to stay home and make our house a place of comfort for him. You know."

"I see." Edith lifted the lid off their desserts. Her eyes widened when they saw the tiramisu. "Yum! Want some dessert?"

"Sure."

They ate in silence for a bit. Millie could almost see the wheels inside Edith's mind spinning.

"What is it?" she asked.

Edith shook her head as she ate. "Just wondering if you have any regrets about quitting your—"

Millie sipped some water. "I loved my job."

The clank of Edith's fork hitting the side of her plate startled Millie.

"But don't think for a moment that Walter forced me to do anything." Millie used her own fork as a pointer. "I made the decision."

But Edith's raised eyebrow revealed her thoughts on the subject. "You mean he didn't try to manipulate you into quitting, you know, by making you feel guilty?"

"No. I made the decision. I mean it, Edith. I know you already dislike Walter, so I don't want this conversation to add to your growing list of reasons." Millie pushed aside the tiramisu.

"No, no." Edith took another bite. "I just wanted to make sure it was your decision."

"It was."

"Do you regret it?"

Memories of her time at the community college flooded her mind.

"I had fun working in the front office, attending classes when I could, and walking around the campus. Running on the track was fun too. But I'm the one who chose not to return. I could have continued taking classes and working at the front office of the campus grounds, but I didn't."

"What about your running?" Edith folded her hands together, intertwining her fingers. Millie thought she looked like a professor asking a student why her homework was late.

"What about it?" Millie played with her fork. "Walter has never complained about it. In fact, I don't think he cares at all about—"

That eyebrow rose again.

"Our marriage is fine, Edith." Millie stood and gathered her plate to place on the tray that room service had brought. But she knew that statement was a lie. Millie also knew that Edith knew it was a lie. She leaned her head back and sighed. "Oh, who am I kidding?"

"Come here and sit." Edith patted Millie's chair.

Millie obeyed her friend's command and plopped into the chair. "How can I love someone who isn't there?"

Edith listened.

With tears forming in her eyes, Millie unlocked her phone and scrolled. "He still hasn't replied to my emails, texts, or voicemails." She shook her head and set down her phone. "He doesn't care."

"Millie—"

"I made us a home. I have hobbies, and I keep busy." Millie leaned forward. "I've done my part. But every time I ask something of him, I'm told to wait, or not yet, or soon. Soon our adventure will happen." She went to her suitcase and removed her running shoes and socks. "Well, I finally did something on my own and for myself, and as usual, he can't understand."

Edith continued to listen.

Millie covered her mouth, remembering how her friend had lost her husband. Millie turned to her. "I'm sorry, Edith. What am I doing? I'm being so insensitive. I mean, here I am complaining about my husband when your Charlie is—"

Edith hung her head and chuckled. "Don't be silly."

"No, really." Millie sat by her. "I'm being so cruel, whining about my husband when I should be appreciating him, shouldn't I?"

"Look here, everyone needs to complain a little. Walt's a good man. He's a survivor. He's proven himself faithful and true. A good businessman, right?"

"Right."

"Charlie wasn't perfect either. I complained about him on our weekly runs, didn't I?"

Millie laughed. "A few times."

"Marriage isn't easy, that's for sure." Edith patted Millie's leg. "It's hard work. Walt's a good man, but he's just . . . well, he's settled."

"Settled?" Millie watched Edith set the dishes on the tray and head to the door.

"Yes." Edith stood holding the tray. "He's settled into the groove. He's comfortable, content."

Millie rushed over to open the door and watched as Edith set the tray onto the floor in the hall.

"He certainly doesn't want to be disturbed. You know?"

"Yes, I know." Millie grabbed her pajamas from her suitcase.

"But now you've disturbed him by heading to Rome without him. He's rattled." Edith jiggled a finger into the air for emphasis. "You've disrupted his normal routine, and now you have his attention." She opened the dresser drawers and pulled out some socks.

"Sometimes you need to leave someone behind to get their attention," Millie murmured as she nervously folded and unfolded her pajama top.

"You've done good, kiddo." Edith sat on the bed and put on her fluffy socks.

"I hope so." Millie headed to the bathroom. "Dinner was perfect. In fact, the entire day was perfect. I'm taking a long, hot bath."

"Enjoy!"

While soaking in the bath, Millie thought more about her life with Walter. The hot water and steam helped relax her body and mind. *Did I do the right thing?* she prayed. *Oh, God, I hope so.*

She sat up and rinsed water from the washcloth. *I hope he's there when I get back home—and I hope he sees me now.*

CHAPTER 8

The morning light snuck through the curtains, waking Millie from her slumber.

"Time to go for a run," Edith said in a singsong voice.

Millie groaned.

"How late did you stay up sending those photos to that John person from the wedding? Make sure he pays you too."

Millie groaned again.

"Well, you'll feel better after our run through Rome. After that, we'll head to breakfast," Edith said as she pulled on her running jersey. "I'm not a breakfast eater at home, but this hotel's bountiful continental breakfast cannot be ignored."

Millie rolled over and saw the digital clock by the bed. "Five-thirty?"

"Wake up, sleepy head. Time for a quick run and then a cappuccino." Edith clapped her hands.

"Ugh." Millie rolled over again and covered her head with her pillow. "I went to bed too late last night."

"Writing to Walt into the wee hours of the night?" Edith chuckled.

"What?" Millie tossed the pillow aside and threw off the covers from her legs. "Oh no! I completely forgot to write to him. He's going to be so angry." She rubbed the sleep from her eyes. "I fell asleep watching some sappy Italian show."

She checked her phone and frowned. Nothing. *He must be busy with work.* She sighed. *Or worse. He just doesn't care.*

"Well, let's get in a quick run, get some coffee into you, and then head to the Vatican City." Edith patted Millie's bedspread. "Let's go!"

As Millie sat on the edge of the bed, her neck ached. "This marathon idea isn't as appealing as it once was."

"I know, but once we get out there"—Edith tossed Millie an energy gel—"and once you get some energy in you, you'll be fine."

"Listen to you being all cheerful and encouraging about running. Who would have thought?" Millie stood and stretched.

Edith playfully jogged in place. "I'm excited. Let's go."

Later in the hotel restaurant, Millie and Edith sat with Joy, Jamie, and Michael, who were already enjoying their breakfasts. With plates overflowing with fresh fruit, eggs, pastries, and jellies, the group thoroughly relished the bounty. Betsy and Hank sat at a nearby table.

"I'm so hungry after our run." Millie winked and bit into a strawberry.

"Oh, yeah. I forgot that you two are running the marathon next week. Wow." Michael salted his scrambled eggs. "How is that coming along?"

"Great." Edith sipped her cappuccino, leaving a white foam mustache on her upper lip.

Michael laughed.

Millie handed Edith a napkin. "We had a wonderful run this morning through the streets as the city was waking up. Some other runners were out there too. They were from Australia, and we'll see them at the marathon." Excited flutters filled Millie's belly. "I have a feeling this will be a wonderful experience."

"Life-changing," Edith said. "And isn't that what you wanted?"

"Agreed." Millie raised her glass of juice, and the two clanked their drinks together.

"I admire the two of you so much," Joy said. "I don't know if I could ever do something so daring."

"Don't admire us just yet." Edith laughed. "We haven't crossed that finish line."

Joy faced Millie. "And you really were an Olympic marathoner?"

"No. I didn't get to the Olympics, just the tryouts." Millie offered her a thumbs-up. "But I completed many marathons in my youth."

"What got you into running?" Jamie asked.

Her father's angry face flashed across Millie's mind. She shook it away. "Uh . . . I thought it was fun to see how far and fast I could go." She decided to stay cheerful and not tell Jamie the real reason. *Maybe there'll be a time for that story later.* "It's a good way to stay in shape and pass the time."

Michael chortled. "I'd rather watch a movie or something."

"Yes well, me too, now that I'm older." Millie chuckled and rubbed her neck. "Much older."

"You'll do fine. I can picture you both crossing that finish line. In fact . . ." Joy turned to Jamie. "We should meet them there at the finish."

"Great idea." Millie sat straight.

"With champagne!" Edith laughed.

"And tiramisu," Millie replied.

The group turned to see who had entered the room when they heard some voices.

"Well, well." Edith nodded as she wiped her mouth. Judith and her husband entered. "Look who's blessing us with her presence."

"Steady." Millie touched Edith's arm. "Be nice."

Edith rolled her eyes. "I'm definitely using her as a model

for the villain in my book." She set down her drink. "Picture a young couple in love, walking the streets of Rome. Enjoying each other's company. Laughing, walking, seeing the sights, when suddenly, a crabby old hag blocks their way and—"

"Stop." Millie nudged her friend and waved at Judith. "Come sit with us, Judith and George." She smiled and scooted her chair down a bit to make room for them at the table.

Judith's wide eyes and crumpled face revealed how she felt about the invitation, but she and George sat down at the table. But no one spoke for a few minutes.

Edith cleared her throat, stood, and returned to the breakfast buffet for some toast without uttering one word.

Millie could sense her frustration at having to sit with the villain of her story, after all.

"So, where is everyone headed today?" Millie asked before finishing her orange juice.

"Well, we're off to see Saint Paul's Basilica and then take the train to Naples. I think we'll also go to see Pompeii. What about you?" Jamie asked.

"That sounds amazing. We're off to see the Vatican City." Millie smiled widely. "And the Sistine Chapel."

"A lot of walking." Joy curled her lip. "Be prepared."

Judith remained strangely silent as she buttered her toast with determination.

"And then we're going to eat at a restaurant on the street," Edith said when she returned. "I can't wait."

"Try the restaurant down the street. We stopped there yesterday, and the pizza was fantastic." Michael turned to Jamie.

"How's your father, Michael?" Edith asked.

Millie had noticed Ben wasn't with them but chose not to say anything.

A slight frown came to Michael's face. "He's a bit worn out today and decided to stay in the room and rest."

"I'll check on him later," Joy interjected. "I don't plan on doing much today."

More silence overcame the table. After a spell of clinking silverware and glasses made odd music, Judith cleared her throat.

"We're heading to Venice for a couple of days, and then we'll be back," Judith said without raising her eyes from her plate.

Edith turned to Millie and pursed her lips and silently mocked Judith.

"Stop that," Millie mouthed to Edith. "Sounds wonderful," she said to Judith. Millie glanced out the window to avoid laughing at Edith's mocking facial expressions. "I hope you all have a nice time."

"We will." Judith took a bite of her toast. "We always do."

"Well, we're off." Edith smacked Millie's arm. "We have to catch the train to the Vatican."

"What's this I heard about you taking photos of a wedding?" Judith methodically set down her toast onto its plate.

Millie sat back down. "Yes. It was so exciting. We happened upon a wedding at the Boboli Gardens in Florence and—"

"I know where that is." Judith's eyes narrowed.

"A wedding?" Joy's face lit up, and she leaned in to listen to the details.

"And the grandmother of the bride asked me to take the photos." Millie tilted her head. "How did you hear about it, Judith?"

George rested his elbows onto the table. By the dark half-moons under his eyes, Millie suspected he was tired. "We stopped at a restaurant in downtown Florence, and the manager there was talking about your photographs."

Millie beamed. "Really?" She turned to Edith and grabbed her arm. "Did you hear that? That's wonderful."

"The photos were beautiful." George smiled, then drank

some coffee.

"Thank you." Millie clasped her hands together.

"They were all right," Judith interjected. "A bit dark."

"Oh, the early afternoon shadows were long." Millie wrung her fingers. "And the sunlight was so bright that it was hard to see my camera screen to view them."

"Anyway, let's get going." Edith motioned for Millie to head out.

Millie rose and thought more about her photographs. "And it was such short notice that it took me a while to set the exposure."

"Goodbye, everyone," Edith said with a wave.

"So I didn't really have time to—" Millie continued.

"I'm sure they were lovely," Joy said as she gave Judith a harsh look. "You'll have to show them to us later."

"Enjoy the Sistine Chapel," Judith cried with a smirk on her face.

∽

The metro ride gave Millie a chance to check her messages and emails again.

Still nothing from Walter. A frown formed on her weary face.

Edith seemed to notice her morose expression. "Don't let Judith ruin your day, okay?"

"That woman?" Millie smirked. "No chance."

"Then what is it? Walt hasn't replied yet?"

"Walter, and no, he hasn't." Millie blew air between her lips. "Why hasn't he? I've called, emailed, texted—and nothing." She put her phone into her purse, then removed her camera to review some of her photos. "He can't possibly be that hurt, right?"

"He's all right. Don't worry about him. He married at age forty. Believe me. He knows how to cook and clean and—"

"I know all that." Millie glanced at her camera screen and studied a photo of a door she had shot in Rome. "It's just that I want to share all these experiences with him, and he doesn't want to participate. He's hurt, I understand that. I do. But why can't he celebrate with me? Lord knows I've celebrated all of his accomplishments through the years. I have been there for his highs and lows. Why can't he be there for mine?"

"Tell him about it." Edith stared out the window. "I can't tell you how many times I should have said things to Charlie but kept them inside."

"You're right." Millie removed her phone and started an email to Walter. "I never told you this before, but he and I went to counseling a few years back."

Edith jerked around. "What?"

"It's true."

"When?"

"About four years into the marriage. We were struggling." Millie typed as she spoke to Edith. "And the counselor said communication is key. We weren't communicating anymore. I'd tell him everything I thought he wanted to hear, and he wasn't telling me anything at all."

"That's not a marriage."

"Exactly." Millie wrote out her email. "So I'm reminding him about what the counselor told us. Communication is key. I need him to tell me what he's feeling, no matter how painful it is. And I need him to understand where I'm coming from." Millie stopped writing and looked up. "In fact, I need to talk to Judith."

"I beg your pardon?" Edith crossed her arms. "What are you talking about?"

"Yes. Judith tried to intimidate me. You came to my rescue by putting her in her place, but I need to talk to her. I need her to see that she doesn't intimidate me."

"Wow."

"What?"

"We've been in Rome less than a week, and you've really grown." Edith playfully shoved Millie. "And maybe that's why . . ." Her voice trailed off.

"Why what?" Millie faced her friend.

Edith shrugged. "Maybe Walt has seen in your emails that you've changed since you left." Edith winced. "And maybe that concerns him? Or . . . even scares him?"

Millie's face softened, and she watched the streets rush by in the window. Her belly tightened.

"Don't get me wrong. I think it's great that you've grown, but it might be a concern for Walt." Edith studied Millie's face. "What do you think?"

"You might be right." Millie continued to stare out the window. "Walter could be concerned."

The metro stopped, and the ladies hopped off the train and walked along the crowded sidewalks until they spotted a line of people along the Vatican wall.

Edith waved Millie over. "I think I've located the entrance to the Vatican City by this line of people."

A worker approached. "Bongiorno. How may I assist you this morning?"

Edith showed him their tickets. "Are we in the right line?"

"Ah, yes. You are in the correct line." He smiled, then walked up to the next confused person.

"Good. We're in the right place."

But Millie's blank stare showed she was deep in thought. She reread the email she had drafted to Walter on the train while Edith placed their tickets into her purse.

```
Dear Walter,
      Since I still haven't heard from you, I
thought I'd let you know how that makes me
feel. I remember how the marriage counselor
told me that I tend to keep my feelings inside
so as not to bother you, but that's avoidance,
and that's not a good thing.
      Walter, the fact that you haven't
```

responded to my emails, texts, or voicemails
has caused me much distress. First, I thought
that maybe you were in an accident or ill. I
had Susan, our neighbor, check on your welfare.
That's how concerned I was. But now that I know
you are fine, I have to admit that I'm angry.
I understand that you are hurt that I went to
Rome without you, but I am hurt that you didn't
see how important it was to me that you come
with me.

"The line's moving," Edith said.

Millie sent the email, exhaled, and placed her phone in her purse. "Okay. That's that."

"You sent it?" Edith walked ahead.

"I did."

"Good for you." Edith turned and smiled. "How do you feel now?"

Watching a few couples in line, Millie's face turned warm. "I feel better, I think."

Edith gave her a side hug. "Well, kiddo, I think it was the right thing to do."

"He needs to know how I feel," she said in an aggravated voice. Her throat tightened. "I'm tired of keeping it all in."

"Now he knows." Edith faced her. "Take a deep breath in."

Millie closed her eyes and inhaled.

"When you exhale, let it all go, because we are about to see something exceptionally beautiful, and I want you to be present during it all, okay?"

With a nod and a smile, Millie slowly exhaled all that frustration out, opened her eyes, and smiled. A blissful look came to her face as she thought about the art and gardens she was about to see.

"Better?" Edith asked with raised eyebrows.

"Ready." With a thumbs-up sign, Millie joined the line.

Once inside the Vatican Museum lobby, the ladies joined their tour group, put on their headsets, and began their adventure.

As they inspected sculptures, paintings, relics, gardens, and more, Millie's eyes greedily drank in the view with wonder and awe. Her camera filled up with photos, so she had to switch to her phone camera.

The sculptures, the history of the paintings, the manicured gardens, and the views of the city, complete with avocado green hills peppered with maritime pine trees of various heights from each window, captured her heart.

Forever.

The two friends located a bench outside in the courtyard and rested for a bit. The air was thick with the scents of jasmine, lavender, and freesia from nearby gardens.

"Just inhale that smell of jasmine . . ." Millie closed her eyes and tilted her head back. "I can even smell the sea. Can you?"

"My feet are killing me," Edith moaned.

Millie laughed. "We'll be prepared for the marathon, that's for sure." Reaching into her fanny pack, Millie removed an energy bar. "Want some?"

Edith shook her head. "Not hungry, just tired. We'll sleep well tonight."

Millie munched on the energy bar. She sat straight, startled by something.

"What is it?" Edith turned to her, then glanced around the bench. "Did you get bit or something? A spider?"

"No." Millie reached into her fanny pack and removed her phone. "My phone vibrated." She scrolled the screen and saw a text message.

"Well?"

With her mouth slightly open, Millie stared at her phone. "It's from Walter."

"What did he write?" Edith gestured.

But Millie stared at the screen, then put her phone back inside her pack. "I don't know, and I don't want to read it right now. I'm enjoying myself too much."

"What if it's an emergency or something?"

"He would've called." Millie watched the tourists meander through the gardens, taking photos of statues and sculptures.

Edith blinked her eyes a few times, then patted Millie's knee. "You're right. Let's head over to St. Peter's Basilica."

Hopping up with a wide smile, Millie felt victorious. "Let's go."

The tour group entered the famous basilica with cameras and phones out, heads tilted back as their eyes admired the elaborate marble ceiling and sculptures set within the walls.

The enormity of the space sent chills over Millie's body. "I can't believe this is real." She spun around with her eyes fixated on the elegant marble designs, the intricately detailed sculptures, and the bronze basilica itself. The massive ornate Baldachin canopy stood in the distance. Millie opened her phone to take a photo and saw Walter's text message notification again.

She sighed and decided to take a photo of the canopy over the altar of St. Peter's Basilica instead of reading it.

"Isn't this magnificent?" Edith stood alongside her with wide eyes following the structure all the way to the ceiling. "All that gold and marble and bronze. Breathtaking."

"I've never seen such a structure like this. Or a place like this. I took so many photos that my camera card is full." Millie laughed.

Edith asked a passerby, "Can you take our photo?" She handed the lady her phone.

The two stood with the massive Baroque canopy behind them and smiled for the photograph.

"Grazie," Millie said to the woman.

"Can you take our photo?" the woman asked as she pointed to her approaching husband.

"Of course." Millie waved for the woman and her husband to pose by the canopy. "Smile."

When the woman saw the photo, her eyes widened. "You

did a wonderful job," she said in a thick German accent.

Two more women peeked over her shoulder and conversed in German.

"Here," one of the women said. "Can you take our photo?"

"No problem." Millie directed them where to stand, ensuring the canopy and some light streaming in through the nearby window made a halo effect around the structure over the altar. "There you go."

The women admired the photograph and gestured wildly as they described it.

"You are very talented," one woman said and hugged Millie.

Edith chuckled.

Soon, many more of the German tourists gathered around Millie to have her photograph them.

Edith sat on a nearby pew and crossed her legs, dangling her foot as she waited.

"And there you go." Millie handed the last tourist their phone.

They nodded and muttered their thanks in German and other languages as they scooted along.

When Millie turned to talk to Edith, she couldn't find her.

"Over here!" Edith waved from a pew.

"Well, that was fun," Millie said as she approached.

"You're too nice." Edith stood and straightened her blouse. "I would have gently sent them on their way."

Millie laughed. "I couldn't do that. Did you see how their faces lit up when they saw their photos? It made my day to see them so happy."

Edith listened as she strolled along the space.

"I thank God that I can use my talent to make people smile." Millie glanced upward at the details of the ceiling. "I want to please Him and also make people happy."

"And you do a marvelous job at both." Edith patted Millie's shoulder. "Now, where are we off to?"

"I want to see the Pieta." Millie rushed off.

Crowds of people stood in front of the Chapel of the Pieta, Michelangelo's famous sculpture of Mary holding the body of Jesus.

Standing on her tiptoes, Millie held her phone up to capture the beauty of the sculpture. The smoothness of the milky-white marble, the way it glistened in the light, and the solemn expression on Mary's face made Millie weep.

"He was only twenty-four years old when he sculpted it," she whispered to herself. "Twenty-four."

She wept because of the beauty. She wept because of the magnificent gift God bestowed upon Michelangelo. And she wept because God had gifted her with seeing the cherished sculpture in person.

She knew it was a once-in-a-lifetime experience.

Wiping her eyes, Millie made her way through the crowd to the front so she could be even closer to the priceless work of art. So realistic, she almost expected Mary to lift her chin or breathe in and out.

She drank it all in, knowing she may not ever get the chance to see such beauty again. *Thank you, Lord,* Millie prayed with her hand across her heart. *Thank you for this amazing gift.*

Outside in the courtyard of St. Peter's Basilica, Millie spotted Edith taking photos of the columns and the piazza, the many tourists, and the dome.

She sniffled and used a tissue to wipe her eyes as she approached Edith.

"What's the matter?" Edith looked up from her phone.

"The Pieta . . ." Millie exhaled and tilted her head back, soaking in the sunlight on her face. "Such magnificence took my breath away."

"Oh, yeah?" Edith grabbed Millie's shoulders and turned her around. "Take a look at that."

Millie lifted her eyes and studied the grandeur of the piazza and the massive St. Peter's Basilica dome rising over the façade.

"No matter where you look, all you see is spectacular beauty that's almost impossible to describe." Millie tossed up her hands. "I give up. If I stay here much longer, I'll keep weeping."

Edith laughed. "It is a religious experience, that's for sure. Come on, then. Let's get the train home."

"Look at that." Millie showed Edith her phone's screen. "15,000 steps today."

Edith rubbed her thighs. "I believe it. My legs aren't too happy with me."

"And to think we still have a marathon to run." Millie gently elbowed Edith.

Glancing down at her phone again, Millie noticed the battery was almost dead, so she decided to read Walter's text message before the phone died.

"I'm fine," was all he wrote.

She turned the phone off, then placed it into her pack.

CHAPTER 9

On the train back to Rome, Millie shifted in her seat, first left, then right, and back again.

"Something wrong?" Edith looked up from her paperback novel and shot Millie a glance that revealed her annoyance.

"No. Nothing's wrong. Why?" Millie crossed her arms and stared out the window at the countryside racing by.

"Something's wrong, or else you've got a rash on your bottom." Edith turned the page in her book. "Sit still, will you?"

Millie sighed and tapped her pack around her waist. "I read Walter's text message."

"And?" Edith removed her reading glasses.

"I'm fine." Millie pursed her lips together. "That's all he wrote."

"That's it?"

"That's it." Millie shook her head. "I'm fine." She used her fingers to make air quotes.

Edith laughed. "Well, at least you know he's fine."

"I suppose."

"He'll never be accused of being verbose, that's for sure." Edith tilted her head. "Right?"

Millie laughed. "Right."

The two friends laughed on the train so loudly, passengers turned to stare at them.

∞

Back in Rome, the ladies sat at a table inside La Vecchia Roma restaurant for a late lunch. After viewing the menu, Millie settled on an order of bruschetta for starters.

Edith ordered chianti and some bread.

"What a day." Millie pulled out her camera and viewed the many photos she had taken. "Another dream realized. Photographing the Vatican Museum was indeed a dream come true. Winning this contest has afforded me the incredible opportunity to photograph Rome, Florence, and now the Vatican City and St. Peter's Basilica. I can't wait to get home and edit these."

"I wonder which ones the publisher will select for their calendar." Edith pointed to the camera. "Ooh, and the coffee table book."

"I don't know, but I still have more to take of the doors around here."

"Scusi, signora," a man said.

Millie looked up to see an older Italian man staring down at her. "Yes?"

"I couldn't help but overhear you say that you are one of the contest winners visiting Rome?"

"Yes. I am." She sat straight.

"Wonderful." He held out his hand. "My name is Luigi Carmalini, and I am the manager of this ristorante. Benvenuto."

"Grazie." Millie smiled.

"I am looking for photographs," he said as he pointed to the restaurant walls. "May I take a look at some of your photos?"

"Certainly." Millie pulled out a chair, and Luigi sat down.

She and Edith waited patiently while he scanned through the photographs. He remained silent through most of them but made the "mmm" sound at a few. When his eyebrows rose, Millie suspected he liked some.

The waiter brought the bruschetta, and Edith grabbed one of the tomato-covered bread slices drizzled with olive oil.

"Well?" she asked the manager between bites.

"I love these." He slid the camera to Millie. "Do you have a business card so I can contact you for the prints?"

Millie's eyes widened. "Uh, sure." She grabbed her purse and scavenged it for her business card. "Here it is!"

She turned it over and wrote her email address on the back.

"Grazie, Signora." Luigi stood. "I've been taking my own photographs to hang in here, but they lack polish. I truly love your work and feel they will add to the ambience of the dining room, no?"

"Yes!" Millie cried. "Absolutely."

"I couldn't agree more," Edith added.

Luigi bowed and headed to the kitchen.

Millie clutched her chest. "Did that just happen?" she asked. "I can't believe it."

Edith raised her glass of chianti. "I can believe it. You are that talented, girl. Cin-cin."

Millie used her water glass to toast. "Cin-cin."

"Hello," Judith said as she approached. Without asking, she pulled out a chair at their table and sat down. She used her manicured fingers to move her bangs away from her face.

"Uh . . . hello?" Millie said with her glass of water in her hand. She lowered it to the table. "Judith."

"Ah, Judith. So nice to see you again," Edith said with a sardonic grin. "What are you doing here?"

"We thought you were headed to Venice today." Millie set down her water.

"Change of plans." Judith leaned back in her chair and smirked. "George is . . . he decided to stay in the hotel room. I told him I wanted to get some—"

"Authentic Italian food, yes, we know." Edith ate more

bruschetta.

"Anyway." Judith pursed her lips so tightly, they almost disappeared. "I saw you two and decided to join you."

"Well, good." Millie turned off her camera and set it aside. "It's been a glorious day. First, we saw—"

"Get good shots today?" Judith asked.

"As a matter of fact, yes, I did get some good shots," Millie answered with a wide smile. Various images she had taken flashed through her mind. A warm feeling flowed over her.

"The manager asked Millie for her business card. He wants to buy some prints from her." Edith nodded and took a bite of the bruschetta. "What do you think about that?" she managed to say between chews.

"Congratulations." Judith waved to the waiter. "Can I have a glass of red wine?" She stabbed the table with her finger. "Put it right here."

The waiter hurried off.

"Millie . . ." Judith began. "Why didn't your husband come with you to Rome? I mean, what's the *real* reason?"

Right before she bit into some bruschetta, Millie froze.

Edith cleared her throat. "My, my, Judith, but that's an awfully personal question, don't you think?"

"Just making conversation." Judith chuckled as she took the wine from the waiter's hand before he could set it down.

Millie remained still, staring at the bruschetta toast in her hand.

"I mean, it just seems a little suspicious." Judith sipped her wine.

"What do you mean?" Millie finally said in a small voice. "I told everyone the real reason. My husband couldn't take time off from his job."

"Does he support your photography business?" Judith tilted her head and leaned forward with her elbows on the table. Her position brought her face just inches away from Millie's.

What was she looking for?

"My photography business?" Millie fiddled with the toast on her plate.

"Yes. Your photography business. Does he support you?" She gulped down some wine.

"Sure, he does." Edith spoke up and glanced over at Millie.

"He's just up for an important promotion and didn't think it was the right time to ask for vacation time," Millie said with as much enthusiasm as she could muster.

"Hmmm." Judith curled her upper lip. "He didn't think it was a good time to leave work. You see? That's where I have an issue." She jabbed her finger onto the table again, shaking it.

Edith reached out and grabbed the candle before it tipped over. "Relax, will you?"

"What exactly do you mean, Judith?" Millie looked at Judith and then at Edith. "I don't understand what you're implying."

Millie thought back to the argument that she and Walter had before she left. *I have an issue with it too.*

"We always support our husbands, don't we? I know I do." Judith crossed her arms defiantly. "George has golf tournaments, business conferences, boring dinner parties for clients . . . I've had to endure all of those events for him."

"Right." Millie squinted as she tried to figure out where Judith was going with all this.

Edith leaned in, and Millie suspected she knew what Judith was getting at. So Millie leaned in, too, pretending to understand.

"So why can't they support us?" Judith waved over the waiter and took the glass of wine from his hand as he approached. She sipped it. "We cook and clean and do laundry, yet when we ask them to support us, they are too busy."

"Too busy." Anger flowed through Millie. But she wasn't

angry with Judith. Her anger burned at Walter.

"She's right," Millie said to Edith. "I do everything for Walter, and the one time I ask him to be there for me, he says now is not a good time." She banged the table with her hands, and several patrons turned to see what happened.

This time, the wine bottle almost toppled. Edith grabbed it in time. "Will you two stop banging on the table? People are staring."

"I mean, I know he's not being truthful. He just didn't want to spend the money," Millie fumed and her face grew warm, and not from hot flashes.

"What money?" Judith leaned closer to Millie. "It's an all-expenses-paid trip to Rome."

"I know!" Millie agreed and the two women laughed. "A free trip to Rome. What is wrong with him?"

"Ladies," Edith interrupted. "I think the problem is—"

"Why can't he just be truthful with me?" Millie held out her phone to Judith and pointed at all the messages. "I've emailed him each day and texted him about the trip, asked him about the promotion, and all I get from him is, 'I'm fine.' That's it."

Judith pursed her lips and shook her head as though disgusted. "I'm fine." She scoffed. "That's their stock answer for everything. We know he isn't fine."

"So, Judith . . . what really happened between you and George?" Edith asked as she folded her hands.

Millie recognized that look in Edith's eyes. She knew Edith was asking questions to gather more information for her book. Or for herself.

"I mean, Walter didn't come with Millie, but you got George to come with you to Rome." Edith narrowed her eyes to mere slits. "That doesn't align with what you're saying about him not supporting you."

Judith rolled her eyes. "He came with me, but I know he doesn't want to be here. We were on our way to Venice when George and I got into a huge fight on the train." Her eyes grew shiny.

Millie gasped. "No. I'm so sorry, Judith. What happened next?"

Judith vented air between her lips. "I'm here, and he's there."

"Whoa." Edith glanced at Millie, then back at Judith.

The waiter tried to set down a glass of wine for Millie, but Judith took it out of his hand. "Thank you." She took another big gulp.

"Easy there." Edith gently tapped Judith's hand, and she lowered the wine glass.

"Sorry. I get a bit dramatic at times." Judith snickered.

"Yes, we know." Edith slowly slid the wine glasses out of Judith's reach.

"Judith, I'm so sorry about what's happening between you and George. I really am." Millie meant it too. She couldn't imagine such an argument causing calm, compliant George to remain in Venice while Judith returned to Rome alone.

"Yeah, well. I couldn't head back to the hotel just yet, so I thought I'd stop in here for a drink." She glanced longingly at her wine glass but sighed. "By the way, the food here is delicious."

Edith smoothed out the tablecloth as if smoothing things out between herself, Millie, and Judith. "Are you going to be all right, Judith?"

But she didn't answer right away. Her light brown hair pulled back into a ponytail revealed some gray hairs at the temples, and her lipstick hadn't been applied with her usual precision.

"Are you ready?" the waiter asked. But when he saw the three unhappy faces, he spun around and departed for another table.

"We're here to help." Millie offered Judith a smile and a gentle touch of her hand.

"Thanks. And no, I'm not all right." Judith rubbed her

forehead as if it ached.

Millie knew that ache well.

"Haven't you noticed that I've been . . . on edge the whole time we've been here in Rome?"

Millie and Edith tried to look astonished as they shook their heads and shrugged.

"No, not at all," Edith replied.

"Oh, come on." Judith chuckled. "You both know it." She leaned on the table and covered her face, heavy with weariness. "He didn't want to come on this trip in the first place, but I convinced him. No, more like manipulated him."

A sick feeling hit Millie's stomach when she heard Judith's words.

"And then when we got here, he seemed to be fine with it. I mean, this free trip and all. We didn't have a vacation last year, so this was perfect timing. Plus, we went to the villa of Carlo Ricci, visited some art galleries interested in my work and . . . I thought he'd be happier for me." She sniffled. "But he seems bored."

"Men," Edith huffed.

"I struggle to understand them at all," Millie interjected.

"They can be enigmas, that's for sure." Edith waved to the waiter. "I think we're ready to order."

It was as if Edith instinctively knew where the conversation was headed, and Millie understood that Edith didn't want to head down that rocky road so soon after losing Charlie. Edith's instinct astonished Millie time and time again. As did her strength.

After dinner, the three women sipped coffee and dug into tiramisu.

"So what are you going to do?" Millie asked Judith.

"He needs some time alone to think. I'm giving it to him." Judith laid out some euros to pay for her meal and wine. "And then I'm going to continue doing what I enjoy doing, which is enjoying the rest of my stay in Rome. Life is too short to care so much about what our husbands think. They don't own us. We are grown women with our own minds, our own wants and desires. I'm not going to give myself up for him."

Millie looked over at Edith.

"What about you?" Judith asked Millie.

"I'm going to enjoy the rest of my time here, keep emailing Walter details about my day, and text him to check on him. What else can I do?" Millie shrugged. "He is who he is. I can't change him. I can only change me."

"Why even tell him about it?" Judith pulled out a compact mirror and lipstick from her purse and touched up her lips.

"Because I want him to feel like he's here with me." Millie smiled a cheeky smile.

Judith mechanically lowered her compact mirror and glared down her nose again. "Millie," she began, "I think we've established that he doesn't care about your time in Rome."

"Judith . . ." Edith glowered at her.

"Well, I don't know about that." Millie shifted in her chair. "All he said was that he's fine. He didn't tell me to stop emailing him."

"Millie knows her husband." Edith crossed her arms.

Judith scooted away from the table, stood, and put her purse under her arm. "He obviously doesn't care. Why waste your time wondering if he cares? Want my advice? Take it or leave it."

"Well, not—"

"I think you should just make the best of the rest of your time here, and to hell with Walter." She spun around to leave but stopped at the entrance. "That's what I told George. I'm too old to spend my days living for someone else." But Judith's eyes shone with tears, revealing her true feelings. "Anyway, thanks for dinner, girls."

Millie and Edith watched Judith storm out of the restaurant.

"Come on." Edith took Millie's forearm. "Let's head back

to the hotel."

The weight of Judith's words held Millie down for a bit, and she couldn't move.

"Mill? You okay? Don't let Judith's words affect you."

Millie inhaled, then slowly exhaled, releasing the grip Judith had on her. "You're right."

CHAPTER 10

On the way back to the hotel, Millie couldn't get Walter's simplistic text message and Judith's comments out of her mind. *After my emails and text messages, that's all he could write? He's obviously angry with me.* Judith had fueled the flames of Millie's anger, that's for sure. It went from a spark to a forest fire in a few minutes.

"I'm going for a walk to take more photos of doors," Millie said.

"I thought your camera card was full?" Edith tilted her head.

"I'll use my phone," Millie snapped, then glanced down an alleyway. "I just need to clear my head."

"Millie." Edith sighed.

"What?" She turned to face her friend.

"Don't be angry at Walt. He is who he is, you know that."

"I'm not angry."

Edith raised an eyebrow.

"Okay, maybe I am angry, but more at myself than Walter."

"That's not true." Edith waved her hand. "Go on, then. Clear your head. Be careful, and don't stay out too late."

"I won't. Thanks for dinner." Millie spun around and

headed down an alleyway past shops, bars, and more restaurants. When she came upon a dark green door, she took a photograph with her phone and inspected it. The composition of the photo pleased her, as did the lighting. The kind remarks of the German tourists filled her with joy, and she beamed with confidence. The anger in her heart began to fade.

Making her way down the street, Millie noticed the violet sunlight illuminated some buildings and cast shadows over others. Passersby were getting off work and heading home or scouting out restaurants to patronize.

She turned down another street and ran into Joy, sobbing by a doorway.

"Joy?" Millie asked as she approached. "Are you all right?"

She shook her head and glanced at the phone in her hand.

"What's the matter? Is it bad news from home?"

"No." Joy lifted her chin and let out a slow sigh. "Jamie heard from Carl tonight."

"Carl?" Millie tried to remember who that was. When she did, her mouth dropped. "You mean her ex?"

Joy scowled. "Yes. Her ex. He texted her, and then she called him and . . ."

"Don't tell me they're getting back together?" Millie grimaced.

"Looks like it." Joy wiped her eyes.

"Oh no."

"Millie, you and I know that she loves Michael. I just know she does."

Millie nodded in agreement.

"And Michael—" Joy cried. "He adores her."

Millie took her hand. "I know he does. I can see it in his eyes when he looks at her."

Joy smiled as she wept. "Yes." Then her face crinkled as if she smelled dog mess nearby. "Let me tell you this. Carl never looked at her that way. Ever." She jabbed her finger at

Millie. "Not once. He didn't love Jamie. And now . . ." Joy covered her face and wept.

Millie hugged her. "I'm so sorry, Joy. Maybe Jamie will surprise you and not—"

"No." Joy pulled away and wiped her eyes. "She spoke with him and is willing to see him. I begged her not to, and then we got into a big fight. I left, and she's in our room calling him."

Millie's shoulders sank. "Wow."

"Yeah. Wow." Joy leaned against the wall. "He said he's willing to fly out here so they can talk."

With mouth dropped open again, Millie staggered back a bit. "How . . . romantic?"

"No. Carl is not romantic. He's manipulative. She mentioned how she and Michael spent time together, and now Carl says he's flying out?" Joy hugged herself. "He's playing her just like he did before."

"Come on, Joy. Let's go for a walk." Millie gently took her forearm and led her down the alley. "I love these little alleyways, don't you?"

Joy wiped her cheeks and nodded.

"The little tables by the restaurants and the tiny white lights glowing above. So romantic." Millie glanced above them.

"What can I do, Millie?" Joy begged. "There has to be something I can do, right?"

"Not a thing." Millie walked on.

"I know." Joy dropped her hands to her sides. "All I can do is pray. Pray that she'll see the light. I've been praying that she'll see right through Carl. He's conniving and manipulative and—"

"Would you take your husband back if he showed up right here in Rome and begged you?"

"Absolutely not!" Joy shouted. Several passersby turned around.

"Joy, you taught your daughter well. You've taught her

that life can go on. You've shown her what a strong, capable woman looks like. You've shown her that there can be a life without a terribly manipulative and deceitful man at her side. Trust her. She'll make the right decision."

"Do you really think so, Millie?" Joy faced her.

"Yes. I do." Millie gave Joy a side hug and turned her around. "Just give her time to process everything and think about it. Okay?"

"Okay."

"Now. Head back to your room, take a hot shower or bath, and breathe. Order something for yourself. A decadent dessert or something," Millie instructed. "All right?"

"All right. Thank you, Millie." Joy touched Millie's chin. "You're a gem."

Right when she walked off, Millie said, "I admire you, Joy."

She tilted her head. "You do?"

Millie nodded. "You've shown me that a middle-aged woman can start again. You've shown me that a woman our age can take charge of her life with dignity and grace. I've learned a lot from you, Joy. You're amazing."

Joy gave her one last hug, then spun around to head back to the hotel.

After Joy left for the hotel, Millie headed down the alleyway until she spotted a lovely wooden door stained with a deep dark walnut brown stain. The brass door kick plates and ornate doorknobs grabbed her attention. As she pointed her phone's camera to the door, Millie hesitated. *I wonder what's behind this door.* She stepped toward it and listened. Glancing upward, her eyes followed the limestone façade until she spotted several windows with flower baskets filled with bright red geraniums attached to the balcony rails. Geraniums. Her favorite.

Lace curtains appeared in most of the windows.

Does this door lead to those apartments upstairs? How amazing would it be to live in Rome? Envy ran through her veins.

She took several photos of the door, then backed away and leaned against a wall, allowing herself to dream a bit. *What would life be like here? What if I could make it as a photographer? I could work at a local college or the community center and then show my photos at a gallery. It could work. Couldn't it?*

Tears formed in her eyes, and the sting shook her from her dream. Millie blinked the sting of tears away.

For the first time in her marriage, she pictured a life without Walter, and it made her stomach sick. She couldn't swallow. The sick feeling made her cough and gag until she hugged her middle.

Why, God? She wiped her eyes. *Why is Walter doing this? Why couldn't he support me in just this one thing? I don't understand.*

That prayer and sting of tears made her wince, because it was all too familiar. She had prayed a similar prayer about her father all through college. And now, thirty years later, she was still praying.

I didn't enter the photography contest to win a trip alone to Rome. I entered for . . . The reasons were catalogued in her mind. *You know my reasons. You know my heart, Lord.*

A flood of emotions overtook her, and she covered her face and wept quietly there on a street in Rome, half crying and half laughing. The release felt good. Millie chortled when she realized she hadn't cried before this trip. Crying made Walter uncomfortable, so she would hold it inside so he wouldn't see.

So he wouldn't be uncomfortable.

Everything's about Walter. I can't even cry when I need to. She exhaled the frustration. *Just like everything about my life before was about my father.* Her mother's weary face flashed in her mind. *Mom did everything for Dad, and look what it got her. She gave up everything for him, and for what?* A memory of her childhood home sent waves of pain over her already tired body. Spotless and organized, it could have been a model home. But it had no soul, no joy, no feeling of warmth.

And no one ever came over to visit.

Millie breathed out slowly, and she glanced upward again. Just like no one ever came over to her house back home.

As Millie's eyes rose to the second story window, the lace curtains animated by a breeze flowed softly in and out of the open window, catching her attention. Her mind wandered as she imagined what it looked like inside the apartment, who lived there, and why. Someone came out of the door, startling her. But the door closed before Millie could look inside. The young woman who walked out looked to her left, then hustled past as if she had an agenda.

Millie watched her stride away with such confidence that her heart sank. *I've been alive for over fifty years, and I've never walked with such confidence. I've never had such confidence.* She looked left, then right as more people passed by. *What must it feel like? Is it Rome? Does living here give you confidence?* An ache filled her soul. Millie had never felt such a craving as she did in that moment. Her eyes fixed on the door again. It called to her and tugged at her to open it. The intrigue pulled at her, and she stepped toward it.

A flashback to when she was six years old stopped her mid-stride. A door had intrigued her back then too. A door at a rest stop in the desert. While her parents argued by the parked car and her siblings ran around the parking lot, six-year-old Millie focused on the door and wondered what was behind it.

"Scusi!" A sudden shout startled Millie back to Rome. A man approaching fast on his scooter rushed by, almost striking Millie. She leapt back in time, realizing she had been in the middle of the road.

"Scusami," Millie shouted to his back. Relief flowed through her. Going back to that time in her childhood wasn't something she wanted to do that evening, not after having seen the glory of St. Peter's Basilica, the Pieta, and the piazza. Instead, she took a few more photos of the door and building, then walked further down the street to find more doors.

That night in her hotel room, Millie opened her laptop to write an email to Walter. Edith slept soundly, and no cheers or music came from the alleyway outside the window.

The quiet room matched Millie's somber state of mind.

Dear Walter-

Edith and I went to the Vatican City today and toured the museum. I couldn't believe all the art! Everywhere we turned, there were magnificent paintings, sculptures, statues, and views outside the windows. I took so many photos, I'll spend most of tomorrow saving them onto my computer.

I think my favorite part of the visit was St. Peter's Basilica. The bronze canopy they built over the place they think Peter was killed is mammoth in size. The photos won't do it justice. I've attached a couple to this email. You'll see some people at the bottom to give it scale. Remarkable, isn't it? Everything here is on such a grand scale. Every way you turn, there's beauty.

Next, we stopped at a local restaurant for a late lunch, and the manager overheard me talking about winning the contest and having to photograph Rome. Anyway, to make a long story short, he asked for my business card so I can send him my photos. He wants to buy some to hang in his restaurant! It's like a dream come true. I can't even imagine my humble photos hanging in Rome. I'm so glad I had business cards made before I left home.

Tomorrow, we head to the Expo to pick up our bibs for Sunday's race. I still can't believe I let Edith talk me into running the Maratona di Roma. That's

Rome Marathon in Italian. Can you imagine Edith and me running through the streets of Rome? I won't believe it until it's happening. Well, tomorrow we will pick up our bibs, and that will make it seem more real.

I'm glad you responded to my text message. I was worried. I know you don't believe me, but I was worried. And I miss you. I wish you were here.

I'm sorry that you're still upset with me. I honestly wish you were here with me in Rome. The most romantic city in the world.

Love, Millie

Before she hit send, Millie opened up a blank Word document and wrote the email message she really wanted to send.

Walter,

I'm writing this because I feel you should know how I really feel being alone here in Rome.

How dare you! How dare you not even try to come with me or show any excitement about my accomplishment?

Yes, that's right. MY accomplishment.

I finally did something on my own, OF my own, and you don't care.

Do you know how many times I've had to show excitement about your accomplishments? How many times I've sat at your work banquets and clapped when they awarded you a plaque or award? How many times I've sat next to your drunk coworkers, listening to them tell the same boring stories repeatedly so you could go sit by the executives and schmooze them? Too many times.

She paused to grab a tissue and wipe the tears streaming down her cheeks.

All those boring banquet rooms filled with boring people talking about the same boring topics . . . year after year. But I put up with it because I knew it was important to you, and I love you. That's what people do when they love each other, Walter.

Then one day, I took a chance and believed in myself

enough to enter a contest, but I guess it was too much for you to handle, wasn't it? Your wife actually did something on her own. Your wife actually has talent. Your wife actually did something that had nothing to do with you.

And you can't stand it.

That's not love, Walter.

I'm here in the most romantic city in the world, and I'm alone, because my husband is so selfish, he can't set aside his own needs and wants to celebrate the wife he claims to love.

"Wait," you always say.

"Wait until we save enough money."

"Wait until I retire."

"Wait until this . . . wait until that."

Well, I grew tired of waiting, Walter. I'm afraid of life passing me by.

I've set aside my own needs and wants for years, beginning with my need to have children. I know we married late enough for it to be an issue for me to conceive, but when the doctor explained our options, you didn't even attempt to seek them out.

I went along with it because I trusted your judgment. I know God gave you to me for a reason, and I believe that reason was to reel me in when my intrigue or curiosity tempted me to go in the wrong direction.

The rest stop door appeared in her mind.

Your steady hand always kept me from doing something outrageous and possibly harmful.

I know God didn't want us to have children, and I accepted that long ago. But I also know that God didn't want me to give up my dreams and toss aside my gifts and talents to just sit at home and support you.

My hope is that one day you'll come to this realization, too, and reconcile the fact that you have an amazingly talented and gifted wife who can have accomplishments of her own, you know?

And that can happen without diminishing any of your own accomplishments or dreams.

-Millie

She sat back and stared at the words on the document. The blinking cursor mocked her, almost daring her to send it to Walter.

It says everything I've always wanted to say. She sighed. *But I'll never send it. I just needed to get that all out.*

Grabbing some tissues, Millie dabbed her eyes and blew her nose, then stared at the wall for a few minutes, wondering what Walter's week had been like. He probably cooked for himself, cleaned the kitchen, folded his laundry, ironed his shirts, straightened the family room, and took out the trash.

All without her.

That little girl painting at the community center table came to her mind. She opened her files on the laptop and scrolled until she found the photos of the little girl.

She painted liberally.

No one stood behind her, shouting orders.

No one told her she was doing it wrong. No one told her she couldn't do it at all. And no one told her to wait.

She painted in total freedom.

Millie saw that door again at the rest stop and her little six-year-old hand pressing on it. It was as real to her as it had been on that fateful day forty-six years ago. She could almost feel it against the skin of her now fifty-two-year-old hand.

On that day long ago, no one told her not to go in there. No one was there to stop her. No one even saw her at all. No one ever did.

Tears streamed down her face again. *Walter doesn't see me. Walter doesn't need me.* She reached up and dabbed her eyes. *He never did.*

"How can you stay with someone who isn't there?" she muttered to herself.

I'm not there. Millie sniffled. *And, just like my father, Walter doesn't even notice that I'm not there.*

She saved the document to a folder on her computer, knowing she would never send it. But wanting to save it just in case.

If you don't invest in love, Walter, you'll lose it. She closed her laptop.

As Millie sat on her bed inside a hotel room in Rome, for the first time in her marriage, she realized that she didn't need Walter.

But she wanted him, desperately.

Please don't lose me, Walter. She leaned back against the upholstered headboard and wept.

CHAPTER 11

The next day, Millie rose early to get some stretching in before the day's events began. *First, we head to the Expo to pick up our racing bibs, followed by more sightseeing, then lunch.* She exhaled. After a shower and change of clothes, she found Edith already dressed and ready to go.

"Twenty-four hours until race day!" Millie clapped her hands.

"I'm starved. Let's get some fruit and croissants." She shot Millie the thumbs-up sign.

In the hotel restaurant, Millie and Edith spotted the rest of the group seated at the tables, drinking and chatting.

Jamie paced in the hotel lobby with her ear pressed to her phone. Her furrowed brow revealed that the conversation wasn't pleasant.

Edith waved, but Jamie ignored her.

"I wonder what's going on?" Edith asked Millie.

"Well . . ." Millie bit her upper lip.

"What do you know?"

Millie pulled Edith aside and told her what had happened. "I don't think Joy would mind me telling you . . ."

"Telling me what?"

"Jamie heard from her ex yesterday, and well, she's—"

"Going back to him?" Edith's mouth dropped open.

"Not sure yet. He offered to fly to Rome just to talk with

her." Millie's face crinkled up. "What do you think?"

"I think she belongs with Michael." Edith frowned. "It's obvious that he cares for her and she cares for him."

"That's what I think."

Jamie ended the call and stared at her phone for a second or two before heading into the restaurant for breakfast.

"I guess we'll find out soon enough." Edith took Millie's arm. "Every book has a plot twist."

"This is quite the plot twist."

"Let's go." Edith pulled Millie along.

"Pretend like you don't know," Millie ordered.

"Good morning, all," Edith said with a wide smile.

Millie waved to the group and then headed for the plates and napkins. Next, she placed strawberries, a croissant, and jelly onto her plate. Out of the corner of her eye, she spied Joy without her usual cheery disposition.

Judith sat with Betsy and Hank, chatting about the famous Stairway to Heaven. "Are you and Edith going to try to climb the steps?"

Millie furrowed her brow as she approached. "Not with a marathon coming up." She patted her thigh and laughed. "I need to save my legs." She sat next to Joy. "Maybe afterwards, if I can walk at all."

"Are you nervous?" Joy asked.

"Of course we are." Millie rose to get some juice. "I hardly slept a wink last night just thinking about it."

"Speak for yourself." Edith sat down. "I'm as ready as I'll ever be, so why be nervous?"

"Exactly." Betsy smiled and pointed to her temple. "I read that running a marathon is more about psychology than anything."

"What's the worst that could happen?" Michael asked as he sat down across from Jamie instead of next to her.

Millie turned to Michael. "Well, the worst thing would be if we are too slow and they pack up the race and finish line before we can even reach it."

"They do that?" Edith asked with wide eyes.

"Yep. If you don't finish by hour seven, they shut the whole thing down, and you're no longer in the marathon. You're just out for a stroll." Millie laughed.

Edith's eyes grew even larger, and she slowly turned her head as though picturing the humiliating moment inside her head.

"But that won't happen to you two, Edith," Joy encouraged her. "I just know you'll finish."

"Yes, we will," Edith replied.

"You never know, though," Michael said with thick sarcasm in his voice. "Sometimes things happen that completely blindside you and leave you feeling—"

"Michael," Joy interrupted.

"Disappointed," he finished.

Jamie remained silent, staring at her plate.

"Eat up so we can head to the Expo, Edith." Millie bit into a strawberry.

"Everything has been so delicious, hasn't it?" Joy said. "I was just telling Claudia."

"I'll treasure this place always. It has helped make my time in Rome perfect." Millie smiled and turned to see Judith smirking at her.

"By the way, Millie . . ." Jamie handed her a note. "Claudia was looking for you earlier. She asked me to give this to you."

Millie took the note and read it. She glanced up and quickly placed the note into her fanny pack.

"What is it?" Edith asked between sips of her coffee.

"Nothing. I'll tell you about it on the train. We'd better head out now."

Just around the corner of the hotel, Millie and Edith hopped onto the metro to head to the Expo.

"Ah, the Expo…" Millie sighed. "It's been a long time since I've attended one."

"What is this event, exactly?" Edith asked.

"It's where we pick up our racing bibs then do a little shopping for racing gear or paraphernalia. It's fun."

The butterflies in Millie's belly made the ride on the train feel like a rollercoaster ride. But the butterflies weren't just about the marathon.

"Michael seemed hurt, didn't you think so?" Edith shook her head.

"I guess he knows, huh?"

"Hopefully, Jamie will see the light and dump her ex." Edith scanned through her phone.

Millie shifted in her seat again.

"I know you're nervous about the race on Sunday, but I really think you—"

"It's not the race that I'm nervous about." Millie removed the note.

Edith studied Millie's eyes for a moment, then took the note and read it. She offered an exaggerated "Hmm," and handed it back to Millie. "What are you going to do?"

"Well, I want to know what you think of it first. And will you go with me?" Millie swallowed the knot in her throat.

"To a seaside villa in Italy? Are you kidding? Of course, I'll come with you. But I want to know what's making you nervous."

"Carlo Ricci, the most famous photographer in Europe, has invited me—us—to his villa to see the work for his new book and to have dinner. That's what's making me nervous." Millie rubbed her neck. "In addition to the marathon."

Edith laughed. "You wanted adventure, dearie. You got it."

"I know, I know. You keep saying that." Millie sighed and reread the note in her hand. "But I wanted Walter to experience it with me."

"He's there. You're here." Edith turned in her seat to face

Millie. "This world-famous photographer wants to talk to you about his work and yours. You can't pass on such an amazing opportunity."

"Say no more." Millie reached over and touched Edith's arm. "I'm not nervous anymore." She thought more about the stroll through town the night before and the secret letter she had written to Walter. "It's a whole new day."

Edith turned to face her. "What happened on that stroll last night? Did you talk with Walter? Did you have, you know . . . *the* talk?"

Millie shook her head. "No. He still hasn't written to me, nor has he returned any of my calls." She gestured like an umpire would calling a player safe at home plate. "I'm done with that. I'm here for me now. The rest of my time here is about me and fulfilling my dreams."

"Astonishing." Edith crossed her arms. "You never answered me. Just what happened last night on that stroll through town?"

"The strangest thing happened, Edith." Millie drew the outline of a door in the air with her fingers. "I saw this beautiful door and stopped to photograph it. As I stared at it, I wondered what was behind it. And that's when I thought more about how Walter is so much like my father. He doesn't see me, you know?"

Edith nodded.

"I'm just there, but I'm not *there*. Not until he needs something. Only then does he see me. I started to approach that mysterious door to open it, but something stopped me, and I'm glad. I don't want to know just yet."

"Understood."

"And that's when I saw her."

Edith crinkled her brow. "Who?"

"I saw this beautiful and confident young woman with flowing dark hair and large brown eyes."

"A younger version of you?" Edith chuckled.

"Yes . . . and no. She passed by me with such conviction

and confidence that I was humbled. She had such determination and purpose in her walk that I—" Millie swallowed back tears. "Edith, I wept."

"Oh, Millie." Edith frowned, reached over, and squeezed Millie's hand.

"I wept because, at age fifty-two, I realized I have never had such confidence in myself. Ever. I envied her."

Edith squinted as though studying her friend.

"And I wept because I need to let go of who I was and embrace this." She pointed to her reflection in the window. "The new me." Millie fanned herself, trying to keep herself from crying. "I wept, but it felt good to get it all out. I needed that release." She patted Edith's leg. "Needless to say, I am more confident now. I'm going to rely on myself to get me through."

"I'm so happy for you."

"Thanks, friend." Millie rested her head on Edith's shoulder for a second, then sat up straight. "And about the race . . ." She raised a finger. "I feel as confident about it as ever. I'm experienced. We've been running every week, and I've been running every day for years."

Edith gave her a playful nudge.

"Besides. I've been running since I was in high school. Muscle memory is a real thing, you know."

"I believe you." Edith offered her a thumbs-up.

"I'll rely on my training and muscle memory. It'll be fine."

Edith opened her mouth to say something but hesitated.

Millie squinted. "What? What is it? You don't believe in muscle memory, huh?"

"Why do you run, Millie?" Edith asked. "I mean, why did you start running?"

The smile on Millie's face crept away as the face of her father appeared in her mind. She turned to watch the city pass by the window.

"I'm sorry. I didn't mean to pry. It's just that, in all these years we've known each other, I never really asked you about it before. Or if I did, I don't remember your answer."

Millie stared at her shoes. "You remember my home life, don't you?"

Edith thought about it. "Oh, yes. Your mom always kept your house so clean and . . ." She chuckled. "I remember how we were never allowed to play out in your backyard, so we'd go to my yard instead."

"Yeah, well." Millie inhaled some courage. "Mom kept the house clean and the yard quiet or else."

Edith furrowed her brow. "Or else what?" Her face drooped. "Ah. I see."

Millie nodded. "When Father would get home, things got loud. My older siblings would take off with friends or drive away in their cars." Pointed to her shoes, Millie shrugged. "I would just head out the front door and run away."

Edith winced.

"I ran and ran until I'd find myself at the school or at the park or at the mall. One day, the high school coach spotted me running around the track and called me over. He said he wanted me to join the track team. When I explained that I was still in seventh grade, he couldn't believe it." Millie laughed. "Anyway. I suppose I ran to escape. It kept me away from home, and I got to see some places I'd never see otherwise."

"Like where?"

"Our team was good, remember? We made it to state championships all over and then nationals. I saw North Dakota, Pennsylvania, New Mexico, California, and Oregon." Millie glanced upward. "Not sure how or why my father allowed me to go on all those trips, but he did."

"For some strange reason, huh?" Edith asked.

"Yeah."

"Maybe . . . now just hear me out on this." Edith gestured. "Maybe he saw your talent and wanted you to have the opportunity?"

Millie jerked around. "Are you crazy?" Her father's face as he shouted to her during the track invaded her mind again. "My father hated my running. He saw it as a waste of time. He wanted me to get a job, get married, have babies." She sat back and vented air through her lips. "He thought that's all women were about. Living for and serving others. Period."

"Sorry. I didn't mean to touch a nerve." Edith sat back too.

In silence, the two stared out the windows. Millie didn't know what Edith was thinking about, but she thought back to the times she ran and won races. Not one person from her family was there to see her win. Her older siblings had married and moved away. Her mother was always at home. Millie never knew where her father was, just that he wasn't there to see her on that winner's podium having the medals placed around her neck.

And then there was Walter.

Millie removed the note from her fanny pack and then scrolled her phone. She dialed a number and waited.

"Hello?" Millie said into the phone. "Yes? I received an invitation from Signore Ricci to come to his villa and—yes. That's me. I'd like to bring a friend. Is that all right? Oh, good. Grazie. See you then. Ciao."

When she lowered her phone, Millie felt the weight of Edith's stare.

"Why not?" she asked. "Life is too short. We'll go see a seaside villa and enjoy the view. Yes?"

Edith laughed and squeezed Millie's hand again. "Yes."

The train stopped and they exited, making their way up the steps out of the metro station and onto the street.

The beautiful April morning embraced them both,

bringing a smile to Millie's face. She inhaled the cool fresh air.

"According to the GPS on my phone, the conference center where the Expo is should be this way." Edith pointed to her right.

After walking a few blocks, the marathon banners appeared and so did the goosebumps on Millie's arms. *Oh, boy. What have I gotten myself into?*

"This is it. Look at the digital clock over there. It says we now have less twenty-one hours until race day." Edith giggled. "I'm so excited."

"Excited is not the word." Millie gulped. "This isn't where the starting line will be, right?"

"No, not at all. We start right at the base of the Colosseum, remember?" Edith grinned.

Millie's eyes widened. "That's right. I had forgotten. This is going to be so…magical."

"The best way to see Rome!"

Rows and rows of marathon participants appeared at the Expo entrance. The more experienced runners were obvious. Their muscularly trimmed bodies made it obvious.

Millie furrowed her brow. She knew Edith had never run more than six miles. She had no idea what she was in for, but Millie did. The sore muscles, aching back, throbbing feet . . . and hitting the proverbial wall. Although it had been over twenty-five years since her last marathon, Millie remembered it like it was yesterday.

As they waited in line to pick up their bibs, Edith tugged on Millie's shirt. "So . . . what can I expect?"

"Pain," Millie said without skipping a beat.

"Oh?" Edith furrowed her brow. "Now I'm worried."

"I'm just kidding." Millie chuckled. "Sort of."

"Terrific." Edith smirked.

"It'll be fun, too. There's also the excitement at the starting line. The thrill of being with all the other runners. The cheers from spectators along the street. Marching bands play as we run by. And because we're here in Rome, I'm sure we'll meet people from all over the world. How amazing is that?"

"Very." Edith listened as she typed some notes into her phone.

"Are those notes for your book?"

"Yes. I'm at the age now where I need to jot down everything, otherwise I'll forget it later."

The line of people moved closer to the entrance.

"It's so crowded. Do you know where we're supposed to go?" Edith craned her neck to see over the crowds of people.

"Yep. Make sure you have your form, doctor's note, and I.D. ready." Millie pointed to Edith's bag.

Finally, after waiting for thirty minutes in line, they made it to registration.

"Millie Devonshire," she said and handed over the papers. When the race volunteer handed her the race packet, a thrill flowed through Millie. She took the packet and removed the race bib and swallowed the rather large knot in her throat. "It's been a long time since I've seen my name on a racing bib."

The volunteer simply smiled.

Millie turned to see Edith waving her bib. "Let's get a photo."

They posed for some photos, then made their way through the line to where the race shirts were.

"These are nice," Edith said as she held hers up. "Run through Rome."

"I love it. You look like a marathoner." Millie took her photo.

Once they had everything they needed, they saw people stopping to have their photos taken with two men dressed as Roman centurions.

"Oooh, let's get our picture taken with these two centurions." Edith rushed over, and Millie joined her. They laughed as the Roman centurions pretended to thrust their spears at them.

The race gear shops called to them, so they went shopping.

"Look, a Rome Marathon coffee mug," Millie said with wide eyes. "I need one of these."

"I need one of these. A Rome Marathon sun visor. So I won't get sunburned." Edith grabbed a visor and a baseball cap, along with a bumper sticker and a button.

"This will probably be the last time I'm in Rome, so . . ." Millie grabbed a "Run Through Rome" T-shirt and cap.

"Are you two ladies running the marathon tomorrow?" a nice-looking older gentleman asked in a thick Italian accent.

"Why, yes. We are. Are you?" Edith smiled, and Millie noticed a sparkle in her eye she hadn't seen in many months.

"Si . . . o no. My son. My son is running in the race. Nico!" he shouted, and his thirty-something son came over. "This is my son, Nico."

"How do you do?" Edith held out her hand.

"I am well." Nico nodded his head to the ladies.

"He is a very good runner. I am very proud of him. My name is Martin." He shook Edith's hand.

With gray hair on his temples and a thin mustache, Millie thought he resembled an older Caesar Romero. Very suave and debonair in his suit and tie. Nico was dressed more casually in a T-shirt and jeans.

Together, the four of them moved through the race shops. Millie and Edith paid for their treasures and stood for photographs in front of the marathon map, pointing to the starting line by the Colosseum.

"The route of the marathon is magnificent, no?" Martin asked as he studied the huge map enlarged to the size of a wall.

"It is." Edith stepped forward. "Look at all the places we'll run by. The monuments, fountains, along the river . . ."

Millie stood before the map, amazed by the route and all the history of the city. The goosebumps returned, and she rubbed her arms.

"Have you run a marathon before?" Nico asked.

"Yes." Millie nodded. "But not for many years. What about you?"

"This will be my third. I love this race. It gives people from all over the world the chance to see my beautiful city." A light in Nico's eyes revealed his love for Rome.

"I still can't believe I am here." Millie clapped her hands together like a child at Christmas. "It's a dream come true."

"Vieni con noi . . . come with us for some lunch." Martin waved to Millie.

"Yes. You must join us." Nico gently took Millie's arm.

"Sure!" Edith walked off with Martin, and Millie knew there was no chance of getting out of this.

CHAPTER 12

As they walked, the two men talked about the buildings they passed by and the fountains, explaining the historical context of each site.

"I work in this building here." Martin pointed to a modern-style glass building. "I am a businessman."

"What kind of business are you in?" Edith asked.

"Computers. I help businesses all over the world with computers and software to connect them together." He grasped his hands together.

"And what do you do, Nico?" Millie asked.

"I am an architect. I work in that building across from the Expo." He pointed to another modern building. "My firm helps build modern structures all over Europe."

"Sounds wonderful." Millie was impressed with the two Italian men. "And your mother?"

"My mother passed away a few years ago. We miss her." Nico looked down as he walked.

"I'm so sorry," Millie said.

"That is all right. She is resting now." Nico pointed to another building. "Let's go eat in here."

At the restaurant, Martin ordered their entrees for them along with bruschetta and some wine.

"What time should we be at the start?" Millie asked Nico.

He glanced upwards as he thought about it. "Probably

eight-thirty would be good enough."

"And it really starts right at the Colosseum?" Millie leaned close with her hands clasped.

"Yes." Nico waved his hands through the air. "The glorious Colosseum. The morning light, the crowds of excited people . . . it is magnificent."

Millie tried to picture the scene in her mind. "I can hardly wait."

The waiter served their lunches. Millie, Nico, and Edith had pasta carbonara for their carb-loading meal. Martin enjoyed a plate of mussels.

"So you are an author?" Martin asked Edith as he sipped his white wine.

"Yes, I am." Edith used her fork to gather some pasta. "And I'm conducting research for my next book. It will be set here in Rome."

"It is a romance, no?" Martin winked.

"Yes!"

"It has to be. This is the most romantic city in the world," Nico said.

Millie noticed a wedding ring on Nico's hand. "Is this where you met your wife?"

He nodded as he drank some wine. "Yes. She and I went to school together. Not far from here."

"She's not a runner?"

Nico laughed. "No. She is home watching our two little girls." He removed his wallet and showed her and Edith the photos of two dark-haired little girls.

"How beautiful." Millie tilted her head. "Is that your wife?" She pointed to a lovely blonde woman holding flowers.

"Yes. My Angela. She is my joy." Nico kissed the photo, then placed his wallet back into his pocket. "She is originally from Spain, but her family moved here when she was very young." He pointed to his hair. "That is why she has blonde hair and green eyes. Our girls have my hair, though."

"You have a beautiful family. You must be so proud."

"I am. They will meet me at the finish line." He spun some spaghetti with his fork. "Thinking of them will help me finish."

"Assolutamente." Martin raised his glass. "Angela and my granddaughters are the best. They are the light of my world."

Millie's eyes shone with tears. "I'm so glad."

"And where is your husband?" Nico asked Millie. "Will he be at the finish line for you?"

"Uh, no. He wasn't able to make it out here. He had to work." Millie managed a fake smile.

Nico and Martin frowned. "Oh no," Nico said. "I'm so sorry."

"Don't be. I'm not. It's going to be a fantastic race and an unforgettable day." Millie raised her glass, and Martin tried to fill it with wine. "—but no more wine, please. I need my legs strong for tomorrow."

"Hear, hear." Edith clanked her glass to Millie's. "Just water for me, thanks."

"So tell us, what is your book about?" Martin asked.

"Oh, that's a dangerous question." Millie chuckled. "Never ask a writer about their book. We could be here all day."

"Haha." Edith scooted her chair closer to Martin. "It's about a young woman who was jilted at the altar, so she travels to Italy to forget."

Martin and Nico stopped eating to listen.

"But she meets a handsome young man touring Rome with his dying father. The young man's bravery and love for his father endears the young woman to him. Soon, they fall in love."

"Che romantico," Martin sighed.

"Here it comes . . ." Millie rolled her eyes and whispered to Nico. "The crisis point of the story."

"Now, now. Every story has one." Edith cleared her

throat.

"What is this crisis point?" Martin asked Nico, who shrugged.

"It's the part of the story where tragedy happens that hits the main character so hard, she feels she can no longer go on." Edith made a splat gesture with her hands. "She is crushed."

"Ah." Martin tossed his head back. "Si, capisco."

"In my story, the young woman's former lover finds her in Rome." Edith wiggled her empty glass, and Martin quickly filled it with water. "He begs her to come home with him. The young man she met in Rome is crushed when he sees them together. He thinks they have reunited, so he runs off to head to Naples with his dying father. But really, the young woman was only telling her former lover that she will not return with him, for she has fallen in love with someone else—a kind and considerate Italian man."

"Oh mio," Martin exclaimed and smacked his forehead.

"Then what happens?" Nico leaned forward.

But Edith, ever the clever storyteller, took a painstakingly slow sip of wine first. "You'll have to read the book."

"Ahh, no!" Nico tossed his napkin into the air, and Martin laughed heartily, almost falling out of his chair.

Millie got a kick out of seeing Edith and Martin together. She noticed he didn't have a wedding ring on his hand, but she didn't want to ask if he had remarried since his wife's death. She figured Edith would find out soon enough.

After lunch, the four headed to the metro station.

"I will see you tomorrow at the starting line, yes?" Martin asked Edith.

Millie pretended not to hear. She stared at a poster on the metro station wall instead.

"Yes, of course. I look forward to it," Edith replied.

Out of the corner of her eye, Millie saw Martin take Edith's hand and kiss it before he and Nico walked off.

"Thank you . . . uh, grazie for lunch. Ciao!" Millie said to the men as they headed up the stairs and out of the station.

When they were out of sight, Millie approached Edith, who stood feverishly scribbling in her writing journal.

"Well, well." Millie sashayed over. "Martin seems to have taken a liking to you, huh?"

"He's a charming man. I'm taken with him too." Edith snapped her pen closed and tossed her journal into her bag.

Shocked by her friend's admission, Millie stepped back. "Wait, what?"

"It's true." Edith raised her chin as though proud. "As we walked and talked, we found that we have a lot in common."

The train approached, so when the two found their seats, Millie nudged Edith to continue.

"Do tell." Millie grinned.

"Well, he lost his wife three years ago," Edith began.

"That's too bad." Millie lowered her eyes.

"He followed his son here for adventure." Edith playfully shoved Millie. "I followed you here for adventure."

"Followed me?" Millie chortled. "I begged you to come along."

"He's going to retire next year. Before he went into computers, he worked for the newspapers for many years. I wrote for the newspapers for years, remember?"

"I do," Millie replied with a smile.

"So now he says he wants to travel more." Edith folded her hands on her lap. "Something I want to do too."

"But I thought you just wanted to stay home and write." Millie furrowed her brow. "I thought traveling was arduous for you now."

"It is. But . . ." A slight smile appeared on her face.

"Not with the right companion?" Millie giggled. "I'm happy for you, Edith. Martin does seem like a very nice man."

"He is, and I'm glad we met today." Edith laughed. "God works in mysterious ways."

The train stopped at the Via Ostiense a short walk from

the Basilica Papale San Paolo.

As they walked toward the basilica, Millie thought more about Edith and Martin. "It is special that you two have so much in common."

"It's rare these days to find someone you connect with right away, you know?" Edith replied.

When they stepped into St. Paul's Basilica, they both stood amazed at the sight of the gilded ceiling, statues, marble columns, and marbled tiled floor. Millie removed her camera from her bag and took dozens of photos of the sunlight streaming through the glistening columns around the gardens.

"It's so quiet and serene here." Millie glanced around. "If I lived here, I'd get a lot of work done."

"It is spectacular." Edith used her phone to take photos.

The ornate gilded ceiling and the paintings on the walls told the history of the popes. They stood before the bronze canopy placed over the spot where Paul was martyred for his faith. Although not as ornate and grandiose as St. Peter's canopy, the canopy over Paul's tomb provided reverence and a sense of profound honor for what he had endured in life.

"To live is Christ and to die is gain," Millie muttered as she stood before the place where Romans believe Paul was buried.

"Amen," Edith said as her eyes followed the bronze canopy upwards to the ceiling.

Paul died to self, all for God. Millie contemplated her thoughts and motives. Guilt gripped her heart. *I need to rethink a few things, don't I, God?*

A somber prayer service was beginning, so the two decided to walk around the grounds. The gardens were more subdued and humbler than the grand gardens of St. Peter's Basilica at the Vatican. But they were just as reflective.

As they made their way outside, they spotted the large statue of St. Paul.

"There he is." Millie took a few photos.

"Being as humble as he was, I don't think he'd be that happy with such an ornate church built over his tomb." Edith smirked. "But what do I know?" She chuckled.

"I love how this statue has him with a sword. The great defender of the faith." Millie squinted. "And the Word of Truth."

"He was ready to defend it to his death." Edith crossed her arms. "Are we?"

"Hello there!" came a cry from behind them.

The ladies turned to see Jamie and Joy walking along the sidewalk with Michael following.

"Why, hello there. How are you all doing?" Edith smiled, then turned to Millie and winked. "At least he's walking with them."

"Fine. How are you two?" Jamie asked.

Mille couldn't help but notice Michael glancing all around, avoiding her and Edith.

"We're finishing up in here. Have you been inside?" Millie pointed to the building behind her.

"No, we haven't. We've been shopping and walking around the parks." Jamie looked up at the statue.

"It's a remarkable place. So much marble and gold and . . . just breathtaking." Edith gestured. "We're going to exit now, and we'll meet you right where you are. Hang tight."

She and Millie did their best to find their way back, but they had to exit through the small shop full of books and mementos.

"Michael looks so forlorn." Millie sighed.

"He does. But at least he tagged along. That's a good sign."

Millie couldn't resist buying a Christmas ornament with the basilica painted on it before they left the gift shop.

Finally outside, they joined Jamie, Joy, and Michael for a stroll.

"Here you go, Michael." Millie handed him the gift bag.

"What's this?" He narrowed his eyes.

"A gift from me to you." Millie smiled.

When he unwrapped the Christmas ornament, he smiled too. "Thank you, Millie."

"You're welcome. I hope it brightens your day." She patted his arm. "You look a little down."

Joy cleared her throat and glared at Millie, who shrugged.

"Yeah, well. We all have our up days and down days." He looked at Jamie when he said that. "Excuse me." And then he strolled off alone with hunched shoulders.

Millie winced, because Michael looked like a deflated balloon.

"So what did you buy on your shopping trip today?" Edith asked to change the subject.

"Mostly books," Jamie replied with a giggle. "I can't help myself."

Joy dangled a plastic bag. "I did find a rare copy of Shakespeare's Hamlet."

"How wonderful. That is a find."

Millie watched Michael stare at the statue of Paul. She leaned over and whispered to Edith, "He looks so tragic."

"I know. I hope these two get together."

"And this journal too." Jamie pulled a leather-bound book out of her bag. "I'm big into journals. I have several from all over the world. Michael showed this one to me, and—" Jamie stopped mid-sentence and stared at the leather-bound book in her hand.

"I see it has a dragon on the cover?" Edith pointed.

Jamie nodded. "Yes. He knows I love dragons."

"She collects them," Joy added.

"Now this one goes into your collection. What a great idea." Edith smiled. "You'll always remember your time in Rome whenever you use it."

"And you'll never forget Michael." Joy spun around and walked away.

Mille and Edith followed her.

"Are you going to be okay?" Edith asked her.

Joy smiled. "Imagine that. Best-selling author Edith Engram is asking me how I am doing."

Edith rolled her eyes.

"No seriously." Joy touched her arm. "Think of a famous person you admire. Now imagine having a conversation with them in-person."

"Well," Edith began. "In my mind, I'm not a famous person."

"Tell me," Joy said. "What made you want to buy your hometown?"

Millie glanced over at her friend, awaiting the answer.

"I love our little town. Always have. Even when I was a teenager and most of my friends wanted to move to the big city, not me. I wanted to stay put. So, when I finally had some money, I decided to fix up the town. But town leaders were giving me pushback. I bought the town and shut them up."

Joy laughed.

"She's done an outstanding job of fixing it up, too." Millie patted Edith's back.

"I think it's great. I remember reading about it in the paper and felt your actions revealed your heart." Joy smiled again.

"But are you going to be—"

"I'm fine. Really." Joy squeezed Edith's arm.

Millie made her way over to Michael, still staring at the statue. "How's your father doing?" Millie asked him.

Michael shrugged. "He's okay. Very tired. He decided to stay at the hotel and—"

A loud shout interrupted Michael.

All five of them froze in place.

A group of young Italian men, shouting at each other, made their way down the street.

"They're angry, aren't they?" Edith narrowed her eyes.

"What are they saying?" Millie asked.

Michael shook his head. "My Italian is rusty, but it sounds

like they're arguing over football teams."

"Soccer?" Jamie rolled her eyes. "You're kidding me. All that ruckus over soccer teams?"

"Look how passionate they are." Millie studied the young men. Their hands gestured wildly, and the vessels in their necks bulged.

"One man says his team will win, and the other man is arguing against that." Michael curled his upper lip. "I think."

The shouting grew louder, and one man shoved the other to the ground, causing several men to back into Jamie.

Jamie gasped and crashed into the chain-linked fence. "Oh—"

"A fight." Michael grabbed Jamie's arm. "Are you all right? Move over here." He placed himself between Jamie and the mob.

The young man on the ground lurched at the other who had shoved him. By the look on the man's contorted face, something else had happened. He turned pale and groaned.

"Oh, dear." Millie covered her mouth.

Blood poured from the young man's mouth, and the other men grabbed the assailant, who screamed and dropped his knife.

"He stabbed him?" Michael asked. He took hold of Jamie's forearm and moved her behind some bushes. "Come over here."

Joy, Millie, and Edith followed.

The bright red blood against the young man's white shirt sent waves of shock through Millie.

Jamie went limp. Michael caught her as she went down.

"Jamie," Joy cried and rushed to her side. "Someone call the police."

Millie fiddled with her phone as the young men squirmed around the wounded man. They gripped the assailant to keep him from running away.

Michael already called 112 and was speaking to the operator in Italian.

The look of anguish on the young assailant's face told them he wasn't planning on running away. He screamed "Paulo!" over and over again.

"What's he saying?" she asked Michael.

"It seems they are brothers. The one shouting stabbed his own brother." Michael lowered his eyes. "Sickening."

"Over a soccer game?" Millie's eyes filled with tears. "I can't believe it."

"Very passionate people, indeed," Edith replied.

Joy fanned Jamie with a book from her bag. "Jamie?" she cried. "Are you okay?"

The police arrived and handcuffed the assailant, still screaming his brother's name.

The other young men gathered around the bleeding man lying on the ground. An ambulance siren sounded in the distance.

One police officer approached Millie and the others. Joy continued to fan Jamie, and Michael explained to the police in broken Italian what they had witnessed.

"Not sure I said it all correctly, but he seems to understand what I meant," Michael said as the policeman took notes.

The police officer asked to see their passports, so each one produced theirs. When satisfied, the officer returned to the scene. The ambulance rushed the wounded man away to the hospital.

"Well, this definitely adds a bit of drama to your next book," Millie said to Edith.

"I suppose you're right." Edith said then leaned over Jamie.

Michael helped Jamie sit up. "Are you all right?" He stroked her hair and gently touched her dampened temple.

She opened her eyes and stared into his.

Joy smiled.

Millie handed Jamie a water bottle. "Here. See if you can take a sip. It's a brand-new bottle."

Jamie twisted the cap open and sipped some water. She

nodded. "Thank you. That does help. I've never seen such a thing like that before. The bright red blood made me dizzy. What happened?"

Michael gently brushed her hair aside. "Unfortunately, the two men were brothers. One brother stabbed the other."

"How awful." Jamie covered her mouth with her hands. "And right in front of St. Paul's Basilica." She nodded toward the statue.

"Well, we'd better get you back to the hotel." Joy helped Jamie stand.

"We'll have plenty to tell the others at dinner tonight, huh?" Millie said.

"Oh no. Please don't say anything. I'm so embarrassed." Jamie grimaced and placed her hands on both sides of her face.

"Nonsense." Michael guided her by gently holding her elbow. "There's nothing to be embarrassed about."

Joy stayed back with Edith and Millie.

"Thank you for helping me. I was so afraid." Jamie squeezed Michael's arm.

"I don't think she's got Carl on her mind right now. Do you?" Edith asked Joy.

Joy bounced up and down on her toes. "Nope. Not at all."

Millie and Edith walked off with a very cheerful Joy as Jamie and Michael continued talking on their way to the metro station.

CHAPTER 13

Later, at the hotel restaurant for dinner that evening, Millie noticed Jamie sat next to Michael and Joy.

She described to everyone the day's events.

"How are you feeling, Jamie?" Millie asked as she pulled out a chair and sat next to a beaming Joy.

"Much better, thank you." She reached up and adjusted her ponytail.

"Did she tell you what happened, Betsy?" Millie asked.

"She did, and I'm so glad that Michael was there. How frightening that must have been." Betsy winked at him. "I probably would have fainted in his arms as well."

"What a day, indeed." Edith sat down with a heavy sigh. "We saw so many things . . . from the Expo to the basilica, to violence on the streets. Today we saw Rome as it is. Not the tourist attractions, but Rome. Raw and real."

"Too much raw and real for my taste." Millie drank some water to calm her nerves. "We'd better order; we have a busy day tomorrow too."

"Race day!" Joy clapped her hands. People in the restaurant turned to see. "These ladies are running in the marathon tomorrow," Joy exclaimed to the restaurant patrons.

A few politely clapped.

Millie beamed.

"Wish us luck." Edith raised her eyebrows and her glass.

"What to order?" Millie perused her menu. "Nothing too heavy, nothing too light."

"Anything but pasta." Edith rubbed her tummy. "I've had my fill of—" When she stopped in mid-sentence, Millie looked up at Edith, who stared over her shoulder with mouth agape.

"What's the matter?" Millie asked, then turned to see what Edith was looking at.

Entering the restaurant was Martin, their new friend from the Expo. Dressed impeccably in a dark blue suit, white shirt, and patterned tie, he looked diplomatic yet approachable.

"What are you doing here?" Edith stood and rushed toward him.

He pecked both her cheeks, first the left and then the right. "I came to have dinner with you."

"Excellent. Come sit with us." She waved for Millie to scoot over and make room for him. "Everyone, this is Martin . . . uh, Martin?"

"Martin Romano. Buonasera. How do you do?" He nodded.

Edith sat next to him. "We met Martin and his son, Nico, at the Marathon Expo today. They were very kind to tell us more about Rome and treat us to lunch. Nico is running the race tomorrow too."

"He's very nervous tonight," Martin explained. "His wife is making him some dinner, so I thought I'd come here to see what you all were doing. This is a very nice hotel and restaurant." Martin waved to the waiter and ordered some wine in Italian. "Excellent food."

"It's so good to see you again, Martin." Millie offered him a wide smile and a raised eyebrow to Edith. Seeing them together sent a warm feeling through her. They looked wonderful side by side.

"It is my pleasure," he replied.

"Uh, this is Jamie and her mother, Joy." Millie waved her hand over to the ladies.

"How do you do?" Martin reached across to shake Joy's hand.

"And this handsome young man is Michael. Where is your father, Michael?" Edith asked.

"He's having dinner upstairs, but he said he will join us for breakfast tomorrow and dinner as well."

Millie grimaced. Ben's health worried her. She made a mental note to stop by and check on Ben in his room later.

"Perfect. Michael entered the contest and won just like Millie did. He was thoughtful enough to bring his father, who is a native of Rome. Isn't that nice?" Edith smiled brightly.

"Very nice." Martin winked. "A native? I'll have to chat with him. Very respectful of you to bring your father, Michael."

"He is a very respectful young man," Joy said. "Very kind and brave."

Jamie glanced at her phone.

"This is Betsy and Hank," Millie continued.
Betsy waved, but Hank was busy eating his spaghetti.

"They're a happily married couple from America." Millie smiled at them.

"Hello," Martin said to them and nodded. "Very nice to meet all of you."

The waiter came with his ordering pad. "What shall I get you this evening?"

"I'll have escargot," Martin said.

When he saw Millie's eyes widen, he laughed.

"You have never had escargot?" Martin asked. "It is made with a garlic butter sauce. Spectacular." He did the chef's kiss with his fingers to his lips.

"Sounds amazing. I'll have an order too," Joy said.

Edith turned to Millie. "You've never tried escargot?"

"No, and I don't intend to. I'm willing to try anything, but

I have to draw the line somewhere. And I draw the line at snails."

Everyone laughed.

After ordering their meals, they each enjoyed the fellowship and delicious food. Millie curled her lip at the awkwardness of eating snails with the tongs and tiny forks. But she had to admit, the smell of the garlic butter and Italian seasonings made her mouth water. But still . . . snails? Her nose crinkled as she watched them indulge in the delicacy.

Jamie abruptly stood and exited the dining room.

"Jamie. What about dinner?" Joy asked.

"I have to take this call."

"Oh, dear." Joy rubbed her forehead.

Michael simply stared out the window.

"Excuse me." Millie followed Jamie into the lobby.

She found Jamie talking into her phone, but before Millie could say anything to her, Jamie ended the call.

Spinning around to return to the dining room, Jamie almost ran into Millie.

"Jamie," Millie began.

"Millie?"

Millie opened her mouth to say something but stopped herself.

"I suppose Mother told you everything." Jamie rolled her eyes. "That was Carl."

"Are you going back to Carl?" Millie clasped her hands together as if praying.

"Not that it's any of your business, but . . . no. I'm not." She wriggled the phone in her hand. "That's why he called. He wanted to fly here to talk with me, but I told him not to. It's over. I don't want to see him."

Millie winced. "I don't mean to intrude, Jamie. I really don't."

Jamie tilted her head and raised an eyebrow.

"Honest. It's just that I've seen how you look at Michael and how he looks at you." Millie gestured as she tried to find the right words. "I see love in your eyes. I've lived long enough to know it when I see it."

Glancing away, Jamie trembled.

"Michael adores you. He'd do anything for you. I think he proved that today."

But Jamie averted her eyes as if she didn't want to hear about it.

"Anyway, I just wanted to check on you." Millie reached up and touched Jamie's arm. "Take care." She turned to head back to the dining room.

"Millie." Jamie approached her. "I thought I saw love in Carl's eyes too."

"I know, honey." Millie's heart broke for the young woman standing before her.

"A few years ago, Carl said he loved me. He asked me to marry him and gave me a huge diamond ring." She glanced down at her naked ring finger. "He said he wanted to be with me for the rest of his life. And look what happened." Jamie's eyes filled with tears. "How can I know what true love is? How can I trust that Michael won't hurt me like Carl did?"

"Because Michael is not Carl." Millie took her hand and squeezed it. "You know?"

Jamie bit her lower lip and nodded.

Reaching up, Millie gently touched Jamie's cheek. "I'll give you some time alone."

"Thanks, Millie." Jamie turned away and sat on an overstuffed sofa in the hotel lobby.

When Millie returned to the table, she felt the weight of Joy's stare.

"Is everything all right?" Joy asked.

Millie nodded.

Joy clutched her chest and closed her eyes. "Thank the Lord."

Everyone at the table watched Joy leave the table and head to the lobby.

"Is she going to be okay?" Martin asked.

"Yes," Millie replied. "In more ways than one." She said that for Edith and Michael's sakes.

Upon hearing that, Edith exhaled.

"Again, we thank you, Martin, for lunch today," Millie said as she finished her meal of salmon stuffed with cheese and spinach.

"It was a pleasure." His eyes ignored Millie and focused on Edith. "I look forward to more lunches together."

The way they looked at each other sent a chill over Millie, and for a moment, she felt as if she were intruding on their private moment.

After a light dessert, each one said their goodnights, then headed to their rooms.

But Millie spotted Edith and Martin walking off together. They decided to sit on the overstuffed sofas in the lobby to chat.

Millie headed upstairs to check on Ben.

"Hello?" she said as she tapped on his hotel room door. "Ben?"

The door crept open. "Hello, Millie. Is everything all right?"

Millie laughed. "That's what I was going to ask you. How are you, Ben? Can I bring you something?"

He smiled and raised his hand. "I'm fine. I just needed to rest today."

"All right. If you say so. I was worried about you and missed you at dinner." Millie grinned, then turned to leave.

"Millie?" Ben cried to her back. "Give me a moment."

She waited by her room door for a minute. Ben appeared in the hallway with his jacket on and cane in hand.

"Ben, are you sure you're up for a walk?" Millie raced to him. "If you need to rest, then—"

He waved a hand. "No, I need to get out. God brought you to my door to remind me."

Millie laughed again and gently took his arm. "If you're up for a walk, so am I."

Outside the hotel, the streets were bustling with tourists, motorcycles, and music from nearby pubs. The air was cool and crisp, filled with the aromas of delicious food being served by various restaurants.

"Let's just stroll for a bit." Ben, glancing left, then right, led the way down a small street. Silently, they walked, and Millie enjoyed not having to think of something to say.

Some restaurants had empty tables set out. Millie motioned for them to sit down. Ben agreed. He sat with a groan, then exhaled as he leaned back.

Millie recognized the look on Ben's face as one of discomfort. She had volunteered for a year at the local hospice center and knew that grimace. "Ben, are you in pain? Are you sure you want to be out here?"

"Millie," he sighed with his eyes closed. "Soon I'll have plenty of time to rest. In fact, that's all I'll be able to do." He opened his eyes, then removed his pipe and lighter. "So let's have a nice chat out here in the cool night among the locals on the beautiful streets of Rome."

"Absolutely." Millie rubbed his forearm.

When the waiter approached, Millie ordered some lemonade and a water for Ben.

"What do you like most about Rome so far?" he asked as he lit his pipe.

The sweet aroma of the smoke brought memories to Millie's mind of happier times spent with her grandfather. "Let's see . . . what do I like most about Rome so far? I adored the tour of the Colosseum and the Pantheon." The famous sites flashed behind her eyes like on a slide presentation. "I wonder what these ancient sites would say if they could talk."

Ben nodded. "Yes. My thoughts exactly. They have seen so much—life, death, destruction, rebuilding, hope. Civilizations come and gone." He snapped his fingers. "Just like that."

"All those Caesars and other rulers. It boggles the mind.

Our country is so new." Millie watched people pass by their table.

"Have you heard from your husband yet?" Ben asked.

Millie jerked around to face him, startled by his question. When she saw the concern on his face, she softened. "No. Not yet."

"When I was a salesman, I had to travel five days out of each week." Ben let some pipe smoke ease out between his lips. "My wife was home alone with Michael and his little sister. I felt bad leaving them, but I wanted my wife to stay home. I felt it was important for our children to have one parent home with them. You understand."

Millie leaned in closer to listen.

"Because we had only one income, it meant we had to go without many things."

"I know what you mean." Millie thought back to her own upbringing.

"My wife, Ella, was frustrated at first, because all her friends had new cars and went on vacations. But we never could because it was hard for me to make sales. When the kids were older, I took over my brother's family bakery for him. He became too sick to work. My wife came alongside me to help me and my sister-in-law run the business."

"That's wonderful, Ben."

"Finally, we had more money. Instead of buying a new car or going on nice vacations, we put Michael and his sister through school. We paid for our daughter Angelina's wedding."

Millie placed her hand over her heart. "That's beautiful."

Ben gestured wildly. "It was a spectacular wedding. And the reception? Fantastico. The food, the wine, the cake . . . my wife made the cake."

Millie laughed. "I can imagine how perfect it was."

Ben leaned forward and gently tapped Millie's hand on the table. "Millie, what I'm trying to say is that a man feels the need in his heart to provide his family a life that is peaceful and filled with memories of joy and happiness. I wanted our children to come home to their mother, not a babysitter. My heart filled with love when I walked into the house at the end of a long day only to see my children playing and my wife coming toward me. Yes, the house was chaos at times. Yes, there were toys scattered all over the room at times. And yes, my wife was sometimes asleep on the couch from exhaustion at times. But . . ." He lifted a finger. "She told me how she never regretted making a home for us. It was in her heart to provide a space where we all could feel safe. That helped me go into the snowy winters and drive for hours to make a sale. That calling of hers helped me when times were difficult and I wanted to quit because I hadn't made a sale in weeks."

Millie blinked back tears as she listened.

"I feel you have that same calling. I know you and Walter do not have children, but you have still worked hard to make a safe space for him. That's what drives him to work so hard for when you both can enjoy being together later in life." Ben smiled.

"I know, but—"

His raised hand silenced her. "I know. What if something happens, yes?"

Millie nodded as she thought of Edith and Charlie.

"You cannot live your life for the what-ifs. You cannot control the what-ifs, Millie." Ben smiled. "You must trust God and your husband. It is hard to do, I know. But you do not want to become like . . ." He jerked his head back toward the hotel. "Her."

"Judith." Millie pursed her lips.

Ben's downturned mouth revealed he agreed with her reply. "I feel she has forgotten what love is. I don't want you to become like her—hardened toward her husband with a calloused heart."

His words struck Millie like an arrow to the chest. She looked at her own calloused hands and wondered about the condition of her heart. Was she becoming like Judith? Had she become blinded to the needs of Walter?

"Thank you, Ben." Millie offered him a slight smile. "I so appreciate you sharing your story with me and your kind words. You're right. I think Judith has become blinded to her love for her husband. Maybe something happened that made her hardened."

"Don't let it happen to you." Ben puffed on his pipe.

The two sat in silence, enjoying their drinks and the bustling streets.

After a few moments, Ben grabbed his cane to stand. "Come. Let's head back to the hotel." He coughed a few times.

Millie paid the waiter, then helped Ben make his way around the small table. As they walked back to the hotel, Millie glanced around the city streets, studying the faces of passersby. But inside her head, she thought more about what Ben had said, her love for Walter, and his motivations for working so hard.

His are godly motivations, she thought. *Are mine? Have they ever been?* Running ahead was something Millie always struggled with. Her coaches in college had chewed her out for running ahead on more than one occasion. One thing about track that Millie loved was how it was an individual sport but also a team sport. Every decision an individual team member made affected their own score but also the team's. Too often, she found herself thinking of her own score and not the team's, so she'd run out ahead in the lead too soon, sustained by the runner's high of being in first place and feeling indomitable—only to tire and lose the lead.

Her motivations were selfish.

Now, in Rome, Millie felt that familiar pain of loss again. She ran ahead and lost the lead.

"You're a blessing, Ben." Millie hugged his shoulder.

"So are you, Millie," he replied as he made his way through the revolving door.

In her hotel room, Millie wrote an email to Walter about the day's excitement.

Dear Walter,
You'll   never   guess   what   happened
today...

CHAPTER 14

On race day, Millie rose early due to a nervous stomach. Fully dressed and ready to pin her bib to her running belt, she nudged Edith's foot.

"Come on, sleepy head. Time to rise and shine . . . and run twenty-six miles through Rome!"

Edith moaned and rolled over. "What time is it?"

"Seven a.m. Bright and early."

"Millie." Edith rose onto her elbows. "We don't have to be at the starting line until eight forty-five. It takes five minutes to walk there." She fell backwards and covered her face with her pillow.

"Come on. If you get up now, we can have coffee and then head to the start." Millie patted Edith's shoulder.

"Oh, all right." Edith whipped the covers off her legs.

"My goodness. Aren't we grumpy this morning? What time did you get in last night?" Millie chuckled.

"Too late." Edith yawned and rubbed her eyes.

"Had a nice time with Martin, did we?" Millie raised an eyebrow.

"We sat in the lobby talking way into the early morning hours," Edith said.

"A hot shower and some coffee downstairs will do you

good. Come on. Let's get going." Millie tossed some socks at her. "Remember—this marathon idea was yours. Not mine."

"Don't remind me." Edith groaned and fell back onto the bed.

∽

On the walk to the starting line, Millie breathed in the fresh spring air. "Perfect weather. We are so lucky. I read that some years it rained, and other years it was boiling hot. Today will be perfect."

Other runners made their way toward the Colosseum, stopping to take photographs of each other with the amazing ancient structure in the background.

"Here!" Millie rushed over to the railing. "Take my photo with the Colosseum in the back."

Edith did as she was asked, then yawned.

"You don't look very excited." Millie directed Edith to stand before the railing for her photo opportunity.

"I am. I am." Edith rolled her eyes.

As they followed other runners around the Colosseum, the starting line came into view.

"Look at all the runners." Millie's eyes grew large.

"Amazing, isn't it?" Edith stood on her tiptoes. "The crowd goes all the way to the street that leads to our hotel."

"That's a half a mile long." Millie turned to Edith. "Listen."

"What?"

"You can hear so many different languages. There are people here from all over the world." She smiled and bounced up and down on the balls of her feet. "So exciting."

"Alo! Buongiorno!" came a shout from above them.

Edith looked up and saw Martin standing at the railing and waving at them below.

"Hello!" Edith waved; her feet almost left the ground.

"How nice that he came to see us off." Millie waved at him too.

"I'll meet you over there." She pointed to a spot on the other side of the fence.

Martin agreed, and Edith quickly departed with a lightness in her step that Millie hadn't seen in many years.

"Don't be too long," Millie said. "The race is about to start."

"I won't be long." Edith rushed off to meet Martin.

Millie removed her phone and took several photos of the starting line, the racers, and spectators cheering everyone on. The time on her phone said eight forty-five. Fifteen minutes before the start. The butterflies in her stomach fluttered, making her anxious.

Hundreds of racers surrounded Millie. Most of them were Italian men cheering each other on and smiling at her.

Standing on her tiptoes, Millie craned her neck to see over the crowd for Edith.

"Alo!" Martin shouted from the railing again. He waved at Millie.

"Alo!" shouted dozens of racers to Martin. He laughed and clapped for them.

"Hello." Millie smiled and waved at Martin again. But then she saw Edith standing next to him.

Millie tilted her head. "Edith. What are you doing over there?" She pointed to her wrist. "The race starts in fifteen—"

"Come here!" Edith waved her over.

Millie hesitated, then elbowed her way through the crowd of racers until she stood next to the railing. "Edith?"

"Um . . ." she began.

"What's the matter, Edith? What's going on?" Millie noticed the racing bib was missing from Edith's racing shirt, and so was her running belt. "Where's your—"

"Something's come up." Edith took hold of Martin's

hand.

"Oh?" Millie glanced at their fingers intertwined, then back at Edith. "Edith…tell me what's going on?"

All the Italian men around them turned to listen.

"Martin has asked me to go with him to Naples today to see Pompeii." Edith's eyes sparkled.

"What? That's wonderful? I'm not sure you'll be able to go after the race, though, because you'll be so tired." Millie laughed nervously.

"I'm not running the marathon with you," Edith said flatly.

Many of the Italians gasped and stared at Millie for her reaction.

"What do you mean you're not running with me!" A rage rose within Millie. Her heart beat faster. "You get down here right now."

Edith whispered something to Martin, then headed toward the start.

Millie crossed her arms and glared at Martin as she waited.

Edith finally appeared before Millie.

"Now we have nine minutes before the start. Where's your racing bib?"

"Mill, I'm not running with you." Edith grabbed both of Millie's shoulders.

"This was all your idea. You have to run this with me," Millie shouted.

The Italian men stared at them.

"No, I don't." Edith stared deeply into Millie's eyes. "This is your adventure, Mill. You wanted adventure, and this is it."

"What? Are you crazy?" Millie tried to pull away. "You talked me into this!"

"You can do this."

"No, I can't. Not without you. I need you there." Millie's eyes rimmed with tears. Her heart pounded hard against her sternum.

Edith shook her head. "No, you don't need me there. You can do this." She pointed to Millie's chest. "It's inside you. You have the courage and ability to get to that finish line. Do you believe it?"

"Si!" several Italian men shouted.

Edith and Millie smirked at them.

"Do you mind?" Edith returned her gaze to Millie. "You have to believe in yourself. I believe you can do it. Do you?"

"Si!" the Italian men shouted again.

Ignoring them, Edith continued. "Take this adventure, Millie. This is what you've been wanting for all your life. It isn't the Olympics, I know, but it is your chance to run again and prove to yourself that you can do it. Look how much you've grown on this trip. Look at all you've done."

Millie thought about it.

"Plus, this will be the best way to see Rome. To see it up close and real. It's your chance to see what's inside you too."

"But . . . " Millie tried to swallow the lump in her throat. "You can't go off with Martin. You don't even know him."

"Yes, I do." Edith smiled with shiny eyes. "He and I are very much alike. We're kindred spirits. We're of the same generation. We have so much in common."

"Are you ready for this?"

Edith nodded. "In so many ways, Mill. This is my adventure. I have to take it."

Millie rolled her eyes as the conflict within her rose to a boiling point. On one hand, she was thrilled for Edith. She was obviously smitten with Martin. But on the other hand, she was furious with Edith for abandoning her.

"I can't believe you're doing this to me. You know what happened to me when I was little. You know how I fear being left behind and abandoned," Millie whispered.

"I do know." Edith hugged her neck. "But one thing I learned after Charlie died is this—you have to conquer your fears. That's the main reason I signed us up for this race."

Millie blinked back hot tears of anger and fear and looked deeply into her friend's eyes. "You never had any intention of running this with me, did you?"

"That's not true. I did plan on running it with you." Edith shook her finger at her. "But now I see that this way is best."

Millie shook her hands as if they were numb. "I don't know, Edith." She stepped side to side, trying desperately to breathe. "I don't think I can do this. I'm not sure I—"

"You have to see it in your mind. You can do this." Edith spun her around to where the finish line would be set up. "Over there. Do you see that finish line in your mind?"

"Si!" the men shouted again and cheered.

Millie cringed.

"Do you see it?" Edith jabbed her pointed finger. "Do you?"

Millie closed her eyes so tightly, they hurt. And then she opened them. "Yes. I see it."

"What?"

"Yes!" Millie laughed.

"Si!" the crowd shouted and hopped up and down as if at one of their beloved soccer games.

"Do you visualize yourself crossing that finish line?"

"Yes!" Millie shouted, brushing aside a tear off her cheek.

"Si!" the men around her cheered even louder.

"Si!" Millie laughed.

"All right then." Edith spun Millie around to face the starting line. "Let's see you do it." Gently shoving her forward, Edith turned and headed out of the running corral.

"Edith!" Millie shouted to Edith's back. "Be careful!" And then she waved to Martin, who cheered her on.

The shouting and singing Italian men grew louder, making Millie nervous, and she felt sweat drip down her neck.

"Here," one woman said as she pulled on Millie's arm. "Come this way." The young woman pulled Millie to where several women stood in the corral.

"Run with us and not by all those sweaty Italians." She laughed. "I'm Elsie. I'm from Australia. This is my friend Tiffany."

"Nice to meet you. I'm Millie, and I'm from the U.S."

"I'm Olivia, and I'm from London." Another young woman waved.

Being with other women helped calm Millie down. "Nice to meet you, Olivia."

"You look nervous. Is this your first race?" Olivia asked.

Millie shook her head. "No. I used to race way back when. I even qualified for the Olympic trials once."

The women stood with their mouths agape.

"But"—Millie raised a finger—"I was injured and didn't make it. So now I just run for fun, and what could be more fun than running through Rome, huh?" She shrugged a shoulder and laughed nervously.

"Yes!" Tiffany and Elsie high-fived Millie.

"What about you all? Is this your first marathon?" Millie asked them.

"This is our first. We decided to make it Rome because it's our favorite city in the world." Elsie laughed.

"This is my fifth marathon, but my first in Rome." Olivia fluttered her eyelashes. "I'm so in love with this city. I don't ever want to leave."

Millie's heart warmed. "Me too."

The countdown to the start began, and the runners inched forward near the start once the elite runners took off.

"Oh my gosh! Here we go . . ." Olivia clasped her hands together.

"We can do this," Millie said.

"Yes!" Elsie shouted.

"You can do this, Millie." The butterflies inside Millie's

stomach fluttered more and more as the starting line grew closer and closer. *I can do this*, she repeated to herself. *I can do this. I have experience, the training, the muscle memory. I can do this.*

Before she knew it, it was time for her to cross the starting line. Millie turned on her playlist, put her earbuds in, and started her running app to count the miles.

And then she crossed the starting line of the Rome Marathon.

As the runners spread out on the Via dei Fori Imperiali, Millie welcomed the extra elbow room. Olivia, Elsie, and Tiffany ran in front of her. Millie knew better than to run out too fast. She purposefully held back a bit and let the young women do their own thing.

Run your own race. She heard her former coach's voice inside her mind.

The magnificent white marble of the Altar of the Fatherland monument came into view, sending chills over Millie as she ran past.

Soon the runners headed into the nearby neighborhoods. The locals sat outside their homes, cheering runners as they passed. Millie waved and smiled to show her appreciation to them. They could be sleeping in or going about their business, but instead they stood along the route to cheer the passing runners.

A high school band played music as runners raced by. The thrill of the scenery along with locals cheering energized Millie, and she moved her arms faster to get her up and over the first hill.

The City of Seven Hills.

Millie shook her head, wishing she had trained for hills—and cobblestone. The first seven miles were nothing but hills and cobblestone streets. She had totally forgotten how hilly Rome could be. The bottoms of her feet ached, and so did her ankles.

Pumping her arms to help her legs move faster got her up each hill. Millie gasped and ran through the ache.

Passing the famous pyramid, ruins, and important buildings, Millie stopped to take photos whenever she could.

Here I am at mile seven! she texted Edith and attached a picture of herself by a fountain.

Next came running alongside the Tiber River and all the impressive architectural structures along the way.

"How do you feel?" Olivia asked as she jogged alongside Millie.

"So far, so good. How about you?" Millie replied.

"Not too bad. I've been stopping to take photos." Olivia wriggled the phone in her hand. "It's just so remarkable. Beauty everywhere I look. I couldn't help it."

"Me too!" Millie laughed. "I hope my phone battery lasts."

The first hour was done. Millie glanced at her watch. *At least two more to go, maybe three . . . I hope.* When the sun appeared from between the clouds, the air warmed. Millie's throat burned with thirst. She stopped to sip some water at a water station and ate an orange slice. Checking the body's condition was essential for success, so Millie did an assessment.

Legs were strong.

Arms were strong.

Back felt great.

Surprisingly, she felt like she could finish.

Just keep doing what you're doing, she told herself. *You've got this. You've been training, and don't forget muscle memory.*

She stopped to take another photo of a bridge, then texted it to Walter. I'm doing it! I'm running a marathon through Rome. She included a smiley face and a heart. Miss you and I wish you were here!

The conversation she had with Ben came to her mind as she ran. Marriage was a lot like running a marathon. It required discipline, endurance, and humility, that's for sure. Both required listening and being proactive. Listening to one's body and listening to wise voices, too. A rush of guilt flowed over her, causing her to almost trip. When she regained her composure, Millie laughed from embarrassment.

Guilt hit her hard for what she was thinking earlier in the week about possibly living in Rome—without Walter. What was she thinking? Ben was right. She was allowing herself to become hardened toward Walter. She loved him and loved building a life with him.

Yes, Rome was beautiful and remarkable, as Olivia said. But it was empty without Walter.

When I get back to the hotel, I'll write to him. After a shower and a nap, of course.

A shower.

A nap on that soft bed.

Millie's mind wandered. She pictured all the food she would eat, the sweet desserts and wine, plus the hot water of that shower flowing over her.

Snap out of it. She shook her head. *Keep your mind in the race . . .*

Running continued.

And continued.

Finally, the mile ten marker approached. The cobblestone had taken its toll on the bottoms of Millie's feet and ankles. They throbbed and slowed her down. *Keep going,* she told her legs. *You can do it.*

Edith was right to remind Millie to visualize the finish line. It did help. But the thought of being sixteen miles away from the finish line made her feet throb even more.

Crossing yet another beautiful bridge over the Tiber, Millie took advantage of the sight and stopped to photograph the river and surrounding architecture. She also took a selfie with several buildings behind her. Then it was back on with the race.

Elsie, Tiffany, and Olivia were nowhere in sight. Millie suspected they were probably close to finishing since hour four was only thirty minutes away.

Millie couldn't remember the last time she'd run more than ten miles, but the marker for mile eleven was up ahead, giving her some energy. The sun was out in full force now, making the air hotter and heavier. Her running shirt clung to her torso and weighed on her like a wet wool blanket draped over her shoulders.

A volunteer handed Millie and other runners wet sponges. She squeezed the sponge onto her neck, and the icy cold water took her breath away, easing her discomfort for a bit.

Turning a corner, Millie stared at the ground, trying to ignore the heat, but it pressed on her relentlessly. Her legs grew heavier and heavier. Around her, other runners were walking or slowing to a jog.

I could always walk for a bit. No harm in that. But her coach's voice inside her head told her not to walk. "Only losers walk during a marathon," she once said. So she kept going.

Each plant of her foot onto the street sent shooting pain through her ankles and knees. But she ignored it and kept running. Like many endurance runners, she was good at ignoring the pain.

Runners pointed to the SWAT teams along the street, and military members dressed in black uniforms made Millie slow down to see what was happening. The uniforms of the police seemed different than the others she had seen earlier in the race. *I wonder why the security concerns?* Shrugging it off, Millie kept running.

A lovely ornate building in front of her caused her to stop and take photos. Something inside told her it was a special building, but she couldn't remember what it was. Heat exhaustion started to fog her mind.

Hundreds of people made their way toward the building, past the guards and shiny black military tanks. The strange sight slowed her down as she tried to figure out what was going on. *Could this be the reason for all the security measures?*

Two jumbotrons displayed a man giving a speech. As she approached the piazza, Millie walked to the barricade. Many runners stopped to listen to the man giving a speech in Italian. They took selfies and videos. But Millie remained in a fog.

She listened to the man for a bit, and when she recognized him and the building he stood in front of, her eyes widened. "Holy smoke," she muttered to herself. The man giving the speech was the pope, and the building was St. Peter's Basilica.

"I'm in the Vatican City," she said to no one in particular. "That's the pope," she said to another runner who nodded and laughed. "You see him too? Oh, good. I thought maybe I was losing my mind."

Quickly removing her phone and juggling it with trembling hands, Millie took a video as the pope started Mass with dozens of his bishops, cardinals, and priests in chairs below his podium. Spectators continued to enter the square to sit in chairs and listen.

Millie took a selfie with the pope behind her. "*At mile eleven,*" she posted to social media. "*The pope!*"

Taking a few more minutes to watch the scene, Millie couldn't believe she was at St. Peter's watching the pope during a marathon. She rubbed the goosebumps off her arms. *It feels like a dream.* Her insides fluttered, and she felt like a balloon floating away. With a lighter step, she continued running through the streets of the Vatican City. The floating feeling stayed with her for a couple more miles, and she passed the halfway point in the race.

CHAPTER 15

Mile thirteen.

A giant blowup number thirteen waved in the breeze as a disc jockey played rock music and cheerleaders danced and waved their pompoms. Millie waved to cheering spectators clapping along with the loud rock music. Music that pumped out of the speakers over ten feet tall.

All right, she told herself. *Thirteen more miles to go.*

A water station ahead had more wet sponges for runners to cool off. Millie gladly grabbed one from a volunteer's hands and squeezed the cold water over her head. She dabbed her neck and chest with the sponge. Relief from the intense heat washed over her just like the cold water did.

But the feeling of elation didn't last long.

The throbbing in her feet and ankles that crept up to her knees now rose to her hips and lower back.

Millie felt every one of her fifty-two years.

She pumped her arms, hoping they would make her legs go faster. It always worked in the past. But her calf muscles revolted and started to cramp up. *Oh no.*

Mile fifteen. The marker practically screamed at her as she ran past it.

The lack of long-distance training had left her body

unprepared for all the pounding her feet and legs experienced. Distance training was about handling being upright for hours and all the pounding.

But her body was not prepared.

Neither was her mind.

At first, her body whispered to her. Then it spoke to her in a loud voice.

That's how it works.

The body will whisper at first, and if one doesn't pay attention, it shouts. If one still ignores it, it will scream until the body finally stops.

Millie knew her body was getting close to that point.

Dangerously close.

The sweltering heat played its tricks on her mind as she tried to concentrate. *Was that mile sixteen back there?* Millie licked her parched lips and tried to swallow, but her scratchy throat tightened and wouldn't let her. Each attempt was like swallowing a prickly cactus. The water in her bottle was warm and made her sick, so she decided to wait for the next water station.

Running and running . . . in the heat and humidity . . . without water was foolish.

She knew that.

Her body laughed at her. She couldn't blame it. *What were you thinking? It's been twenty-eight years since your last marathon, and you hoped that muscle memory would help you cross the finish line?*

After what seemed like an eternity, the next water station came into view.

Mile sixteen.

The road blurred. Was it the sweat in her eyes? Millie wiped them with her shirt, but things remained blurry.

No longer caring what others thought about her, Millie slowed to a walk . . . more like a limp. When her coach's voice came to her mind, she shook it off.

Her back seized, making running nearly impossible.

Her left calf muscle cramped so tightly, she could barely limp, let alone walk. When chills flowed over her sweaty body and the road underfoot seemed to rise and fall, causing her to zigzag across the road, she knew what was happening.

Heat exhaustion.

Bumping into other runners as they reached for water from volunteers, Millie apologized and took a water bottle from the volunteer's hand.

Millie knew it wasn't normal to have chills on such a hot day. She recognized possible heat sickness and winced at the thought of becoming sick right there on the road.

And at the thought of having to quit the race.

Quit the race?

How did it come to this? She shook her head. Although it had been decades since she ran a marathon, Millie knew what was happening to her. She just couldn't believe it.

The Wall.

The psychological obstacle many distance runners experience that many say is fake, but runners can describe as if it were an actual brick and mortar obstruction, it was that real.

Millie never expected to hit the wall this soon. Mile nineteen? Maybe. Mile twenty-one? Usually.

But not mile sixteen. It was too soon.

What could she do?

Millie spotted a curb. *I'll just rest for a bit,* she told herself.

Don't do it, her mind told her. *You know if you sit down, you won't get back up again.* Her back seized up again, making it impossible to take one more step.

She had to stop.

I'll just sit for a moment, I promise, she bargained with her body. But her mind fought it. Back and forth the argument went on for what seemed hours but was only minutes.

The Wall won, though, and Millie sat on the curb and

massaged her back and calves. Her mind, dizzy from the heat, struggled to do anything but sip water.

And think.

Millie massaged her calves and averted her eyes with embarrassment as runners passed her. What a disgrace. Her mind took over, calling her every name it could summon.

Loser.

Failure.

Has-been.

Quitter.

Defeated.

What have I gotten myself into? She covered her clammy face. *I can't believe I allowed myself to be talked into this. You've really done it this time, Millie.*

What else blurred her vision besides sweat and exhaustion?

Envy. Images of Betsy and Hank holding hands returned to her mind.

Impatience. Sending the contest entry form in without telling Walter made her grimace.

Pride and arrogance. *Yes.* Millie nodded. To think she could rely on herself alone and make it to the finish line made her lower her eyes in shame.

Fear. She swallowed the large knot in her throat.

Millie knew her fear of missing out had caused her to head to Rome without Walter.

Look where it's gotten me. Stuck again, watching runners pass me by, just like in those college races.

She missed the comfort of home, the welcoming front porch with the swing Walter had made for her. She missed her kitchen with its window overlooking the side yard fence and Mrs. Wilson's barky dog. The window box Walter had made for her and filled with flowers. The recent rain made the pansies and petunias thrive . . .

She missed Walter.

More runners passed her, so she lowered her head in

humiliation. When a recent church sermon came to mind, Millie teared up. The priest explained why Paul often compared the Christian life to endurance running.

"Run your race with endurance," he had said. "It takes discipline but also reliance on God."

"God," Millie whispered and brush a tear off her cheek. "I never even prayed about this." When she realized she had thought about the trip, the photography contest, the tour of Rome, and the race—everything except God—the tears flowed.

Millie had considered her wants and needs above everything else, even her husband. Worst of all, she had relied on herself and not God.

Accusing Walter of becoming blind to her needs, it was Millie who had become blind.

Sitting on the curb, a tug on her heart made her bow her head.

Oh God, she prayed. *I'm so scared.* The footsteps of more runners passing by made her glance up. *Look how strong and confident they are. I'm such a fool to think I could do this with little training.* Fear gripped her gut even tighter, and she found it hard to breathe.

I'm afraid, God. I honestly don't think I can finish this race. Her back tightened. *I don't think I can get up, let alone run ten more miles.* She sighed. *Ten more miles. I need your help, God, please.*

And then the guilt flowed over her like a crushing wave. She squinted her eyes and bowed her head again. *I know . . . I know. I'm such an idiot to think I could do this alone. I'm so sorry, God. Please forgive me.* Millie rubbed her face, sticky from sweat. *I relied on everything except You.* She winced from the words. *I relied on my experience, training, muscle memory, pride—everything except You. And now everything I relied on has failed me, and I'm crying out to You. Please hear me.*

The fear pressed down on her as did the afternoon sun.

What if God rejects me? Her body shivered. *What if He abandons me here? What if He doesn't see me like my father never did?*

That door she saw as a six-year-old returned to her mind yet again like a pesky rash that never heals or goes away. She wiped the hot tears from her eyes.

Please, God. Please hear me. Please help me. Millie sighed. *Please see me. Amen.*

"Dai! Andiamo! Let's go!" came a shout from her left, startling Millie.

She looked up in time to see a fellow runner walking toward her with an outstretched hand. "Up! Up," he ordered in broken English. "Walk with me."

Millie cringed and shrugged. "I . . . I don't know if I can get up and walk."

"Come." He wriggled his outstretched hand. "Walk."

Millie took his hand, and he pulled her to her feet.

"Walk. Don't run," he commanded and shook a finger at her. "Walk."

And with those words, Millie exhaled, more than happy to obey that command. Relief washed over her when she realized how her body and mind needed to hear his words. She needed someone to give her permission to walk.

She grabbed a cold bottle of water from the water station and walked with the man.

"I am Sal," he said. He looked at Millie's racing bib. "You are Millie?"

"Yes. Nice to meet you." She gulped down the water and her back loosened. Millie began to feel better.

She knew many distance runners feel that walking during a race is akin to giving up. It's considered defeat. But Millie no longer cared about those opinions.

She knew Sal was God's answer to her prayer.

God had heard her.

God saw her sitting there on that curb. He hadn't abandoned her.

As Millie walked with Sal, he went on to tell her about his life, oblivious to how he had answered someone's prayer for help. Tall, thin, and balding a bit, Sal seemed a few years older than her.

Millie smiled as he spoke.

"Over there is my neighborhood where I grew up," he explained. "I worked with the U.S. Navy in Naples, and that is where I learned English."

"How wonderful." She craned her neck to see the nearby neighborhood.

The mile nineteen marker appeared.

They stopped so Sal could take a photo of Millie. She texted the photo to Walter. Making progress, she texted and then sent it.

A few minutes later, Sal pointed to some nearby apartments. "This is the Olympic Village from when they were held in Rome."

Millie admired the old apartment buildings and other structures, trying to imagine what it must have looked like in 1960.

Next, they passed a fountain and an obelisk that Sal explained. Millie found the historical context fascinating.

"What is it that you do now, Sal?" she asked.

"My family owns a restaurant in town." He smiled.

"Your whole family works in the restaurant?"

He nodded. "Si, si. My son is the chef, and his wife helps run the place. I host, manage the wine, and do whatever my wife tells me to do." He laughed. "That's my specialty."

"And your wife runs the place?" Millie asked. "That's amazing."

Sal gripped his hands together. "She is the glue that holds everything together." He winked. "She also makes the best desserts."

"Tiramisu?"

"Of course, of course!" Sal laughed again. "You and your friends will dine there tonight, yes?"

"Absolutely."

After walking and talking for four miles, Sal turned to Millie. "I have told you about my life. Now tell me about yours. Who is Millie?"

Who is Millie, indeed. She couldn't even answer that question anymore. But she managed to offer Sal a fake smile as her heart sank. Her life story wouldn't take much of their time. Nothing exciting had happened to her before her trip to Rome.

"Well, I was born in Rhinelander, Wisconsin, then we moved to Independence, Missouri, and finally, my family settled in North Carolina when I was a teenager." She lowered her head as she thought of her dysfunctional family. "I have two older siblings and two younger siblings, but I don't see much of them since both our parents have passed away. I've been married to Walter for almost fifteen years."

"Do you have any children?" Sal asked.

Millie blinked back tears. "No, we married late, and I wasn't able to have children."

"Oh, mi dispiace." He grabbed his heart. "I am so sorry."

"Thank you." Millie fiddled with her water bottle. "It's all right. We have a nice life together."

"Is he waiting for you at the finish line?" Sal motioned forward. "I would like to meet him and—"

"No." Millie pursed her lips and removed her phone to check for text messages. But no messages were waiting. "He's back in the United States. He couldn't come with me to Rome."

"He couldn't come to Rome?" Sal jerked his head around. "What is this? Crazy man. Nothing could keep me from coming to Rome."

Millie agreed.

As she walked, she thought about her past and her life with her family. Knowing her family of origin had made her who she was today—a hesitant, tepid woman—made the anger rise within her. Her mother had called her incurious once.

Yet that six-year-old Millie staring at the door at the rest stop would beg to differ. She was curious. She decided on that fateful day to take a chance and open that door.

But what good did it do to be curious?

The door led to the bathroom. A smelly old bathroom. Big deal.

Opening doors didn't add anything to her mundane life.

Six-year-old Millie left the women's bathroom and raced to the parking lot. But the family car was gone.

She walked around the rest stop parking lot that afternoon, searching the cars to see if maybe her father had moved the vehicle to another part of the lot.

But she couldn't find it. Millie's heart raced just thinking about it.

"Mother!" she had cried. She knew better than to shout for her father. "Mother?"

Young Millie's heart raced as she made her way from car to car and person to person.

But her family wasn't around, and no one had seen them. When one woman wanted to take Millie into her car, she refused and ran away.

She did what any small child would do. She returned to the restroom, crawled under the sink counter, scooted into a corner against the wall, and wept.

"They left me," she whispered to herself, pulling her knees up to her chin and hugging them. "They must not have seen me come in here, and they left me here."

Now walking with Sal along the marathon route in Rome, the pain of that little girl in the bathroom shook Millie. She remembered weeping desperately for her mother.

Hours had gone by, and no one entered the women's bathroom looking for her. *Don't they miss me? Don't they notice that I'm not there? Don't they care?* Unable to move from fear, little Millie hugged her knees even tighter. *What if they never come back?* There was nothing she could do but wonder where her family was and how she would get home.

Home.

Maybe she would never see home again. Or maybe she would have to find her way home on her own.

Darkness fell in the bathroom window where sunlight had once streamed in, so little Millie stood and straightened out her dress. She pulled up her socks and inhaled some courage. *I'll show them. I'll head home, and when I walk through the front door, then maybe they'll remember. They'll feel bad for leaving me behind.* Millie pushed on the bathroom door, but jerked forward when her own mother pulled it open.

"Millie!" she cried. "Richard? I found her." Her mother's eyes, wide with fear at first, softened with relief when she saw her daughter. "Millie, where have you been? You frightened us. Your father is very upset."

She used her hand to lead Millie out of the restroom to the rest stop parking lot, now completely empty and dimly lit. When her eyes saw her father storming toward her, Millie winced and braced herself for his anger.

Millie knew this event was cause for rage, and her typically angry father would not settle for anything less. He seemed to relish using moments of his children's disobedience to teach them life lessons.

He grabbed Millie's arm and pulled her toward his reddened face. "Where were you, young lady?"

Millie winced from the pain in her arm. "I had to go to the bathroom, so I—"

"You're supposed to let us know where you're going. Do you know what trouble you caused?" he barked.

Behind him, leaning against the car doors, were her siblings, smirking at her.

"Do you?" Her father jerked her around. "Do you know the trouble you caused?"

"No, sir."

Millie remembered the pain of holding in a flood of tears in her eyes that day. She fought them because she didn't want her father to see her cry. He despised crying.

"We drove for over an hour before we noticed you weren't in the car. And then we had to turn around and drive back. Do you know how much time and gas we wasted? How much money?" He turned her around and swatted her backside.

"No, sir." Millie bit her lip to keep from crying out. She knew crying out would make him even angrier.

Her siblings pointed and snickered.

"Get in the car!" her father ordered them, and they hurried, not wanting to experience any of his wrath.

He raced to the car as Millie's mother held her hand and walked with her. Millie sniffled, so her mother handed her a tissue.

They didn't even miss me. Millie refused the tissue in her mother's hand. *They didn't even notice I wasn't there.*

"And I've been invisible ever since," Millie explained to Sal. "I grew tired of just existing and not being, you know?"

Sal listened.

"You know, that's the first time I've told anyone that story except Walter, Edith, and a counselor."

He placed his hand over his heart and bowed. "I am honored that you trusted me with such a personal story."

Another mile marker appeared alongside the route. Sal motioned for her to stand by one of the road marker signs. "You have come a long way since that restroom, Millie."

"I have." She smiled and waved as Sal took her picture. "Thirty-two kilometers." Millie pointed to the sign.

Sal took the photo. "There. Now people will know you were here, huh?" He laughed. "They will know you existed."

Millie laughed out loud, too, and patted Sal's shoulder. "Exactly."

∽

They continued walking along the route. Millie gained strength, and her back stopped aching. Soon she and Sal entered the fashion district. Embarrassed by her sweaty appearance, Millie walked through it as quickly as she could but noticed Edith was right. The wealthy people sipping their cappuccinos and lattes didn't even notice the slow runners and walkers.

She laughed and picked up the pace. *I worry too much about what others will think.*

After almost seven hours of running and walking, the mile twenty-one marker stood alongside the path. The last leg of the marathon had come.

Millie reflected on what she had seen along the route. The Trevi Fountain, the Pantheon, obelisks, bridges, the river, monuments, locals cheering them on, St. Peter's Basilica, and of course, the pope holding Mass.

And now it was finally coming to an end. Edith, always right about everything, called it perfectly. This was the adventure Millie's life had been lacking. It wasn't what she thought it would be, but it was quite the adventure.

A realist who labeled herself as tepid, Millie allowed herself to become cautious. There was comfort in caution. She grew to despise her humdrum life back home, but now she craved it. Adventure was nice, but definitely uncomfortable.

The busyness of her life, guided by duty and habit, was pleasant and filled with joy. Sitting on the front porch of her house on a spring afternoon appealed more to her than walking on the streets of Rome. Swinging on the front porch swing Walter had made for her seemed more desirable than some silly adventure in Italy. Millie understood this now.

Yet she was grateful for her curiosity. It made her want to know more about other people's lives. Volunteering at the food kitchen of the homeless shelter gave her perspective and appreciation for her own home.

Home.

Glancing upward at the apartment buildings she strolled by, Millie reflected back to when she dreamed of living in one. She had wondered what lay inside one of those apartments. The windows adorned with flower boxes bursting with bright red geraniums smiled down on her.

The house with Walter wasn't a mansion, but it was a home. It wasn't designed as a showcase but a shelter for a family. What was the matter with that? Nothing.

Millie knew that now. *Stop being so curious about closed doors,* she told herself. *Start being content with open doors.*

But Millie didn't regret her time in Rome. The vigorous city had taught her so much, like how to experience everything around her—the sights, the smells, the tastes, the feelings. It taught her how to embrace all Italy had to offer, yet at the same time, appreciate home.

Thoughts of seeing the statue of David for the first time, the Colosseum, the art at the Vatican Museum, the gardens in Florence, and the wedding she photographed returned to her mind like a favorite season.

The wedding . . . Millie sighed as memories flooded over her. *Such a beautiful moment. Such a loving family.* The weeping commenced at mile twenty-one and continued to mile twenty-five. She wept for her foolish impetuous actions. Actions that included leaving Walter behind. She tugged at her damp shirt—damp from sweat and tears—and used it to wipe her eyes. She wept for not having a loving family any longer and grieving what might have been. Looking down at her empty hand, she wept for not having Walter's hand to hold through Rome, like Betsy and Hank had each other.

"Millie!" came a shout from the sidelines, jolting her from her weeping state. Raising her tear-swollen face, she saw Jamie, Michael, Joy, Betsy, Hank, and even Judith waving at her, holding a sign with her name.

"Woohoo! Keep going! The finish line's right around the bend," Jamie shouted.

Millie laughed at them, her friends, and made her way over to them. Michael patted her back.

"How are you feeling?" he asked.

"So proud of you, honey. Keep going," Joy said.

"You've got this. Not much further." Jamie waved.

And right before Millie backed away to re-enter the route, Judith chimed in.

"Hey, Millie. I'm proud of you too. Your courage inspires me." Her eyes rimmed with tears.

"Thank you, Judith. I'll talk to you all at the finish." Millie waved goodbye, then turned to Sal. "How about we try to run the last mile to the finish line?"

He gave her a thumbs-up, and they took off running in front of the Altar of the Fatherland with the Colosseum directly ahead, almost calling out to them. All roads lead to Rome, after all.

The loud music and cheering of spectators urged them to keep going all the way to the finish line.

Her time on that curb and the last nine miles of walking humbled her. Her new-found friends inspired her. And God's faithfulness strengthened her. The last bit of adrenaline in her aching body flowed strongly enough through her veins to help her pick up her knees and pump her arms toward the finish.

And almost seven hours after the start, with a wide smile across her face that nothing or no one could erase, Millie Devonshire, a middle-aged American housewife, ran across the finish line of the Rome Marathon.

A race volunteer placed the medal around her neck, and she grabbed a cold water bottle off the table and guzzled the water down her dry throat.

"Congratulations," Sal said.

"You, too, my friend." Millie held out her hand. "I

217

couldn't have done it without your help." He took her hand and shook it.

"My pleasure." Sal laughed. "You'll never forget this for the rest of your life." He turned her around to face the Colosseum and ancient ruins of Rome. "Look at that."

"You're right." Millie exhaled. "You're absolutely right and in so many ways."

A race photographer took a picture of them both holding up their medals.

"We did it!" they shouted together.

"There she is!" Jamie shouted as she approached the fence with the others next to her. "Millie! You did it!"

She jogged over to them, holding up her medal. "Thanks for being here." She pointed to Sal as he approached. "And this is my new friend, Sal. He helped me get here, trust me. I don't think I would have made it across that finish line had he not stopped to assist me at mile sixteen."

"Really?" Jamie tilted her head. "What happened?"

"It is a long, wonderful story, but one for later tonight at my restaurant." Sal patted Millie on her shoulder. "You all are invited to dinner for the celebration."

"Salvatore!" They all heard his name.

Farther down the fence was a group of people hopping up and down.

"That is my family. I must go now." He bowed to Millie and her friends with his hand over his heart. "Mille grazie."

"Thank you so much, Sal." Millie kissed his left cheek and then his right. "I owe you so much. God used you to answer my prayers."

"Prego," he said with a bow, backed away, then reunited with his excited family.

"I can't wait to hear the story." Michael walked over to where the fence ended and faced Millie.

She hobbled along. "I can't wait to get to the room and take a hot shower and then take a long nap."

"I bet! You've earned it." Joy hugged her shoulders.

"Come on, marathoner," Judith said. "Let's get you to the hotel."

"There she is!" came a shout.

Millie looked up to find Edith and Martin waving to her. In Edith's hands was a bouquet of white roses. "For the champion marathoner." She held them out.

"Yes! Veni, vidi, vici!" Millie smiled and Martin laughed.

"Very good," he said.

Millie took the roses from Edith and inhaled the scent. "Thanks for showing up."

"Our pleasure," Martin said.

Edith shrugged her shoulders up to her ears. "Forgive me?"

"For abandoning me?" Millie playfully punched Edith's arm.

Edith hugged Millie. "Yes. Please forgive me?"

"Only if you tell me you both had a great time together." Millie grinned at Martin.

"We did." Edith grabbed Millie's elbow and helped her along the street. "Let's get you back to the hotel so you can rest."

"Shower, nap, then eat…all the food in Rome." Millie cringed with each step.

"Absolutely. You've earned it." Martin pecked Millie's cheek and took her other arm. Together, they made their way to the hotel.

CHAPTER 16

Millie stood before the steps of the hotel entryway, cringing. Although just a few steps, they might as well have been the Spanish Steps, as far as she was concerned. Sixteen miles of running followed by ten miles of walking had made her legs like noodles.

"Well?" Martin asked. "What do you think? Can you make it?"

"I think it might as well be Mount Everest." She chuckled.

"You all right, Millie?" Michael tilted his head as he approached.

She winced. "Not really. I think I'm going to need some help up these steps."

Michael offered her an arm, and, with the help of Martin, Millie made her way up the steps one painful step at a time all the way to the hotel revolving door. Once inside the hotel lobby, Millie rested for a bit. Claudia turned to see Millie coming through the revolving door.

"Scusi," she said to the hotel guests she was speaking with. "Millie?" She approached her with arms open wide. "You ran the marathon today?"

Millie raised the medal on her chest. "Yes, I did."

Hobbling along on her noodle legs, she managed to smile. "I sort of did, yes."

Claudia, the hotel managers, Edith, and the others clapped for her, and she did her best to bow as she made her way to the elevators.

"Grazie," she said with a wave, but even lifting her arm was painful. She grimaced and bit her lip through the pain.

"We'll leave you alone to get showered and rested." Edith patted Millie's back.

"Thanks. Be back in time for dinner, all right?"

"Sure thing. Martin has to get back to his place, but I will be here." Edith hugged her friend.

Finally in her room, Millie removed her medal and racing belt and gently placed them onto the bed. She stared at them for a moment, almost expecting them to talk to her. "We did it. It's over," she said as she glided her finger across the medal.

When she remembered her phone, she removed it and took a photo of her bib and medal right before the phone battery died. She plugged it into the charger, grabbed a change of clothes, then limped to the shower.

As the warm water ran down her face, the day's scenery passed through her mind. So did the pain and anguish.

But the water rinsed not only all sweat and dirt down the drain but the negative memories as well. After drying off and managing to somehow blow-dry her hair, Millie fell onto the bed for a nice long nap. But before she could fall asleep, she heard her phone ping, jerking her awake.

Could it be? She rose onto her elbows. *Walter?*

Grabbing her phone, Millie scrolled to open it and noticed a text message notification. But when she opened it, she saw it was a message from Edith.

So proud of you. Edith asked her. You ran through Rome!

Millie chuckled and sent her the photograph of the medal next to her racing bib.

Edith replied with a series of explanation points.

`Nap time,` Millie texted, then shut off her phone and fell asleep on her bed.

∽

"Wakey, wakey," Edith said as she gently nudged Millie. "Time to wake up for dinner."

"Dinner?" Millie rolled over and stretched. "Ow!" She grabbed her leg. "Cramp."

"I brought you some ice. It's almost seven p.m. Time to get some calories in you. Come on. Let's get going." Edith opened the curtains. "It's a lovely evening out."

Millie slowly sat up in bed with a groan.

"Sore?" Edith chuckled.

"Ha ha. Very funny. I'm doing rather well, considering."

"Oh?" Edith inspected her hair in the mirror. "What happened? Let's go to dinner, and you can tell me all about it."

"How was your day at Pompeii?" Millie rubbed the sleep out of her eyes.

A smile slowly crept to Edith's flushed face.

"That wonderful, huh?" Millie threw the covers off her legs and stretched her arms.

"It was . . . magical. Yes." Edith fixed her lipstick. "I'll tell you all about it at dinner. Let's go."

"Dinner . . . oh, yeah. We're going to a new restaurant tonight. Salvatore is treating us all to dinner." Millie made her way to the bathroom.

"Who?" Edith squinted as though trying to remember if she had met the person.

"Long story that I'll share on the way to the restaurant."

But before they left, Millie removed a business card from her fanny pack and made a phone call.

"Who are you calling now? Let's go eat."

"One minute." Millie winked. "You're going to want to hear this . . ."

∽

Outside the hotel, the group gathered around and took turns hugging Millie.

"I am so impressed," Ben said. "Twenty-six miles. Unbelievable."

"She's amazing." Joy pecked her cheek. "You give us middle-aged ladies some hope."

Millie laughed.

"You inspire me to take up running," Betsy said. "Whaddya say, Hank? This time next year we'll do the Rome Marathon?"

He rolled his eyes and spun his wife around. "Let's go to dinner."

The group laughed as they walked.

"Where is this place again, Millie?" Judith asked.

"Right this way." On the way to the restaurant, Millie explained to Edith all that happened at mile sixteen. "It was crazy. I have never hurt so badly in all my life. My legs cramped, my feet were killing me, and my back seized."

With her hands over her mouth, Edith gasped.

"What happened to listening without reacting?" Millie chuckled.

"Oh, Mill, I am so sorry you endured all that." Edith shook her head. "I had no idea. What did you do?"

"The only thing I could. I sat down at the curb to rest and massage my aching calf muscles and feel sorry for myself."

Edith grimaced. "I regret leaving you. I should have stayed with you and—"

"No. Had you been there, we both would have been stuck on the side of the road feeling sorry for ourselves."

Edith hugged Millie's shoulder. "Okay, then. I won't

regret it."

"Me neither." She laughed heartily. "And just so you know, I'm not sorry. Not at all." Millie faced her. "God met me there at that curb."

"Oh? How do you mean?" Edith put her arm around Millie, and the two walked on.

"He needed my complete and undivided attention, and he got it," she said.

"Why did he need your attention?"

"To scold me. To admonish me." Millie laughed again. "I was such a fool to think I could rely on myself to get me to the finish." She shook her head. "I was foolish to run ahead to Rome without Walter. Foolish to even consider a life here by myself. I've been so foolish about so many things. But . . . God was gracious and heard my humble prayer of desperation and answered me immediately. I'm so grateful for Sal."

"Sal? The owner of the restaurant we're headed to?"

"Yes. When I said 'amen,' I looked up, and there he was, offering to help me off my bum and back into the race."

"Amazing."

"You see, he told me to walk and not run. I needed to hear that more than anything. I needed that permission." Millie exhaled. "And we walked for miles. That's when he told me about his life here and about his family, the restaurant, friends—the history of this place, the ruins, the monuments. Everything."

"Wow, what a treat. To have a native give you a tour of Rome."

"It really was." She thought back to it. "But most of all, we ran across the finish line."

"What a story, Millie. I may have to include that in my book and—"

"No way! That's my story. If you want it, you have to run the marathon to earn it." Millie playfully shoved Edith.

"I guess so."

"So how was Naples?" Millie whispered. "And Martin and everything?"

Edith grabbed Millie's arm and squeezed. "He's absolutely perfect. An ideal gentleman. I haven't laughed so hard in years."

"I'm so very happy for you, my friend." Millie hugged Edith. "I mean it."

"Me, too."

"I owe you so much."

"Nonsense." Edith waved her hand through the air.

"I do. Because of you, I took a chance. I entered that contest to show you that I, too, can be adventurous and unguarded. I wanted to try something new to be . . . to be more like you."

Edith sniffled. "And you did it."

"I did it."

Millie did do it. She did something she never thought she could do. She ventured to a foreign country, met foreign people and their culture. They made her feel welcome, loved, and wanted. Millie took Edith's hand. "Thank you for coming with me."

They walked toward the restaurant and were greeted by the maître d' outside.

"Benvenuto," he said and waved them inside the warm space filled with many aromas from wine to spices to garlic.

"Millie!" Sal came from the kitchen with his arms open wide. "You made it!"

"Of course we did." She pecked his cheek. "We wouldn't miss it."

"How are you feeling, eh? A little sore?" He nudged her.

"Yes." She rubbed her thighs and grimaced. "Very sore."

"And very hungry, yes?" Sal led them to their tables.

"Very hungry!" Edith replied.

Millie introduced him to Edith and the rest of the group.

"How do you do? And this is my beloved wife, Francesca," Sal said as his wife approached.

"Bona sera," she said with a glint in her eyes.

"This is our crazy group from America," Millie said as she waved her hands over the gathering of friends.

Sal showed the group to their table in the middle of the restaurant. He graciously pushed several tables together to form one long table.

"What a lovely restaurant." Edith glanced around the dining room. "I love the ambience. The exposed brick, candlelight, vines dangling from a lattice on the ceiling." She nudged Millie. "And plenty of space to hang photographs, huh?"

Millie winked. "Maybe . . ."

"Ben!" Edith pointed. You're here. I am so glad you decided to join us tonight," Edith said when she sat down at the table.

"I wouldn't miss our last night in Rome." He smiled.

"Can you believe it? Our last night together, and then we all fly out tomorrow?" Betsy placed her hand over her heart.

Hank read the menu. "I know what I'm having for dinner." He leaned over and pecked his wife's cheek.

"Lasagna. I know, I know." Betsy laughed and playfully smacked his shoulder.

Millie sat across from Edith and noticed Jamie wasn't smiling or talking. Michael seemed a little tense.

"Hello, everyone," Judith shouted, startling everyone.

"Hello, Judith," Edith said without emotion. Then she turned to Millie. "Look, Millie. Judith's here."

Millie waved cheerfully. "I'm so glad you made it."

Judith stepped aside to reveal a smiling George behind her. "Look who I found."

"George!" Ben clapped. "So good to see you again. Sit." He scooted out the chair next to him, and George gladly sat down.

"I'm starved," George said. "This is a nice place."

Judith sat down across from him. He poured her some red wine. "Here, Judith. Have some."

She held up her glass and raised an eyebrow. "He's trying to get me hammered," she whispered to Edith, who sat with her mouth open.

"Here's to Millie." Judith lifted her glass. "Finishing the Rome Marathon."

"Cheers!" Joy said.

"Congrats, Millie," Michael toasted her.

But Jamie remained silent as she lifted her glass.

"Thank you, everyone," Millie said as she stood. "And here's to Sal for his assistance. I honestly don't think I would have made it across the finish line without his help."

The group clapped, and Sal bowed.

"Antipasti on the house, eh?" Sal clapped his hands, and the servers brought out platters of antipasti and bruschetta.

As everyone clapped and served themselves, Edith leaned over to Millie. "What's going on?"

"What do you mean?"

"With Judith." Edith nodded to her left. "And George . . ."

Millie giggled. "She's a new woman."

Joy clasped her hands together "This is wonderful! This food is delicious. Isn't it wonderful, Jamie?"

But Jamie sipped her wine and stared at her plate.

"Something's wrong with Jamie," Millie whispered to Edith. "She's not her usual chipper self."

"Hmm . . ." Edith leaned onto her elbows. "Watch them closely."

"Did she change her mind about Carl?" Millie asked.

"Millie." Sal waved her over. "You come see the kitchen. Come . . ."

Millie made her way over to the busy kitchen, where Sal's son and other cooks were making delicious Italian dishes.

"Smells wonderful in here." She glanced around at the various dishes set out with garnishes.

"This is my son, Luca. He's an award-winning chef."

The young man bowed.

"Grandpa." A little girl approached and tugged on Sal's pant leg. "Can I help?"

He picked her up and kissed her cheek. "And this is my Angela. Our beautiful granddaughter," Sal said.

The little girl with large brown eyes and dark hair set in ringlets around her shoulders reached out her hand.

"How do you do?" Millie shook her hand.

"You need to go sit over there, Angela." Sal put her down.

Millie watched the little girl run to a stool in the corner of the kitchen. She climbed onto the stool and sat there, watching everything. Millie's heart broke. She hated the idea of the little girl sitting alone when she wanted to help out.

"Maybe she can help in the kitchen?" Millie asked.

But Sal held up a finger. "No. Children are to be seen and not heard in the family restaurant."

"Understood." Millie nodded.

Sal showed her around the kitchen and the wine cellar. Millie noticed the artwork on the walls, etchings of Rome from 1800s, and marveled at some of the framed photographs of various parts of Rome. Chills ran over her as she thought about the restaurant that wanted to buy her photographs.

"You have a beautiful restaurant, Sal." Millie patted his shoulder. "You should be very proud of your family."

Back at the table, Millie sat with Edith and tried the bruschetta. She enjoyed the tomatoes drenched in olive oil and listened to the conversation between Edith and Judith as they spoke of Pompeii and other adventures in Italy.

Ben and Michael discussed the stabbing Michael witnessed with Edith, Millie, and Jamie. Ben couldn't believe how it happened.

Betsy explained to Joy all the photographs she had taken of the ancient ruins, showing Joy some of her work on her phone. Millie smiled as they oohed and aahed at each other's photographs.

All strangers just a few days ago, now they were good friends who had shared so many memories of Rome.

Moments later, the waiters brought their meals out along with some bread and more wine. Millie raised her plate of lasagna to her nose and inhaled. "Heavenly."

"It feels good not to have to worry about what to eat and whether it will be too heavy. No more running until we get back home," Edith said.

Millie smiled and ate a bite of lasagna. "Exactly."

"And be sure to have dessert." Edith lifted her glass of wine. "You've earned it."

"Chocolate cake." Millie tapped the dessert menu with her fork. "I already saw it."

"Tiramisu," Edith replied.

Millie's eyes widened. "Oh my goodness. Yes."

"Well, which one? Chocolate cake or—"

"Both!" Millie tossed her head back and laughed.

"Why not?" Edith joined her in laughing.

"No," Jamie said and threw down her napkin, startling everyone silent. "Now leave me alone." She loudly scooted out her chair and left the restaurant, leaving a distraught Michael behind.

"Che' successo, Michele?" Ben asked him. "What is happening?"

But Michael ignored his father and stared at his plate for a minute, then headed out the door after her.

"Joy, what's going on?" Millie asked quietly. "Don't tell me she changed her mind about Carl."

Joy sat with her hands over her tired face, shaking her head.

"Joy?" Edith asked. "What is it?"

Joy lowered her hands, revealing shiny eyes. "Michael

asked her to marry him earlier today, but Jamie said no."

Ben lowered his head and sighed heavily.

"What?" Millie and Edith scooted their chairs closer to the table and leaned in. "When did he ask her?" Millie asked.

Joy craned her neck to check the door. When she saw Michael hadn't returned, she leaned in close. "Before dinner, he and Jamie went for a walk to the Trevi Fountain, where he presented her with a ring and a proposal."

"Wow. How romantic," Millie said. "I can't imagine."

"It was . . . just lovely." Joy wiped her eyes. "But Jamie just can't—" She exhaled. "She just can't forget about what happened back home."

"I'm so sorry." Millie rested her folded hands on the table.

Judith scooted closer too. "What was it that happened?"

"Tell, tell," Betsy said.

"It's quite the story." Edith squinted as she listened.

"A few months ago, Jamie was left at the altar by her long-time boyfriend, Carl." Joy shook her head. "It was awful."

Betsy covered her mouth. "Oh my goodness."

"One hundred and fifty guests were there waiting for the groom. Jamie and I were in the back with her bridesmaids, pacing back and forth in the foyer until Jamie's phone vibrated. Her maid of honor took the call, and just by the look on her face, we knew who it was." Joy rolled her eyes. "He told Jamie that he changed his mind. Marriage was something he just couldn't do."

Edith gripped the table. "That son of a—"

"It gets worse." Joy rubbed her hands together nervously. "Later that night, after we got home and started packing up her dress and the gifts she'd received, her father, my husband, announced to us that he was leaving."

Millie's eyes widened. "What?"

"Nice timing, huh?" Joy blinked back tears. "He went upstairs, changed out of his tuxedo, packed a bag, and told us he was leaving."

"Good Lord," Judith replied.

"It was probably the worst day in both our lives. Her fiancé leaves town, and then my husband leaves town. We sat there on the couch and just cried and cried." Joy used her napkin to dab her eyes.

"Joy, I cannot even fathom such a day of emotions." Edith covered her mouth. "No wonder Jamie's having a hard time saying yes to Michael."

"She loves him, I just know she does. She's just . . . afraid to take a chance on love again." Joy sniffled. "But Michael is so sweet. He's so special."

"He isn't Carl." Millie patted Joy's hand.

"No, he isn't. Thank God for that." Joy managed to smile through her tears. "He's wonderful. Why can't she see that?"

"Love is hard." Edith shrugged.

"Yes, it is." Judith sighed.

"But it can be so beautiful too." Betsy smiled and hugged Joy's shoulders.

"She'll come around," Ben said.

"I hope so." Joy managed a weak smile.

More wine was brought to the table and so were desserts. Millie sank her teeth into the chocolate cake, closing her eyes as it melted in her mouth. "Pure delight."

Sal came around to check on his guests. His little granddaughter, Angela, followed close behind him, peeking around his legs from time to time.

Millie wriggled her fingers at her. "Hello," she mouthed.

The little girl covered her mouth and giggled.

"Back to the kitchen, Angela," Sal ordered.

With a frown, the little girl turned on her heel and headed back to her stool in the corner of the kitchen.

As she watched the little girl, Millie couldn't help but sympathize with her. She knew what it was like to be seen and not heard. In fact, Millie knew what it was like to not be seen nor heard.

Something tugged on her heart. She couldn't figure out what it was. It wasn't anger or pain, but wisdom. Millie knew how Angela felt. And she also knew she couldn't let what had happened to her happen to little Angela.

CHAPTER 17

"I'll be right back," she said to Edith. Millie made her way into the kitchen and made eye contact with Angela, who sulked atop her stool in the corner of the kitchen. Busy workers passed in front of her and even sometimes accidentally backed into her.

Millie waved to her and called her over. But Angela, ever dutiful, shook her head and stayed on her stool.

"It's okay," Millie mouthed, but Angela didn't budge. So Millie went to her and crouched down before her. "Hi there." She reached up and placed some strands of Angela's dark hair away from her face and behind her tiny ears. "It's okay, Angela. I know what it's like to be told to sit still and say nothing. It isn't fun, is it?"

She shook her head.

"I don't think a little girl should be invisible. You're too important and kind to be invisible. The world needs to see you. Okay?"

Angela smiled.

"You can come sit with me and my friends. We're having cake."

Angela's eyes widened.

"Want some?" Millie stood and held out her hand.

Angela took her hand and hopped off the stool.

"Angela," Sal said. "Where are you going?"

"She's going to sit with me and have some cake." Millie smiled.

"All right, but don't be a bother, okay?" Sal patted his granddaughter on the head.

Millie pulled out the chair next to her and helped Angela sit down. Then she cut some of her cake and placed it onto a small saucer. "Here you go."

"Who's this cutie?" Judith smiled widely.

"This is Sal's granddaughter, Angela. Say hello to my friends, Angela." Millie hugged the little girl.

"Hello there," Edith said.

"You're a big girl now, sitting with us." Joy waved to her.

Angela nodded and blinked her large brown eyes.

"Such a beauty."

"She was sitting alone in the kitchen, and I just couldn't take it, watching her sit there all by herself. People passed her like she was invisible. I know all about being invisible." Millie watched Angela enjoy her cake. Her cheeks were smudged with chocolate frosting.

As everyone finished their desserts and Angela made friends with the doting adults at the table, Millie spied Sal leaning against the kitchen wall, watching the scene.

He waved to little Angela, who scooted away and ran to her grandfather.

Millie nodded to Sal, and he nodded back with a wide grin.

Millie knew it was time to make her announcement. She stood, then used her fork to tap her water glass. "Uh, excuse me. Can I have everyone's attention?"

The conversation at the table stopped, and all stared at Millie smiling down at them. Clearing her throat, Millie raised a wine glass and began her announcement.

"I want to thank all of you for your friendship. These

last few days have been more than remarkable, but life-changing. In fact, I know I'll leave Rome as a new person. I raise my glass to all of you. First, Betsy and Hank. I thank you for showing me what a loving marriage can look like after thirty years together. You inspire me."

Hank pulled Betsy to him and kissed her cheek. Everyone clapped.

"Joy, thank you for teaching me that even if something terrible happens in life, I can go on living. You have definitely done so with grace and courage. You inspire me."

Joy raised her glass and smiled through her tears.

"Edith, what can I say? You've been my best friend since childhood and never cease to surprise me. Thank you for getting me here and challenging me in ways I couldn't dream were possible. I look forward to our next adventure together."

"Prego!" Edith laughed and clapped along with everyone else.

"Ben . . ." Millie choked back tears. "Dear Ben. I want to thank you for reminding me to—"

Ben's eyes filled with tears as he listened.

"To remember my husband and why I married him. And how I love him." Millie brushed aside a tear. "Because of you, I now appreciate my husband so much more than when I boarded the plane to Rome. You reminded me to see him for who he is and not what I want him to be."

Edith wiped her weepy eyes.

"I selfishly had forgotten who Walter is and why he does what he does. He loves me." Millie's face contorted from crying. "And I love him more than I can say."

"Prego. Di niente," Ben said to her. "You're very welcome."

The restaurant guests joined in and clapped too. Millie's face warmed and she knew it was turning red from the attention. With trembling hand, she raised her wine glass higher.

"And to Judith . . ."

Judith jerked her head around. "Me?" Her eyes widened as a serious look came to her face.

"Uh-oh," Edith muttered to herself and averted her eyes by looking down at her dessert.

"I want to thank you for motivating me to be a better photographer and—"

"Motivating?" Edith muttered again without looking up.

"Shh." Millie waved her hand at Edith. "Challenging me to work harder at my photography."

"My pleasure." Judith raised her glass.

"And challenging me to be a . . . friend, even with someone I disagree with."

Judith and George chuckled.

"It can be possible to look past those things that make each other different and focus on those things that make us the same, right?"

"Absolutely," Judith said.

"I thank you and George for reminding me of the importance of listening to one another and being patient with one another in marriage."

George took Judith's face into his hands and gently kissed her lips.

"Awww," Joy said.

Clapping and cheers from those at the table made more heads turn.

Judith's eyes became shiny.

"Sal?" Millie waved him over. "He has a surprise for you, Judith."

Edith looked up and turned around in her chair.

"Judith," Sal began. "Millie was so kind as to show me your lovely photography on your website."

"What?" Judith placed her hand over her heart.

"I would love to have you display your photographs in my restaurant." Sal bowed, then waved his hand over a wall nearby.

"Seriously? Me?" Judith pointed to herself. "I thought they wanted you to—"

"Nope." Millie shrugged. "Not when I showed him your amazing work."

Judith covered her mouth. "I don't know what to say." She turned to George, who pecked her cheek.

"Say yes!" Millie laughed.

"Yes." Judith stood and offered Sal her hand. "I'd love to display my work in your lovely restaurant."

Millie set down her glass and applauded Judith.

George joined in the applause and whistled.

"Excellent choice," Ben cried as he clapped.

"To friends!" Millie picked up her glass again and raised it high.

"Friends." Edith stood and joined in the toast. "Cin-cin."

They all stood and clanked their glasses together.

Judith's eyes met Millie's. "Thank you," she mouthed.

"Everyone!" came a shout from the doorway.

All heads turned to see Michael and Jamie race to the table. He held up Jamie's left hand, where a sparkling solitaire diamond reflected the light. "She said yes."

Millie and Edith gasped and rushed toward them. "Congratulations!"

Joy stood with her hands over her mouth and tears streaming down her face. "Is it true?"

Jamie nodded and embraced her mother. The two stood holding each other and laughing through their tears.

"This is incredible," Edith said to Michael. "What happened?"

He raised his hands. "I ran after her, and we walked and talked about everything. And then we found ourselves by the Colosseum, so I knelt and asked . . . no, I begged her one more time to trust in love and spend the rest of her life with me." He lifted Jamie's chin with his finger and stared into her teary eyes. "Because I love her more than anything in this world. And thank God above, this time she said yes."

"Because I knew I was being ridiculous before." Jamie wiped her eyes. "I knew I was allowing my fears to ruin the best thing I ever had, and that's a life with Michael." She took his face into her hands. "Michael, you are the best man I have ever known. You're the best person I have ever known."

The two looked directly into each other's eyes and saw it.

Hope.

A bright halo of light coming from the lamp above shone around Jamie's chestnut hair, making her look angelic, Millie thought. Yes, the look in Jamie's eyes said love. Hopeful love. And that love made her willing to take a chance . . . again.

Tears formed in the corner of Jamie's eyes. Her head rested on Michael's shoulder.

Michael turned to his father. "What do you think, Pop?"

"Sono fiero di te." Ben stood and embraced his son. "I'm so proud of you," he cried. "You have found love in Rome. You have found romance."

Michael kissed Jamie hard on the lips. "I sure did." Everyone cheered.

"You both have made me so very happy. We must call your mother," Ben said.

Michael dialed his phone, and a concerned voice came on. "Michael? What is it? Is everything all right?"

"Mom?"

"Yes, Son. What is it?"

"Mom . . . I asked Jamie to marry me, and she said yes!"

"What?" Her voice came through loud and clear.

Ben took the phone from Michael and began to explain in Italian what happened.

"Champagne for all," Sal ordered. Once everyone had their champagne flutes filled, they cheered for Michael and

Jamie.

For a second, Millie thought about calling Walter to share the good news, but as soon as the thought appeared, it was gone. She knew such news would be confusing to Walter back home. After all, he didn't know any of the people at the table. But it would be nice to celebrate with him.

Millie sat with a loud exhale. Her mission was accomplished. She was able to thank each one for what they had given her: glimpses into what love should be.

The empty wine bottles sat open on the table. The waiters cleared away the plates and glasses, signaling it was time to head back to the hotel.

∽

On the walk back, Millie and Edith reviewed the night's events as well as their time in Rome.

"I was mad at you for leaving me at the marathon starting line, but . . ." Millie smirked.

"I know." Edith gestured as if trying to find the words. "I didn't handle it well. I should have—"

"No. You did the right thing." Millie stared at the sidewalk as she walked. "I asked for adventure, and you gave it to me."

"I'm glad you see it that way."

"I do. And I meant what I said back there. I thank you for giving this to me." Millie hugged her friend's shoulder. "I needed this. I've craved excitement and adventure for so long that I have no idea what I'm going to do when I get back home."

"You have those photographs to send to that other restaurant manager. Don't forget about that." Edith wagged her finger at Millie. "The wedding photographs will lead to something, I can assure you of that. And you need to read the rough draft of the book I'm going to write when we get home."

"Absolutely. I can hardly wait." Millie rubbed her hands together. "I'm just so glad that Michael and Jamie provided you with the perfect happy ending."

"I don't think it could have been written any better than how it unfolded right before our eyes. Brilliant!" Edith replied.

"Happy endings are what your readers want, right?" Millie asked.

"For my romances, yes. I got away from happy endings when I started writing suspense. I have to admit, it was a lot easier writing those books than the romances."

"Why?"

"Happy endings are hard to write when life isn't going well."

Millie knew Edith spoke of the time when Charlie was ill.

"Scary brutal endings come naturally to me," Edith said. "But this trip? This trip has inspired me again to try writing those happy endings." Edith hop-skipped. "I'm back in the saddle. The stories I heard and witnessed on this trip are perfect for my book."

"Except my story, right?" Millie chuckled.

Edith stopped and turned to her. "What do you mean?"

"My story doesn't have a happy ending." Millie sighed. "At least not one that makes romance novel readers fall in love with the story." Millie kept walking. "My story is pathetic."

"Stop it." Edith gently shoved her.

"Emails and text messages every day these two weeks, and he still hasn't responded." Millie raised her arms and dropped them at her sides in defeat. "I give up, Edith. I really do."

"No, you don't." Edith caught up to her and spun her around. "Don't give up on love. It can surprise you. Look at Judith and George, huh? If those two can make it work out, then you and Walt can."

"Walter." Millie inhaled and slowly exhaled. "I suppose you're right. Ben, Betsy, Joy, and Judith have all helped me to see that. I will make it work. When I get home, things will be different."

"Edith!" came a shout from across the street.

They turned to see Martin walking toward them.

"Martin." A wide smile came to Edith's face. "So good to see you."

"Hello, Martin," Millie said. "What are you doing here?"

He kissed Edith on the cheek and squeezed her tightly to him. "Are you ready?"

"Yes." Edith turned to Millie. "We're going for a stroll."

"What?"

"He texted me at the restaurant and asked me to meet him here." Edith gripped Martin's arm.

"How romantic." Millie clicked her tongue. "Go make a happy ending."

Edith hugged Millie's neck. "Don't give up on love, okay? Make your happy ending, all right?"

"I will." Millie kissed Edith's cheek, then watched her and Martin walk off together, arm in arm.

When they disappeared around the corner, Millie stood alone there on Cavour Street for a moment, listening to the sounds of Rome. The people passing by, the mopeds and scooters zipping along the street, and the cheers coming from a pub around the corner made her heart sad because she knew it was her last night in the magical city.

With a heavy sigh and tears in her eyes, Millie said her goodbye to Rome there on the street. The next afternoon, she would board a plane and head home with Edith. Joy announced she was heading to Venice. Judith and George were heading to Prague. Jamie and Michael were heading to Milan. Ben was flying home to New York.

As she walked up to the hotel, thoughts of the first day she arrived in Rome returned to her mind. Claudia introducing herself, meeting each one in the group, and learning their stories . . . All of it brought a smile of sadness to Millie's face. She learned to love them all and wondered if she'd ever see them again.

It begins with me, she thought. *I have to make the effort to keep in touch with them.*

Millie was excited to be that person. A person who made an effort to keep in touch with her new friends. A person who looked to the future with hope.

She entered the revolving door of the hotel no longer the woman she was when she had first arrived in Rome. She was glad that person was forever gone.

"Hello, Millie." A voice startled her.

When she heard his voice, her heart skipped a beat.

CHAPTER 18

Standing in the center of the hotel lobby in a wrinkled sports coat, was Walter holding a small bouquet of roses. He swiped his graying hair, messy from sleeping on a plane, away from his forehead.

Millie stared at his face, unable to move. "Walter…what are you doing here?"

"Scusi, signore," a man said as he came to the revolving door. Millie hadn't realized she was blocking access to it.

"I'm sorry." She scooted out of the way without looking away from her husband.

"I thought I'd surprise you," he said with his arms out. "So . . . surprise. Here I am!"

Blinking back tears, Millie opened her mouth to speak, but nothing came out.

"I've missed you, Mill," he said. "The house is a mess. I ruined my white T-shirts when I accidentally left a red dishcloth in the washing machine. Now everything's pink. I burnt a meatloaf the first night, so I've been eating fast food every day. I feel sick." He grimaced.

Millie took a step toward him as he spoke.

"I'm lost without you." Walter looked down at his feet. "What can I say, Millie? I messed up. I should have come with you."

She covered her mouth and cried. "You do notice me. You do need me."

"Of course, I do, Mill. I need you more than anything, and I've been such a fool. My pride kept me from replying to your messages. Can you ever forgive—"

Millie ran to her husband's waiting arms, embracing him and almost knocking him over.

"Oh, Walter," Millie cried as she wrapped her arms around his neck. His arms around her waist tickled her heart, and she laughed again. She couldn't remember the last time she felt the warm pressure of her husband's arms around her. "I can't believe you're here. How? When?"

"I know." He chuckled. "I can't believe it either. I can't remember everything. It's sort of a blur. All I know is that I got your messages, bought a ticket, then hopped on a plane. And I've been on a plane for a long, long time."

They parted, and Walter curled into her, looking deep into her eyes, reigniting the flame that had almost burned out. Romantic flutters filled Millie's belly.

Walter reached up and gently stroked his wife's cheek as if touching a rare porcelain doll, wet with tears.

"I may not have been there for you before, but I'm here now, Millie." He kissed the tip of her nose. "I'm really here for you, and I do see you, my sweet Millie girl."

Millie pressed her lips to his and pulled him close. When they parted again, she wiped her eyes and face.

"These are for you." He handed her the bouquet of roses.

"Coral pink. My favorite color." She hugged the bouquet to herself and inhaled the glorious scent. The flowers fulfilled their destiny of bringing such unmitigated joy to its owner. She inhaled the roses with freesia mixed in along with violets and creamy white carnations. "They're lovely, Walter. When did you get here?"

"Not too long ago." Walter spun around. "My bags are

over there. I was about to ask them what your room number was, but then I remembered you're with Edith, so . . ."

"We'll get our own room." Millie led him to the front desk. "I fly out tomorrow, so we'll have to see about your flight and then—"

But he stopped her and took her hands into his. "Well . . . actually, there's been a change of plans."

She tilted her head.

"It's true." He motioned to the front desk. "I made reservations last week for us to stay here another four days so you can show me Rome." Walter smiled.

With wide eyes, Millie couldn't believe what she'd just heard. Her knees became weak. "You what?"

"Your emails were so descriptive. I could picture everything in my head. So, I want you to show me the city."

Her head spun around like that revolving door. Millie stepped back to study this man before her.

"Who are you, and what have you done with Walter?" she asked.

He tossed his head back and laughed.

"I . . . I can't believe this. I'm speechless." Millie laughed through her tears and embraced him again.

"But . . ." Millie swallowed. "Can we afford it?"

"I got the promotion." Walter beamed.

Millie gasped as Walter twirled her around, then danced with her there in the hotel lobby.

"I'm so proud of you, Walter."

"Come on. Let's get our room, and then we can go gather your things." Walter motioned to the manager, who wriggled his eyebrows and smiled at Millie.

"You knew?" she asked the manager.

"I was sworn to secrecy, signore," the manager said as he handed them the key cards to their room.

In her room, Millie tossed all her clothes into her luggage and then scooped all her bathroom supplies and makeup into her handbag. Walter patiently waited for her and chuckled as he watched. Then she opened her laptop, found that letter she had written to Walter, and joyfully deleted it.

"Where's your medal?" Walter craned his neck to see into the room.

Mille grabbed it and held it up.

"Wow." He shook his head. "You did it, Mill."

"I know, right?" She clutched her chest. "It was hell, but I crossed that finish line."

Walter continued to stare at the medal with wide eyes.

Millie tossed it into her bag. "But the real prize is seeing you here with me in Rome, Walter."

A hopeful smile appeared across his face.

"Are you hungry? We can get something to eat if you'd like." Millie pulled her luggage through the door and followed Walter to the room down the hallway.

He swiped the key card and opened the door. "Actually, how about we order some room service, huh?"

"What?" Millie laughed.

"I've never ordered room service before, and the way you described it in your email the other day, I think I'd like to try it." He held the door open for her.

Millie shook her head. "I'm in shock. I think I need to sit down for a moment and—"

Her mouth dropped open when she saw the size of the room. The suite included a sofa, loveseat, and a fireplace.

Filled with bouquets of flowers at every turn, the room's floral scent made her dizzy with joy. More bouquets of carnations, the color of the sea, greeted her, as did azaleas and violets a foot long set inside crystal vases. Roses of every color imaginable smiled at her from vases resting on the bedside tables. And then her favorite—white anemones and red geraniums in a ceramic pot sat on the coffee table, reminding her of the Boboli Gardens in Florence. She rushed over and inhaled their sweet scent.

"The flowers of the wind." She spun around. "I don't

know what to say. I've never seen so many lovely flowers. How did you—?"

"Edith."

"Edith." Millie laughed. "She knows everything, doesn't she?"

He raised his shoulder. "She knows how to get things done, let me tell you. When I told her I was flying out, she took care of everything for me. Here. Read this." He handed her a card.

"Thank you, Millie!" she read. "Without you, I don't think we would have gotten together. Love, Jamie and Michael . . . wait. When did everyone have the chance to sign this card?" Millie looked up at Walter.

"Earlier this evening, I think. Edith said she'd take care of it, and she did."

Millie was thankful that Jamie and Michael did make amends and get together after all. Deep down, Edith must have known. Millie chuckled. *Edith knows everything.*

"Enjoy the precious time with your husband. Love, Ben. You two deserve true happiness. Love, Betsy and Hank. Many more adventures await you two. Love, Joy. You're the example of true class, dignity, perseverance, love, and friendship, Millie. We admire you so. Love, Judith and George." Millie wiped her eyes. "And last but not least— Cin-cin. Love, Edith."

Millie covered her mouth as more tears flowed. "Whatever did I do to deserve this?"

"Now . . . go take a peek over there." Walter jerked his thumb to the large sliding glass door. Millie's eyes grew large when she saw that it led to a balcony. "Oh, wow."

"Did I do good?" Walter took off his blazer and tossed it onto the king-sized bed.

Millie spun around. "You did very good, dear. Come take a look."

Together, Millie and Walter stepped onto the balcony that overlooked a walkway below that led to the Piazza della

Modanna dei Monti in the distance.

"Wow," he said. "What a lovely view." He rubbed his wife's back.

"Isn't it amazing?" Millie studied his face as he took in his first view of Rome.

"It is. It's just like you described." Walter planted a deep kiss onto Millie. Her knees grew weaker, and she staggered back a bit.

"Walter." She giggled, and her face grew warm.

In the room, Walter pointed to a bottle of champagne resting in an ice bucket. He removed it and popped the cork. Millie turned on the fireplace and lowered a few lights.

Walter poured the champagne into the two glass flutes the hotel had provided. "Here you go." He handed her a glass.

"Thank you." Millie inhaled the scent of the champagne.

"To my wife. A fantastically gifted photographer, a brilliant woman with a generous heart so big, even the Colosseum would fit inside it."

Millie smiled so hard, her cheeks ached.

Walter raised his glass to Millie. "You take my breath away; you really do."

"After all these years?"

"Yes."

They drank the champagne and sat on the sofa across from the fireplace.

Walter took her hand and squeezed it. "I stopped listening." Walter kissed her hand. "I'm so sorry, Millie. I should have celebrated your winning this contest with you. I should have dropped everything to come to Rome with you. And I'm sorry I didn't."

"But you're here now." Millie held his face in her hands. "And that's all that matters to me now."

Walter pulled her close. "Oh, Millie girl."

She smiled when she heard him say those words.

"Wow, it's been a long time since you've called me your Millie girl."

"Too long." He moved some wisps of her hair away from her eyes. "You are my Millie girl. You'll always be my Millie girl."

∽

The next day, Millie and Walter headed downstairs for breakfast inside the hotel restaurant when they ran into everyone loading their bags into the van.

"Hello, everyone," Millie said to the group.

"Hello," Joy replied. She straightened when she saw Millie with Walter.

"As you know, this is my husband, Walter." Millie rolled her eyes. "I can't believe you all kept the secret from me."

"It wasn't easy." Michael came over to shake Walter's hand. "So glad you made it, Walter."

"Me too." Walter smiled at him and the rest of the group.

Millie made eye contact with everyone. "And thank you for the card."

"It was our pleasure." Judith grinned. "What are you two going to do while you're here?"

"I'm going to show Walter Rome, and then we may head to Florence for the day. Not sure yet." Millie shrugged.

"Goodbye, Millie," Judith said with shiny eyes. "Keep in touch."

"I will." She hugged her close. "I promise."

The two women parted, and Millie stood amazed at Judith's sentimentality. She remembered all too well how critical Judith was when they first met, but now she was sweet and genuinely saddened by their goodbyes.

"Your wife taught me a lot," Judith said. "She's the best."

Millie nudged her. "Oh, stop."

"So long, Millie," Jamie said. She and Michael both kissed her cheek, then turned to Walter. "We owe so much to Millie."

"She taught us to never give up on love." Michael hugged her.

"Good luck to you both." Millie held her young friends' hands in hers. "I wish you both so many blessings."

"Thank you." Jamie looked at Michael. "We're headed back to New York. We have a wedding to plan."

"How romantic." Millie turned to Walter. "These two met and fell in love here in Rome."

"I read about it in your emails." He held out his hand. "Congratulations."

"Thank you." Michael shook his hand and kissed Jamie's forehead. "I can't wait to start our life together."

"I'm so very proud of them." Ben patted Michael's back.

"You headed to New York, too, Ben?" Millie asked.

"Back to the bakery." He pecked Millie's cheek and shook Walter's hand. "Walter, sir. So glad to meet you. Very good of you to come. Take good care of this angel."

Millie and Walter stood on the steps of the hotel as the group climbed inside the van. Once the doors shut, the van started and pulled away from the curb.

They waved to Millie and Walter from the windows.

"I'll miss them all," Millie said in a soft, teary voice.

"You'll see them again."

"I will?" Millie turned to him.

"Yes. They love you, and you love them. You're friends. That's what friends do."

She beamed with joy.

"Where's Edith, though?" Walter asked.

Millie texted her friend. "She's supposed to fly out today."

When she read her reply, Millie laughed, then handed

the phone to Walter. "I guess Edith has other plans."

Edith had sent a photo of herself with Martin on the train. "I checked out of the hotel early this morning. We're heading to Venice and then who-knows-where . . ."

Walter raised an eyebrow. "I suppose she knows what she's doing." He rubbed his hands together. "So . . . what should we do first today?" Walter stepped onto the sidewalk.

"I want to show you the ancient ruins, the Colosseum, and then the doors of Rome."

"Sounds good."

Holding hands, the two strolled down the streets together. Millie showed him the ruins and the Altar of the Fatherland. As they walked, she pointed out the marathon route and told how Edith had left her at the starting line. Walter chuckled when she told him that story.

For dinner, Millie took Walter to Sal's restaurant.

"So good to meet you," Sal said as he shook Walter's hand.

"Thank you for helping my wife." Walter gave Millie a wink. "I probably would have left her there to wallow."

"Oh, hush." Millie smacked his hand. "You would not have."

Sal laughed. "You two look wonderful together. I'm so happy that you made it here, Walter." Sal placed his hand on his chest and gestured widely. "Rome is the most—"

"Romantic city in the world. Yes, I've been told." Walter chuckled.

Millie wriggled her eyebrows at him. "He's about to find out just how romantic it is."

Sal brought over a bottle of champagne to their table and toasted. "Salute, Riccezza ed Amore!" he said. "To your health, wealth, and love. May you have time to spend them all."

"Cin-cin," Millie said as she raised her glass and Walter touched his glass to hers.

During dinner, Walter shifted in his seat and adjusted

his shirt collar.

"What's the matter?" Millie asked with a raised eyebrow. She wondered if he worried about the cost of the dinner or champagne. "The champagne was on the house, so no need to worry about the cost."

Walter shook his head. "It's not that."

"What is it then?" Millie set down her fork.

When he pulled out an envelope from his pocket, Walter sighed. "Millie, I have something to give you, but I'm hesitant . . ."

She tilted her head.

"I don't want to resurrect hurt feelings. My intention is to bring healing and not hurt."

Intrigued, Millie scooted closer to the table. "What is it, Walter?"

He set the envelope down. "When you won the contest, your name was in the paper that week. Did you know that?"

She furrowed her brow. "No. I had no idea. I wonder how that—"

"Edith." Walter smiled.

"Edith." Millie rolled her eyes, then laughed. "Who else?"

"Well, your older sister saw the announcement and . . ."

"Sharon?" Millie straightened.

Walter nodded. "She called the house, but I told her you were already in Rome. Anyway, Millie, she came over to deliver something she received from your father."

Her eyes widened. "From my father."

"And we both agreed that you should have it." He handed her the manila envelope.

When Millie took it, she noticed its weight. "What is this?"

A medal fell out, along with a newspaper clipping and a note.

Dear Millie,

I read the newspaper article about you heading

to Rome to take photos and run the marathon. I want you to have this. Dad gave this to me right before he went into hospice care. He said not to give it to you until he passed. I admit I hesitated for a while, because I know you and Dad had a tumultuous relationship. I'm still not sure why he wanted me to wait, and I remain unsure if this will help you or hurt you. Call me when you get back. I think it's time we talk, you know?

    -Sharon.

With teary eyes, Millie stared at the medal resting on the table. She picked it up and read the inscription. "It's a track medal that my father won when he was in high school."

Walter bit his lower lip as he listened.

"I guess his high school team went to state. I never knew this. I never even knew he ran track." Millie ran her finger across the medal's surface, and then she read the newspaper clipping.

"This is from the town paper when I won entrance to the Olympic trials back in 1991."

She sniffled.

"I know." Walter handed her his handkerchief.

"Local track star Millie Howard won the marathon and has earned a chance to qualify for the Olympic trials in Louisiana this coming June . . ." Millie glanced up at Walter.

"Your father had an entire scrapbook of newspaper clippings about your high school and college track accomplishments, Millie." Walter reached out and took her hand. "And Sharon wants you to have it."

Millie shook her head. "Why?"

"Keep reading." Walter pointed to the article.

"I see where I was interviewed by the reporter. I remember that." She wiped her eyes.

"Please keep reading."

When she saw her father's name in the article, Millie wept. "'Our entire town is so proud of our daughter,' said Martin Howard, Millie's father. 'I know she can go all the way. She's that capable. I've seen her race since she was in high school. She can do this. I ran track in high school, so I know what I'm talking about. She's got it. She's that good . . .'"

Staring at the words, Millie's head fogged up. "I don't remember this at all. I mean, I guess I never read the article in the paper."

"Apparently, your father saved everything. I saw the scrapbook, Mill. It's amazing."

"But why, Walter?" she asked with weepy eyes. "Why didn't he ever tell me this? Why didn't he ever show me the scrapbook? All he ever told me was that running was a waste of time. He said it would never amount to anything worthwhile." She shoved the medal away from her.

"I don't have the answers, Millie. I've never been a father, so I can't say what was going through his mind. All I do know is that he tried for a track scholarship in order to go to college. But unfortunately, it never happened. I guess, in his mind, your endeavors weren't going to amount to anything either."

Millie glanced away.

"So I guess by his actions, he did support you, and he was proud of you." Walter sighed. "He just didn't know how to say it to you."

Millie squeezed her eyes closed when she heard those words.

"Did I do right by showing this to you? I really struggled with it. On the plane, I prayed about it and—"

"You did right." Millie turned to him. "And I will call Sharon when we get back. I promise."

∽

After dinner, they walked through the neighborhoods and turned down the alley where Millie first spotted the special door that had intrigued her. She stood in front of it.

"What do you think?" she said as she inspected it.

"It's unique." Walter stared at it, then looked at his wife. "What made you want to photograph the doors of Rome?"

"I don't know. They are all so beautiful." Millie pointed to the other doors nearby. "I find them to be mysterious. What's behind them? Who lives in the building, and who are they?"

"Interesting."

She felt the sting of tears in her eyes when she remembered the conversation, she had had with herself.

"Walter," she began. "I need to tell you something."

"What is it?" He stood in front of her, holding her hand.

"Just a few days ago, I stood here, wondering about this door and what's on the other side. I was angry with you." Millie looked away.

"I know."

"I was hurt, and so I thought some angry thoughts about you." An emotional knot choked her throat. "My friend Judith told me to forget about you and what you want and go after what I want."

"I see."

"I know now how foolish I was being. I know now that it's wrong to think and feel that way, and I'm so sorry." She reached for his hands and squeezed them.

"No, you weren't being foolish. I was being foolish." Walter pressed his lips to her hand. "You were dreaming, that's all. I tended to pour cold water on all your hot ideas."

"You were being safe, and I need that."

"I was being too safe, Millie."

"How could I ever imagine a life without you?" She shook the idea from her head.

Walter leaned against the wall and stared at the door across from them. "All I could think of was waiting for retirement to do all these adventurous things. I should have listened to you. I should have replied to your text messages. I was just sulking."

"I love you, Walter." Millie rested her head on his chest.

The door they were admiring opened and startled them. Millie frowned, as though resenting the intrusion. This was their time in Rome.

But then she saw through the doorway. "Whoa," Millie said as she peeked inside before it closed. "I was wondering what was behind that door."

"Well? Let's go in and find out . . ." Walter reached out and put his hand on the wooden door before it closed.

"No, Walter." Millie grabbed his arm to stop him. "We can't do that. That's trespassing." She wrung her hands together.

"Sure, we can." He smiled at her before he disappeared into the doorway. "You know you want to. Come on, follow me."

"I can't believe how adventurous you're being." Millie giggled as she followed him into the mysterious doorway.

When her eyes adjusted to the darkness, her mouth dropped open when she saw the sight. "Wow."

They stood within a courtyard illuminated by tiny white lights draped from one end of the courtyard to the other. Ceramic pots filled with petunias with purple petals and yellow centers and bright pink geraniums sat at each corner of the courtyard.

Above them were rows of apartments with balconies overlooking the courtyard.

"This is so beautiful." Millie spun around in the glow of the lights. "I never imagined it was like this. The lights are like stars in the sky."

Walter watched her, then removed his phone and took some photos. "The light's reflecting off your eyes and hair."

Millie used her hands to cover her hair. "Oh, don't take my photo." She winced. "I look terrible."

"Nonsense." Walter lowered his phone. "You look amazing. You look like you did when I first met you."

She pointed to her hair. "Grayer on top."

He pointed to his balding head. "Less hair on top."

Millie laughed.

Music from one of the apartments filtered down. Soft jazz music played, and Walter took Millie's hand and twirled her around. He grabbed her waist and pulled her close.

"Dance with me," he whispered.

Millie gladly gave in and looked deep into his kind, sincere eyes. "I'm not the woman you married. I'm thicker around the middle, have more wrinkles, and graying hair."

"I love you, Millie girl." He pecked the tip of her nose. "Just the way you are."

She smiled. "I'm so glad we didn't wait until retirement to do this."

"Me too."

Millie and Walter danced in the courtyard behind that door in Rome.

As they danced together, Millie realized that both she and Walter had the courage they never knew they had. They opened a door that led to a new adventure and closed the door to their former stagnant ways.

∽

Doors open and doors close.

That's what doors do.

To open a door without knowing what's on the other side takes courage.

To close a door that never should have been opened requires faith.

THE END.

Authentic Italian Lasagna Bolognese Recipe

Prep Time: 30 Min
Cook Time:2 H and 30 Min
Servings: 8
For a 13×9 inch lasagna pan:

For Bolognese Sauce (Ragu alla Bolognese)

300 g (10 oz) of coarsely ground beef
150 g (5 oz) of sliced pancetta (you can replace pancetta with minced pork)
300 g (1 1⁄4 cup) of tomato passata or crashed peeled tomato
1 small carrot (about 50 g)
1 celery stalk (about 50 g)
1 small onion (about 50 g)
100 ml (1⁄2 cup) of dry white wine
100 ml (1⁄2 cup) of whole milk
300 ml (1 1⁄2 cup) of meat broth
3 tablespoons of extra virgin olive oil
fine salt
freshly ground black pepper

BÉCHAMEL

5 tablespoons unsalted butter
¼ cup all-purpose flour
4 cups whole milk, warmed
Pinch of freshly ground nutmeg
Kosher salt

Preparation:

Heat butter in a medium saucepan over medium heat until foaming. Add flour and cook, whisking constantly, 1 minute. Whisk in warm milk, ½-cupful at a time. Bring sauce to a boil, reduce heat, and simmer, whisking often, until the consistency of cream, 8–10 minutes; add nutmeg and season with salt. Remove from heat, transfer to a medium bowl, and press plastic wrap directly onto surface; let cool slightly.

BOLOGNESE SAUCE
Step 1
Pulse onion, carrot, and celery in a food processor until finely chopped.

Step 2
Heat oil in a large heavy pot over medium heat. Add beef, pork, pancetta, and vegetables; cook, breaking up meat with a spoon, until moisture is almost completely evaporated and meat is well browned, 25–30 minutes; season with salt and pepper.

Step 3
Add wine to pot and bring to a boil, scraping up browned bits from bottom of pot, about 2 minutes. Add milk; bring to a boil, reduce heat, and simmer until moisture is almost completely evaporated, 8–10 minutes. Add tomatoes and 2 cups broth; bring to a boil, reduce heat, and simmer, adding water by ½-cupfuls if sauce looks dry, until flavors meld and sauce thickens, 2½–3 hours.

Step 4
Let sauce cool, then cover and chill at least 12 hours or up to 2 days. (Letting the sauce sit will give it a deeper, richer flavor.)

ASSEMBLY
Step 1
Reheat the sauces. Combine Bolognese sauce and remaining 1 cup broth in a large saucepan over medium

heat, and heat until sauce is warmed through.

Step 2
Meanwhile, if you made the béchamel ahead of time, heat in a medium saucepan over low heat just until warmed through (you don't want to let it boil).

Step 3
Working in batches, cook fresh lasagna noodles in a large pot of boiling salted water until just softened, about 10 seconds. Remove carefully with tongs and transfer to a large bowl of ice water; let cool. Drain noodles and stack on a baking sheet, with paper towels between each layer, making sure noodles don't touch (they'll stick together).

Step 4
Preheat oven to 350°. Coat a 13x9" baking dish with butter.

Step 5
Spread ¼ cup béchamel in the prepared baking dish. Top with a layer of noodles, spread over a scant ¾ cup Bolognese sauce, then ½ cup béchamel, and top with ¼ cup Parmesan. Repeat process 7 more times, starting with noodles and ending with Parmesan, for a total of 8 layers. Place baking dish on a rimmed baking sheet and bake lasagna until bubbling and beginning to brown on top, 50–60 minutes. Let lasagna sit 45 minutes before serving.
Source: Bon Apetit Magazine (2013) https://www.bonappetit.com/recipe/lasagna-bolognese

Gustare!

ABOUT THE AUTHOR

R.A. Douthitt is the award-winning, multi-published, author of fiction and non-fiction books.

Because Ruth is also an award-winning artist, she illustrated her fantasy-adventure books.

When she isn't writing, you'll find her running, gardening, or creating art in her home studio. Ruth lives in Arizona with her husband and their little dog.

To learn more about Ruth, visit her website: www.artbyruth.com

Made in the USA
Monee, IL
03 October 2023

43878291R00152